Praise for the Nick Madrid Series

"Bringing intelligence and caustic ... been Guttridge's specialty ... in ...
—T...

"Original and highly readable ... but a word of warning: never let this
man house-sit if you value your pets."
—Lynne Truss, author of *Eats, Shoots & Leaves*

"Peter Guttridge has ... the kind of mordant wit and cold-eyed social
observation to make his Nick Madrid mysteries de rigueur reading."
—*Good Book Guide*

"Jokes are delivered with the speed and accuracy of a Gatling gun."
—*Daily Telegraph*

"Brilliant."
—*Shots*

"Few British crime writers can match the outrageousness of their American
counterparts but Peter Guttridge is well on his way ... the satire is spot on."
—*The Guardian*

"Wacky ... Hilarious ... A great read."
—Minette Walters, author of *The Sculptress* and *Fox Evil*

"Brilliant ... Peter Guttridge is a fresh, stimulating new talent."
—Peter James, author of *Faith*, *Host* and *Possession*

"Madrid is a highly engaging hero."
—*Daily Mail*

"Brilliant one-liners, lightning action, lots of suspense and very funny—
self-deprecating Madrid is fast becoming my favorite crime hero."
—*Good Housekeeping*

"A plot that engages and amuses to the end."
—*Crime Time*

"A fast moving, laugh-a-line frolic."
—Reginald Hill, author of the *Dalziel and Pascoe Series*

"Sharp and sassy."
—*Birmingham Post*

"Peppy plotting is Guttridge's stock-in-trade."
—*The Times*

"An extremely likeable hero ... Agatha Christie on laughing gas."
—*Colchester Evening Gazette*

"The funniest crime novel of the year."
—*Publishing News*

Other Nick Madrid Mysteries
Now Available or Coming Soon

A Ghost of a Chance
Two To Tango
The Once and Future Con
Foiled Again

NO LAUGHING MATTER

PETER GUTTRIDGE

speck press
denver

First published in the United States by *speck press* 2004
Printed and bound in Canada
Book layout and design by *Magpie*, magpiecreativedesign.com

This book is a work of fiction. Names, characters, places, and incidents
are either the product of the author's imagination or are used fictitiously.
Any resemblance to actual events or locales or persons, living or dead,
is entirely coincidental. Although the author and publisher have made
every effort to ensure the accuracy and completeness of information
contained in this book, we assume no responsibility for errors, inaccura-
cies, omissions, or any inconsistency herein. Any slights of people, places
or organizations are unintentional.

Published in Great Britain by Headline Book Publishing 1997
Copyright ©1997 Peter Guttridge

Library of Congress Cataloging-in-Publication Data
Guttridge, Peter.
No laughing matter / by Peter Guttridge.
p. cm.
ISBN 0-9725776-4-5
1. Journalists--Fiction. 2. Comedy festivals--Fiction. 3. Montréal
(Québec)--Fiction. 4. Edinburgh (Scotland)--Fiction. 5. Los Angeles
(Calif.)--Fiction. 6. Women--Crimes against--Fiction. I. Title.

PR6107.U88N6 2004
823'.92--dc22

2004016221

10 9 8 7 6 5 4 3 2 1

To my mother and father

The author gratefully acknowledges the financial assistance
of South East Arts in the completion of this book.

MONTREAL

ONE

I was trying to figure out how to scratch my nose when the naked blonde flashed past my window. She looked surprised to see me, judging by her wide eyes and waving arms. And I *was* pretty surprised to see her. It wasn't that I knew her, although she did look vaguely familiar. And it wasn't because she was naked. I'd seen naked women before. I was surprised because my room was on the fourteenth floor and I was pretty sure the hotel didn't have an outside elevator.

Her fall was badly timed if she was expecting help from me. I couldn't even get at an itch. I was in an advanced yoga posture, technically known as *uthitha kurmasana,* less technically, for reasons unclear to me, as the "balancing tortoise" or "corpse position."

Balanced on my hands, I'd lifted my legs back under my armpits and over my shoulder blades and crossed my ankles at the back of my neck. As you do. It is one of those postures that is hard to get in to, even harder to get out of.

I felt sorry for the blonde, catching sight of me in her hurried descent. Instead of her life passing before her, her final moments would be spent puzzling over the sight of this naked man whose big ears, sticking out either side of his head, had toes on them. She'd be glad to hit the ground.

It was the first time I'd managed to get into this posture and, aside from my itchy nose, I had been feeling quite comfortable. I'd chosen as my *drusty,* or gaze-point, a silhouette of a person I could see in a lighted window in the building opposite. I'd been staring fixedly at it when the blonde whizzed by and broke my concentration. Startled, I lost my balance and toppled over.

I landed heavily, trapping my ankles beneath my head, my legs under my arms, and my wrists under my buttocks. It took a moment or two to realize I was stuck. My body weight was on my feet and hands and I couldn't immediately work out a way to free them. When I tried to lift my head to release my ankles, my buttocks pressed down on my hands. When I tried to raise my buttocks, my weight shifted on to my ankles. Either way, the pain was agonizing.

It was three hours before the maid found me. By then I'd lost all feeling in my body. I had tried to free myself but all I'd succeeded in doing was wiggling my ears for the first time in my life. So I'd laid still, concentrating on keeping my breathing steady. I was worried mostly because my posture encouraged flatulence. I didn't want to be asphyxiated by my own … well, you get the idea.

I passed the time perfecting my ear wiggling and thinking about the woman who had fallen to almost certain death. Even upside down, she'd been a real looker.

The maid screamed when she saw me. I think at first she thought I'd somehow been chopped in half. Then she thought there were two of me doing something very rude. I croaked for help and she looked more closely. When she saw I was alone, naked, and in a strange self-embrace, she curled her lip in disgust.

I asked her to turn off the air conditioning, cover me with a blanket, and ring for help. I asked her to be discreet. I was sharing this Montreal hotel with some 250 comedians taking part in "Just For Laughs," the largest comedy festival in the world. If any one of them heard about this I might as well leave town.

The maid flung a blanket over me and went out of the room, leaving the door wide open. I'm sure I heard the word *pervert*. Out of the corner of my eye I saw one or two people walk along the corridor. They looked in, saw me wrapped in a blanket, looked again, then hurried on.

"Would you shut the door?" I called weakly to the maid just as Loud Lenny Finnegan walked by.

"Hi fella," he said, coming to a dead stop. "You okay?"

I groaned. I may as well leave town. Lenny, a motor mouth stand-up comic from Seattle, stepped into the room. He looked down at me. Sniffed suspiciously. Wrinkled his nose.

"Somebody die under there?"

In response I broke wind for the fiftieth time. He took a quick step back.

The blanket was tucked up to my chin so all he could see was my head resting on a pair of crossed feet. He indicated the feet.

"Aren't you going to introduce me to your friend?"

I smiled thinly. "Ain't nobody here but us chickens, Lenny."

Lenny frowned. He seemed lost for words, which must have been a first for him. He was a permanently *on*, stick-it-there, how-ya-doin' kind of guy. I'd met him on my first day as I was getting in the elevator. He'd shouted after me, "Don't take that elevator—I had a dream." That's the thing about sharing a hotel with 250 comedians, there's no rest from the witty.

He walked over, pulled the blanket off me. His eyes widened.

"Jeez, Nick, you really take self-gratification seriously, huh? A solo *soixante neuf*. I'm impressed." I could almost see his mind racing behind his eyes. Comedians aren't like the rest of us. In any situation they're always looking for the punch line. "Is this what you Brits call having a leg-over?"

Lenny was just getting started, I could tell, but thankfully the maid came back in with one of the deputy managers. He joined

Lenny and stared at me blankly. Sniffed suspiciously. I wiggled an ear in greeting.

"This is shaping up to be a very strange day," he eventually said.

"You've found the girl who jumped out of the window?"

Lenny looked down at me. "Somebody jumped out of your window?"

"You know her?" the deputy manager said sharply.

"The broad who did this to you?" Lenny said. He looked reverential. "Who did this *with* you?"

"I saw her. She went past my window as I was doing my yoga."

"Ah, yoga," the deputy manager said, looking slightly relieved. Then he peered at me suspiciously. "The maid says you've been like that three hours. You were doing yoga at five in the morning?"

"Jet lag. My sleep pattern's all to pot. But listen, do you think you could help me here?"

"Where'd she land?" Lenny asked the deputy manager, ignoring me.

"In the pool." The deputy manager looked sorrowful. "It's a tragedy."

"Yeah, poor woman," I said in commiseration.

"We only had it retiled last week. She's made a real mess in the shallow end."

"Landed in the pool," Lenny murmured, already working on ways to get this stuff into his act.

"People will be most unwilling to use it now. Especially with the other death."

A dreamy expression crossed Lenny's face. "The other death?"

"The man in the pool," the deputy manager said.

"The man in the pool?" Lenny beamed. "She landed on someone doing his fifty laps? Whoa. At five in the morning, must be another Brit, right?"?"

"She didn't land on him. It seems he died of a heart attack when the young lady joined him in the pool so precipitately. As I said: a very strange day."

"Ah well, another day another *doleur*," I croaked, rather pleased with myself for making a bilingual joke in this bilingual city. The two of them just stared at me. I became conscious again of the indignity of my position.

"Look, could you kind of roll me on to my side and then unhook my ankles?"

Lenny and the deputy manager didn't move.

"C'mon guys. I'm not contagious. But go slow. My muscles have seized up."

Two hours later I was lying snug in bed. The deputy manager had summoned the physio from the health club to massage my body back into life. Loud Lenny had gone on his way by then. As he left I called after him hopelessly, "I'd appreciate it if you'd keep this to yourself, Lenny."

He didn't give me so much as a backward glance.

I woke at five in the king-size bed that could easily sleep three but sadly never had since my arrival. I was still woozy with jet lag and had a few aches and pains, but overall I felt pretty good. As usual I was due to meet Bridget and Frank in the bar at six. I wondered what the chances were I would get down there without being the recipient of a little impromptu rib tickling. Sometimes it was no joke attending this festival.

I'd been here twice before, freelancing for *The Sunday Times* and *The Guardian*. This year the tag round my neck, bearing an unflattering photograph, at least I hoped it was unflattering, simply said Nick Madrid, British Press. I'd been commissioned to write a 2,000-word, color piece for one of the posh Sundays, and I was looking for interviews with Bradley Stokes, Jim Carrey, and Steve Martin.

Stokes, the fat star of the popular *Hitman* movies, was hosting one of the gala evenings. The other two were rumoured to be attending, though that, of course, was no guarantee I'd be able to get them.

Bridget and Frank were the two other British hacks covering the festival. Bridget Frost was my best friend in journalism. "The Bitch of the Broadsheets," she was loud, pushy, opinionated, grudge bearing, drunken, vindictive, and tacky, but she had her good points. Actually, those were her good points.

She and Frank Wyatt had been friends ever since they worked on *The Ham and High* together an age ago. He'd been chief sub on a middle-market magazine for years now and the trip was a bit of a lig for him since he only had one piece to write and his editor probably wouldn't even ask for it.

Spending a week at the festival wasn't exactly arduous for any of us. In fact the hardest thing to do was occupy ourselves during the day without getting too drunk. As a freelancer who only got paid for what I could sell I was busier than the other two, but that wasn't saying much.

I phoned the festival press office from my bed. I'd been trying for three days to get someone to confirm the rumour that Carrey and Martin were coming to town. So far I'd got diddly. The woman in the press office passed me on to a freelance public relations guy called Steve Hewitt, a young Canadian who claimed to be in contact with the film superstars. He was also handling Bradley Stokes.

I'd spoken to him already and realized he was a master of the art of prevarication, like most of his U.S. peers over the border. The difference between British and American PRs is that the British want you to interview their clients, the Americans don't. Hewitt was in the American mold. I knew I would have to go around him to get anywhere, but I had to make the call.

"Steve Hewitt? Nick Madrid. How are you today? Wondered

what the word was on Carrey and Martin. How are they fixed for interviews?"

"Nick. Busy day. Well, Carrey and Martin are coming in but so far as interviews go, who can say? Carrey is a definite no-no. He isn't doing anything. Frankly we're lucky he's coming at all."

This came as no surprise. The Toronto-born physical comedian, who had spent fifteen years on the stand-up circuit, had been on the front page of every magazine and newspaper for the past four years as his salary rocketed from $250,000 for *Ace Ventura* to $20 million for *Cable Guy*. Recently he'd been getting serious in a Peter Weir film, but he was expected to get back to comedies soon.

"What about Bradley Stokes?"

"He's possible. But see the tabloid journalists have been harassing him about his divorce for months."

"I'm not tabloid, and I'm not interested in his divorce." I wasn't really interested in Stokes. I'd hated the three moronic *Hitman* movies that had made him famous. "Steve Martin?"

"If he comes I doubt he'll do press. He's not booked to appear or anything, it was just that he expressed interest in taking a look up here. He doesn't really perform live any more. Shame."

"I'm not doing too well here, am I?"

"Well, what about Phyllis Diller or Billy Cash. Cash is going to be hot."

The manic Diller I knew: I'd interviewed her once before.

"Who's Billy Cash?"

"Kind of a foul-mouthed guy, but very funny. Used to be a musician. Started doing stand-up then got his own show on cable. Prize Cash. It's phenomenally successful. Won a bunch of awards. He's a good color piece—pushing fifty, hell raising, drugs, tomcat past. He's had a makeover and just signed a three picture deal for sixteen million dollars."

"Impressive. But nobody in Britain will have heard of him."

"You could be ahead of the game. Plus he loves publicity so

getting him would be easy. I'm not handling him but I'll talk to Juliette Smith."

"Juliette's his manager?"

"Yeah. You know her?"

"Only by repute."

I thanked him and asked him to keep pushing for me. He said he would. Liar.

It was six thirty before I got in the elevator with a short guy in a dark linen suit. The jacket sleeves were rolled up to his elbows revealing tanned, immensely hairy forearms. He looked at my chest then studiously ignored me. I looked at his tag. He was from a west coast agency. Everyone from his agency had swapped the standard issue string on their identity tags for silk cords. Is that prissy or what? Comic Billiam Coronel (a great guy to have at an anagram party) said it looked like they'd bought them from Hermans of Show Business.

Journos were no good to this guy and anyway he didn't like me being bigger than him. I'm six four and, thanks to yoga, I'm a fine figure of a man, aside from my childbearing hips.

The elevator stopped on seven and a skinny young guy in a white T-shirt and black jeans got in. He checked my tag, saw the magic word 'Press,' and went to work.

"Hi, I'm Jackie Cosmo. You should write about me."

"What do you do?"

"I have this wild visual thing, a telescope that goes up my nose and out my mouth. I do a bunch of other stuff too. I finish by cutting off my tongue with a razor blade. After I've set fire to it, of course."

"Of course," I said, willing the elevator to go faster.

"I'm doing Club Soda tonight on the late, late show. You should come down."

"I'll do my best," I said out the elevator doors as it reached the mezzanine.

The hotel bar was packed. I spotted familiar faces from the British contingent. We'd flown over with a bunch of English comics, Channel 4 execs, producers, agents, and an independent production company filming the wraparound for the footage of the live gala evenings that Channel 4 brought in every year.

The comedy festival was, quite apart from anything else, a giant trade show. Cable channel execs, movie producers, casting directors, major agencies, comedy club chain owners, flim-flam men, groupies, and liggers had all made the flight from Los Angeles or New York. For the duration of the festival, Montreal was Deal City.

The deals went down all the time, any time. All day and all night, taking in pre-gala drinks, the VIP tent at the gala and the post-gala party, you'd find guys with business cards in one hand, mineral water in the other, working the room, schmoozing. Also known as schmoos, schmoozl, or even shmoo.

There was a whole lexicon of schmoozing. First, the Schmooz Intentional: a wave across the room to indicate the intention to meet up and have a chat. Second, the Schmooz Proper: the mutually advantageous chat and exchange of business cards. Third, the Postschmooz Squeeze: a little pinch of the arm to say 'we've had our schmoo but I'm still aware of you.'

The big news over the past couple of years was that after ten years of boom, comedy in the U.S. was going bust—clubs closing down, ratings falling, live audiences dwindling. On my first evening here—I'd only been there three days but it seemed like forever—an L.A. woman in production told me, "I didn't mind when the cash cow, 500-seater theaters in the suburbs closed. But it's sad to see the pearls have gone. The rooms that Eddie Murphy and David Letterman started in. I tell you, comedy in America is death."

If it was true that stand-up was on its last legs, then, judging by the people in the bar, there was going to be a hell of a wake. Everybody who was anybody or wanted to be anybody in comedy was here. I walked past Charles Joffe, Woody Allen's manager and former agent of Robin Williams and Steve Martin, as he was saying to a bunch of younger agents, "Comedy is tragedy with timing." They all nodded sagely. A guy I recognized from Jay Leno's *Tonight Show* was laughing loudly with a group from David Letterman's show.

I passed Bruce Hills, the festival's programmer, and British comic Lee Evans. Evans was the funny Norman Wisdom who'd broken into movies with *Funny Bones,* then played alongside Bruce Willis in *The Fifth Element*, the Luc Besson film. I stopped to speak to them but I was distracted by the shambling arrival of a German comic.

Every year there was always one—a willy waver—and more often than not it was this bloke. He was naked from the tip of his bald, slightly pointed head to the top of his long brown socks. Heads turned as he walked over to a table of power players and dangled his penis and notoriously large scrotum in the bowl of olives.

"Bet Billy Cash hasn't got one like this," he said, with a slight accent, to a woman with too big hips in a too tight skirt. The woman smiled thinly.

"Werner. How nice to see you," she said coldly.

He removed his penis from the olives and sat, uninvited, on a stool, draping a napkin coyly across his lap. He offered the bowl of olives around his new friends. All declined.

I looked at the woman he had addressed. So that was the legendary Juliette Smith, Billy Cash's manager. Werner wouldn't faze her. She was tough. And was believed to have laughed only once in her life, out of politeness. I wondered whether to go over and introduce myself so I could set up the interview but a big guy with a dork knob came over and whispered in her ear. She excused herself from the table.

Bridget arrived alongside Eddie Izzard. Izzard had on bright red nail varnish and lipstick, tight leggings, high-heel shoes, and a sports jacket. Bridget was also dressed down, as usual. Flame red velvet miniskirt, black tights, low-cut black top, thick seventies platform shoes. Her long, bleached blonde hair was scooped up into an extraordinary beehive. Post -*Ab Fab* irony or the real thing? It was hard to say with Bridget, whose notion of good taste was ... well actually she had no notion of taste, good or bad.

Izzard went over to a Channel 4 commissioning editor. I followed Bridget as she tottered to the bar. Unasked, the barman put a large vodka in front of her.

I used to think I could drink until I met Bridget. She could—and often did—drink me under the table without exhibiting any apparent signs of drunkenness. And however much she consumed, she was never, ever late with her copy. Although she was in her mid-thirties now, the only effect of the years of booze seemed to be a bit of additional weight on what had always been a curvaceous body.

I squeezed in between Bridget and a redhead whose name tag was lodged so deeply in her impressive cleavage it was required reading for any man who passed by. She was part of a crowd from one of the big TV comedy shows.

There were always a lot of beautiful women here and I was never sure what they did. Correction: I was very sure what a number of them did. Comedians these days collected groupies like rock stars used to. There was even a joke about it, as there was about almost everything in Laugh Land. A beautiful girl goes up to a comedian and tells him how wonderful his act is and how she wants to sleep with him because she admires him so much. "Did you see the first or the second show?" he says.

"So Yogi Bare," Bridget said. "What's this I hear about you making the beast with one back? That brunette you were talking to last night not come up with the goods?"

Before I could answer we were both distracted by a loud protest from the other side of the horseshoe-shaped bar. I looked across in time to see Stevie Smith swallow an ashtray. The promoters and producers who were with him went bug-eyed as the ashtray disappeared down his gullet. Stevie, a professional regurgitator, regurgitated billiard balls, Rubik cubes, small change, butane gas, goldfish, and light bulbs. I'd seen him swallow hand soap, inhale cigarette smoke, and bring back smoke-filled bubbles. The ashtray would be up again in five minutes, which was just as well for the one smoker in the group who had missed the stunt and was looking around grumpily for somewhere to stub his cigar.

"What have you heard about the girl who jumped?" I asked.

"Only that you saw her whilst engaged in a probably illegal sexual act. Have you filed a story yet?"

Bridget was soft hearted, too.

"I don't know who she is. Besides I've been a little preoccupied."

"No excuse. God, if perverts couldn't write for the press there'd be some pretty thin newspapers. You're in the company of the top people. When Andrew was—"

"I'm not a pervert. I was doing some yoga."

"Sure, kid. So everyone's saying."

"Everyone?"

"People do talk. So no story, huh?"

"I don't know who she is. Was."

"When has that ever stopped a journalist?"

"Bridget, desist. I'm feeling a little fragile."

"Okay. But you're always grumbling you're not making enough money. Here's a story that's fallen into your lap, well, almost."

"That depends who she was."

Bridget sighed.

"It was Cissie Parker."

"Ah yes, Cissie Parker." I nodded slowly. "Who's Cissie Parker?"

"You're the film buff. English wild child turned TV pop program presenter comes to America after she scores a bit part in a cult director's next movie."

"Shit, yes. I knew she looked familiar. How did you find out?"

"I'm a journalist, sweetie. I asked somebody."

Cissie Parker. Around twenty-five with a lifetime of experience behind her. But she didn't just want to act. She'd been trying to make it as a comic on the circuit, built her act on jokes about dating older men.

"What floor was she on? I mean, did she fall a long way?"

"She wasn't staying here. She had an apartment across the road. The police are still trying to find which window she fell out of. But if you want to file a story you'd better get a move on. We're five hours behind here remember."

"I'm not an ambulance chaser," I said. "How cynical do you think I am?"

Bridget shrugged.

"I couldn't be so ruthless," I said. "Besides I don't know how to do news stories."

Bridget shrugged again.

I phoned the obituaries editor instead.

Every evening we had a choice. We could either go to the VIP tent behind the Theatre St Denis to watch the nightly four-hour gala on TV monitors whilst drinking cheap red wine, or we could go to Club Soda on the other side of town where most of the acts in the televised galas tried out their material. If an act scored there, the chances were it would score on its gala appearance.

There was a wodge of big British names that year—Paul Merton, Vic Reeves, Jo Brand, Ben Elton, Jack Dee, Lee Evans, and the others. Bridget, for whom the word *pushy* had been invented, had invited herself to dinner with them. I headed down to the tent. The festival provided courtesy mini-buses to take you to the venues but I liked to walk, to get a feel for the city and to catch the street performers.

Montreal is a bilingual, some would say schizophrenic, city. It is split very distinctly between the Anglophiles and the Francophones. The only thing they have in common is taking the piss out of Toronto. In the festival, performers from all over the world did either a French- or an English-speaking set. And because the French tradition of humor is more visual than verbal, a good many of the acts did some kind of performance art.

Within moments I was skirting trick cyclists, jugglers, stilt walkers, clowns, and mimes who were getting an enthusiastic reception from a large crowd of people munching on pizza slices or *chiens chaud* (no, really) and drinking Labatt Bleu out of styrofoam cups. It was a humid evening and I was sweating when I flashed my tag at the security guard outside the VIP tent. There were only a couple of dozen people hanging out there, watching the opening acts on the television monitors. They didn't laugh much. I'd noticed this before. When industry people heard something they liked they'd say: "That's funny," without cracking a smile.

A South African comedian I vaguely knew stood by me at the bar. We watched one of the monitors together. "They look so confident up there," he said. "I can't believe these are the same people who were throwing up in the toilet half an hour ago."

There were a number of other comedians in the tent, although no headliners. I could hear a senior guy from one of the big late night shows talking to a group of younger people. "I don't want prop acts, magic acts, comics who juggle chainsaws, or comics who fart bubbles out of their ass."

"He's going to be hard-pushed to find anyone then," my companion murmured.

He was right. The acts usually split into the verbal, the visual, and the very weird. This year the very weird predominated. Some acts once seen are never forgotten, however hard you try. So far I'd seen something even more boring than a drum solo, a mimed drum solo. I'd seen a man play Chopin with his nose and Mozart with one hand whilst spinning a plate with the other and balancing a violin on his chin. A midget impressionist performed as Elfin Presley (I remembered him as Micro Jackson in an earlier year). A cowboy rode on stage to recite comic poetry. Everyone agreed the horse had the best lines.

The tent began to fill up. The industry folk preferred the tent to the theater because they could see who looked good on screen for when a performer made that switch from stand-up to sitcom. Ambitious performers never knew where to pitch their act. They knew they needed the energy of the live audience but they also needed to score in the tent. The snag was that the people in the tent weren't always watching. Usually the big shots were schmoozing while some poor ignored schmuck seltzered on the television monitor.

I was watching a Canadian comic who was pretty funny. "In my home town of Kirkland Lake, Ontario, the best looking girl was inflatable and group sex was when you had a partner. You married the first thing to come along that didn't have antlers." I heard something I'd never heard in the tent before. A real laugh. A yelping, uninhibited laugh from the table where the *eminence grise* was sitting. I looked across to see a woman with her black hair cut in a Louise Brooks bob splutter her drink all over the table, rock backwards, and fall off her chair in a flurry of limbs.

She lay on the floor, giggling uncontrollably, her dress up over her waist, showing a skimpy pair of white panties and long, brown legs. A few of the others in her group were laughing despite themselves and I felt myself grinning from ear to ear. I was about to walk over and help her up in my most gallant manner when Lenny Finnegan threw an arm round my shoulders.

"Yogi, didn't recognize you with your legs back on the right way. Do you know Vera Verna from *Global Village*? Vera, Nick. He's a journo from the London something-or-other."

Lenny moved to one side to make way for a short, slight woman, dressed entirely in funereal black, even down to her beret. It was perched dead center on her head, its little stalk pointing straight up in the air. She was very skinny and in that outfit looked just like an unlit candle. She had a sour look on her face. She nodded.

"Vera here is upbraiding me—hey, and they say I'm not an intellectual? You like that word? *Upbraiding* me for being anti-gay. But no, no. I'm not anti-gay. I just tease them a little. Do you have a problem with that, Nick?"

"The only problem I have with you, Lenny, is that some of your jokes will upset people."

"I don't want to upset anyone. I see myself as a cartoon guy, a Fred Flintstone. That's all."

Vera drifted away, scowling. She was right to get upset about many of the stand-up acts. Stand-up comedy is predominantly a male form. Some of these guys were *very* male. They would have been happier if the mike was called "Dick." Most of them were sexist, racist, and homophobic—and that was just the liberals.

"So what's the dope on this Parker dame?" Lenny said.

"Did you know her?"

"No, but I respect her memory, as one performer to another," he said.

He looked gloomy and I realized why, he wasn't going to be able to do any jokes about her now he'd found out who she was.

"Hi, Lenny." The woman with the Louise Brooks bob

punched Lenny playfully in the bicep. "Aren't you going to introduce me to your journalist friend so he can make me famous?"

Sometimes I love this job.

Her name was Amanda Colgate. French mother, American
father, New York born, California based. A secretary until she
was thirty, then she started doing open-mike nights in the L.A.
clubs. Within a year she was on the road. For the past, well, let's
say the past little while, she'd spent forty weeks a year criss-
crossing America playing the clubs in the comedy chains and
the little one-offs. Even as a relative unknown playing third or
fourth billing she was making $60,000 a year.

I learned all this within ten minutes of Lenny leaving us. I'd
like to pretend it was in response to my sensitive questioning but
it was actually an unsolicited monologue. In fact it was impossible to shut her up.

I should care. She was gorgeous—six one, lithe, and slim.
And she seemed to like me. Not because I was a journalist, we
don't rate highly enough for sexual favors. But I could read the
signs, I've had an unhealthy interest in body language since my
youth. She was standing legs apart, hips facing forward, only
inches away from me. If that doesn't mean she's offering her
body to me, I thought, then I'm a Dutchman.

"It's a good living," she said. "But I'm ready for top or at least
second billing. I'm ready for the shot on television that gets you
that billing."

Usually that meant Letterman or Leno. Conventional
wisdom had it that one appearance on either David Letterman's
show or Jay Leno's *Tonight Show* made you a star. That wasn't
necessarily true. Steve Martin appeared with Johnny Carson
when he was doing the *Tonight Show* maybe fifty times but he
didn't become a major star until he switched to movies.

"Have you ever been to bed with someone with a sexual
deformity?" Amanda said, between swigs from her beer. She and

I were about the only two people drinking alcohol. The drink of choice for everyone else was mineral water with a twist.

This sounded like a leading question. But leading to what? An admission or was it code? Was she actually a man? I'd got nothing against men in dresses; I just didn't want to go to bed with one. I was trying to formulate a response when she said:

"I slept with a guy once whose erect cock instead of pointing upwards was curved downwards."

"That must have presented one or two practical problems," I said, relieved but bemused.

"On the contrary, it opened up all sorts of possibilities."

I was waiting for a punch line or an explanation. Instead she said "I'm prepared to sleep with Billy Cash to get on his show. Do you think that's wrong?"

I recalled my conversation with the PR Steve Hewitt about Billy Cash and his womanising.

"Is it essential?" I said.

"I would think so. See I need to advance my career. And soon. I'm not getting any younger. Got to strike whilst the bod is hot."

As she said this she flexed her body unselfconsciously. Ouf.

"Would you like to come back to my room after the show?" I murmured, my heart beating like the mimed drum solo.

"For sex?" she said, rather loudly. I reddened. "With you?" She let out another yelp of laughter. I thought tulip fields, clogs, and windmills.

"Oh Nick, I'm sorry." She stifled another giggle, leaned over and gave me a soft kiss on my burning cheek. "I didn't mean it to come out like that. I have to meet Juliette for a drink right now."

"Juliette?

"Billy's manager. To get the show on the road."

She kissed me again on the cheek, gave me a big smile, handed me her bottle.

"You finish this. And wish me luck. I'll let you know which way his willy points."

I hung around for ten minutes sipping the tepid beer. It was almost eleven and the tent was filling up. Performers from tonight's show appeared. They were speeding, pumped up, egos bared, alert for compliments. It would take them a couple of hours to come down. The hotel bar was usually packed until four in the morning.

A courtesy bus was leaving for Club Soda so I took the ride. According to my program I would be in time for the late night Danger Zone. Not to mention Jackie Cosmo.

I was lounging on the seat behind the driver gazing out of the tinted windows when the driver suddenly said: "Whatsamatter? You're too famous to talk to a driver?"

I looked up to see him staring at me in the rear-view mirror.

"Me? I'm not famous at all."

"Oh yeah? This is an ex-parrot. It's defunct. This parrot is deceased. Suppose that doesn't sound familiar?"

"It's Monty Python—"

"I fart in your general direction in a French accent that from where I'm sitting is actually racist."

"John Cleese in—"

"I'm not famous, he says, trying to patronize me because I'm just a driver. Well I won't always be a driver and when the future catches up with my past I just hope you're present to see it."

He jerked to a halt outside Club Soda, staring straight ahead, revving the engine. I slid open the side door and climbed out. I looked back, bewildered, as he pulled immediately away.

Inside Club Soda the stage was empty and Frank was attempting to chat up the barman. Since the barmen here chose to speak only French and Frank's knowledge of the language seemed to be restricted to yes, no, and faster please he wasn't getting very far.

"Nicholas!" he shouted above the hubbub. "Let me buy you a beer. *Deux biere bleu*, Philippe."

"I see your French is coming on in leaps and bounds."

He fixed me with watery bloodshot eyes, leaned close so I could smell the combination of wine, beer, and whiskey on his breath, then bellowed in my ear:

"I've got a little hush-hush gossip to share with you."

Half a dozen people at the bar turned to listen. I picked up our beers and led him along to an open area near the toilets where we habitually stood during the shows. All the tables were usually occupied and here you were equidistant from bar, toilet, and exit.

"I'm all ears," I said, leaning against the cigarette machine.

"So Lenny tells me," Frank said. "You must demonstrate this yoga for me some time, Nicholas. I didn't realize you had such hidden talents."

I ignored the innuendo in his voice. Frank was outrageously camp and unrestrainedly promiscuous but I was a good ten years too old for him. In his early fifties, he was about to take early retirement. He had a property in Spain with his long-term partner, Alec, up in the hills near Granada. They were supposed to retire there together. But they'd had some falling out a few weeks before. Bridget blagged him this freebie to get him away from his woes.

He was a portly man with a red face, baldhead, and trim white moustache. In the three days he'd been here he'd drunk a heroic amount and importuned as many young males as he came across. He and another member of the British contingent went off on regular midnight cottaging jaunts together.

"Cissie Parker," he said.

"Don't come at me with any more yoga jokes," I warned him.

"The police are assuming it's suicide."

"Seems likely."

"But I heard something very peculiar on the eighteenth floor last night."

"Your room's on the eighth, isn't it?" I said, unable to control a smirk.

"Nicholas, I saw this darling boy in the bar who I swear was queer. We engaged in conversation and I judged by those little signs that pass between people that our evening would end in mutual satisfaction. Those lips, that mouth, that tush."

"And …"

"And then he disappeared. That bitch Bridget got into an argument with some Channel 4 oik and I had to rescue her. And when I looked round my boy had disappeared."

The loud rock music that had been blaring over the sound system was abruptly silenced. Julian Clary was on stage in a mauve suit. A voice boomed out: "Please welcome Julian Clary, who is here to tell you big boys don't cry … if you use a lubricant."

There was uncertain laughter. Most of these people preferred to laugh at gays not with them.

"Do you fancy him Frank?"

"Don't you?" Frank said, without taking his eyes off Clary.

He had a point. Clary was a very beautiful man. I turned my attention back to Frank.

"So what about the eighteenth floor?"

Frank put his hand on my shoulder and his face close to mine so that he could speak in a normal voice.

"My darling boy lives there. I went to look for him. I didn't know the room number. So I went from door to door listening."

"And you heard Cissie Parker?"

"Possibly. I heard a man yelling terrible abuse at someone, then I heard a cry when he hit her."

"It was a woman crying out?"

"Exactly." Frank looked sheepish. "Now I wonder if it was Cissie Parker. If maybe I should have done something."

"Nothing you could have done," I said, patting his shoulder. "You couldn't burst in on a private argument. Did it sound like he was trying to kill her?"

"I didn't hear enough. Just sounded like he'd started beating her up." Frank's lower lip started to tremble. "I'm not a physical man, Nicholas. I hate violence."

"Frank, it's okay. There's nothing you could do. Did you hear her say anything?"

"No, she just cried out. But it was definitely a woman."

"What room was it?"

Frank shook his head. "I'm not sure."

"Did you recognize the man's voice?"

"No, but I would if I heard it again."

"You know, this may be something or it may be nothing, Frank. But you should go to the police with it."

Frank nodded non-committally, his next remark drowned out by the arrival of Lea Delaria on stage. She was a short chunky woman in a man's suit waving a two-headed dildo over her head like a battle-axe. "It's the 1990s," she bellowed, rampaging from one side of the stage to the next. "It's hip to be queer and I'm a bi-i-i-i-g DYKE!"

"God I hate dykes," Frank shouted under her onslaught. He looked at her and sniffed. "She looks like a carpenter."

"She was a carpenter," I said, "in some all-lesbian construction outfit."

"Dykes building houses? There wouldn't be a straight line in the place."

Frank chuckled at his own joke.

"Come on," he said. "let's go back and check the eighteenth floor. See if I can find the room again."

"Or your darling boy."

"You see through me so clearly, Nicholas."

"I see you're a randy old bugger."

"That I am, Nicholas, that I precisely am."

"The thing about me is that it's not that I don't like penises," Delaria was saying as we left. "I just don't like them on men."

Bridget was having an altercation on the pavement outside the club. She was searching through her capacious bag, muttering angrily at the big doorman who was blocking her way. She saw us approaching.

"It's all right you French Fuck," she snarled at the man towering over her. "I don't need to come in. I've found what I'm looking for."

"Bridget, we're just headed back to the hotel to do a little Miss Marpling," Frank said. Bridget grabbed his arm and said to me:

"Come on, we need somewhere to get a quick drink."

"What's been happening?" I said, following her as she dragged Frank down the street.

"That fucking clown wouldn't let me in without seeing my identity tag. As if he hadn't seen me here the past three nights."

"Bridget, listen," Frank said, squirming out of her grip. "We have to go back to the hotel."

"Frank has a line on Cissie Parker's death."

Bridget hauled Frank to a stop so abruptly I barrelled into him from behind. He raised an eyebrow at me.

"Didn't know you cared for the tradesman's entrance, Nicholas."

"Is it about Phil Peters?" Bridget demanded, suddenly flinging out a hand and shrieking "Taxi!" so loud I swear I heard half the taxis back in London screech to a halt. "I know a bar near the hotel," she said. "It'll be quiet at this time of evening."

We piled in the taxi, which did a U-turn to a chorus of car horns, and set off back into town.

"What's this about Phil Peters?" I said. Peters was a British stand-up who'd been on the circuit for donkeys' years. In his early forties now, he was never going to make it big but seemed content enough to be working regularly.

"I had dinner with Paul and Jack and the others," she said smugly. "They were talking about Cissie."

Bridget rummaged in her bag and came up with a pack of cigarillos and a lighter. She looked defensive when she caught me watching her.

"It's a time of stress. And I've only had a couple today. Maybe five."

"Certainly no more than ten," Frank said, making a spluttering sort of noise, which I realized with pleasure could only be a chortle. I felt privileged. I'd read about chortles hundreds of times but until now had doubted they really existed.

Bridget blew smoke down her nose and out of the corner of her mouth at the same time.

"You're so adept," Frank said. "I expect smoke to come out of your ears, too."

Bridget smiled mirthlessly. "Only steam, sweetie, only steam."

The taxi drew to a halt outside the iron frontage of what looked like a punk cafe. Inside, all was steel sheeting and glass. It was virtually deserted. Bridget led us to a corrugated iron booth and ordered a bottle of wine.

"Phil Peters has had a thing for Cissie for years. Accounts differ as to whether they've ever shagged but Phil can't stop talking about her."

"What floor is he staying on?" Frank said.

Bridget didn't hear. "Phil used to be Cissie's supplier. They used to get high together."

"You're doing one of your elliptical narratives, Bridget. How does this tie in with Cissie's death?"

"The drugs."

"The drugs?" Frank and I said together.

"Haven't you heard the latest? Cissie was drugged up to the eyeballs."

"So it was accidental death? Trying to see if she could fly?"

"Maybe. It still could be suicide. But my feeling is Phil tricked her into getting high to get her into bed and either she went weird or accidentally fell. But Phil's to blame. Has to be."

"What if they just took some drugs together?"

"Cissie wouldn't do drugs. She was clean. I had a drink in the bar with her two nights ago. She told me she was finished with all that. I'd have known if she'd lied."

Bridget was unmovable on her assumed insight into people, her intuition about them. Nobody could lie to her.

"Frank heard a violent argument on the eighteenth floor, not long before Cissie died."

"Your room's on the eighth," Bridget said quick as a flash. "I suppose you were up there looking for that little bumboy you were fondling in the bar the other night?"

"Bridget, that was rather a low remark. Is this Phil character staying on the eighteenth floor by any chance?"

"No idea but we can easily find out. Then we can cross-check it with what Nick told the police."

"I haven't told the police anything. Nobody's asked me to. Anyway what can I tell them? I only saw her flash past the window."

"And you call yourself a journalist?" Bridget snorted. "What's your room number?"

"1414."

"Okay. Assuming she fell in a straight line and assuming the hotel is symmetrical, she must have fallen from room number fourteen on any floor between fifteen and twenty-six. What room did you hear the row in, Frank?"

We had by now started on a second bottle of wine. Frank,

cheeks and forehead flushed a deep red, eyes slitted, had started to tilt. Bridget pulled him back to the vertical.

"Frank, dear, which room did you hear the row in?"

"I don't remember," he said, his voice suddenly beginning to slur under the influence of who knows how much booze.

"Come on, Frank," Bridget said, tugging at his sleeve. "We've work to do."

"Marpling to do. Quite right, Bridget. The very thing."

We got Frank out from behind the table without too much difficulty. The revolving door proved a trial but once we'd freed his hand he was okay. He wrote with his other one anyway.

We picked up a cab and hustled Frank into the back. Bridget and I exchanged glances. The dent across his hand had started to turn purple but he hadn't noticed so we saw no reason to tell him. He dozed off and began snoring, slack mouthed.

"This thing with his partner has really hit him hard," I said. "Judging by his drinking."

"What do you mean? He always drinks like this. What's killing him is chasing sex every night. He's not used to it. A man of his age."

Frank woke up when we pulled up in front of the hotel and came alive as we hurried him through the lobby. There had been a reception there earlier and the leftover food still littered several tables. Frank lunged for a bowl of crisps, missed, and put his hand into an avocado dip up to his wrist.

At the elevators Bridget shushed him. Just before the doors opened she said, "Listen we've got to be discreet about this," unconsciously scratching at her thigh where the ladder in her fishnet tights was evident.

"Discretion!" Frank bellowed. He reached out a hand to lean against the wall, missed the wall but hit the elevator doors with his outstretched palm just as they shot open.

Frank disappeared sideways. I heard a screech. When I looked into the elevator there was a glamorous woman in a long, low-cut turquoise dress. On her impressive embonpoint there were avocado fingerprints and a green trail to her crotch. Frank lay at her feet, one arm outstretched.

"H–he attacked me!" the woman yelped indignantly.

"Not intentionally," I said, joining her in the elevator.

"He put his hand on my … my …"

"So we can see, dear," Bridget said, joining us. "If you'll get out of the elevator we'll see he does no harm to anyone else."

"But my dress …"

"Frankly, dear," Bridget said, ushering the woman out of the elevator, "it was probably the dress he was after." She trod on Frank's leg with her clumpy heel. Frank cried out and pulled his knees up. "Wasn't it, Frank?"

Bridget punched nineteen and the doors closed on the still protesting woman.

"Help me up," Frank spluttered. He brought the hand with the dent in it before his eyes. "My God. Look what that woman's cleavage has done to my hand. They must be concrete not silicone."

He struggled to his feet.

"She'll have the hotel management alerted to the existence of a *sex pest* in the hotel," Bridget said calmly. "We haven't much time. If we get off at the nineteenth and nip down the stairs that should do the trick."

We got out of the elevator and Bridget clomped her way ahead of us down to the eighteenth floor.

"Can you remember anything about this room, Frank?" I said gently.

"It was a long walk."

"Which way did you turn when you came out of the elevator."

"Sensible question," Frank said, patting my arm. "No idea. I vaguely thought I would follow the scent of his aftershave."

"How much had he put on, for God's sake?" Bridget protested. "Or are your olfactory senses so good?"

"All your senses are heightened at such a time," Frank said with a certain dignity.

"So which way did you go from the elevator?" I repeated.

"I think it was right or was it—"

"Don't say it. Okay let's start from the right."

"Any distinguishing features?" Bridget said. "Ashtrays, torn carpet, windows, fire extinguisher?"

"Yes!" Frank said. "There was a room service tray right outside the room. I remember thinking it was a bit late for breakfast."

Frank looked pleased with himself until he saw our faces.

"I don't think the tray will still be there, Frank." I smiled at him. "So that's not much use, I'm afraid."

"Hang on though," Bridget said. "We can check with the hotel which rooms had room service that night."

Frank looked supercilious.

"That's what I meant." He stopped at a service phone in the wall, picked it up. Bridget took it from him and put it back.

"Not now. Later."

"The phone. There was a phone nearby," Frank said triumphantly.

"That's good," I said to Bridget. "That narrows it down considerably."

We walked the whole floor. It went in an L shape. It seemed miles. There were six phones. One was two doors away from 1814.

"How near to the door was it?"

"Can't remember," Frank said. Sleepiness setting seriously in.

"Was it to the left or right?"

"Can't remember."

Just then the deputy manager walked out of room 1809. He was surprised to see us.

"Oh, Mr. Madrid, it's you," he said in an unnaturally loud

voice, glancing at Frank slumped against the wall. "One of our guests has complained about being molested by a ... I believe she used the words *sex fiend*."

We all looked at Frank, who chose that moment to slide down the wall. He lay at its base, one leg sprawled out, the other bent under him. Unconscious. We all saw that his fly was open.

"Our friend here isn't a sex fiend," Bridget said, her eyes flickering to the deputy manager's nametag on his lapel, "Beatrice." She ducked her head closer, frowning. "Beatrice?"

The deputy manager blushed, looked down, and clapped his hand over his nametag. "Gerard, madame," he said, patting his lapel. "Do go on."

"Our friend here is merely a little the worse for wear—if your name is Gerard why does your name tag say Beatrice?"

"A mix-up, madame, simply a mix-up." Where before he had been patting his lapel now he tried quite casually to take the tag off, fumbling with it as he spoke. "I must have picked up my colleague's name tag by mistake, that is simply all."

"When?" Bridget said.

The deputy manager looked from one to the other of us, panic in his eyes. "When?" he repeated.

"Bridget, how Gerard got ... Beatrice's tag is neither here nor there. The main thing is our friend here whose reputation has been maligned," I urged.

"He tripped and accidentally brushed against this woman," Bridget said. "It was all quite innocent."

"I'm sure it was. I'm sure it was," the deputy manager said, looking down at Frank's open fly. He darted glances up and down the corridor. He took my arm. "Perhaps we could discuss it at our leisure downstairs. We don't after all want to disturb anyone who may be sleeping here."

"You're the one who's been shouting," Bridget said. "Who's in the room you've just come out of?"

"Nobody," the deputy manager said abruptly.

"Really?" Bridget said, walking over to the door and rapping on it.

"Madame!" the deputy manager squeaked, rushing over to the door.

"Beatrice," Bridget called. "Come out, sweetie. Gerard told me to tell you the manager's on his way. He knows everything."

The door sprang open and a plump young woman in high-heeled shoes stood there, tucking her blouse into her skirt. I leaned towards her lapel. Her badge said Gerard Laput, deputy manager.

Beatrice looked perplexed, Gerard looked mortified.

"I regret this incident," he said. "But we are both single peoples."

Bridget put her arm round his shoulders, gave him a quick squeeze, and smiled solicitously. I trembled for him. She was at her most lethal when she was smiling.

"I know I speak for Mr. Madrid when I say our lips are sealed. As a favor to you. As a favor to us we need a list of occupants of every room on the eighteenth floor and details of who had room service the night Cissie Parker died."

"I can't possibly—that's privileged information."

Beatrice spoke very quickly in French.

"There's no need for your husband to find out, Beatrice," Bridget said, bestowing her sickly sweet smile on the woman.

"Oh, you speak French, madame," Beatrice simpered.

"Fluently," Bridget said shortly. "We're going to take our colleague to his room then we'll be in Mr. Madrid's room. You can either phone the information through or bring it to us there."

"It's very late, madame."

"Mademoiselle. We'll wait."

We carted Frank down to the elevator. He was at least on his own two feet again.

"Evolution," I said. "Frank learns to walk erect."

"So I see," Bridget said, gesturing down at Frank's crotch. Frank's semi-erect penis protruded from the still open fly.

I heard the whirr of the approaching elevator.

"Bridget," I said weakly.

"So do something," she said.

"I'm not touching it. I don't know where it's been."

"On the contrary, dear," Bridget said. "We both know exactly where it's been, which is why I'm not touching it either. I must say I'm impressed there's still life in the old boy after the amount he's drunk today."

The light pinged above the elevator door, the doors slid open, and the woman in the low-cut turquoise dress stood there, her eyes fixed on the stub of Frank's penis poking up at her, her mouth a perfect O of surprise.

Just kidding. The elevator, thank God, was empty. Frank was sort of asleep at his post, standing up—or rather swaying—as the elevator descended, gazing blankly at the ceiling. His erection had diminished now and his penis, nestling in its folds of fore-skin, merely peeped from his zipper.

"Your fly is undone, Frank," I said, hoping he'd look down.

"Sorry, old chap," he said slowly, reaching down and giving his zipper a firm yank with his one good hand. His face con-torted and he bent double. "Christ!" he screeched, flapping both his hands helplessly. "Jesus Christ!"

Bridget looked at me in bewilderment. I winced.

"For God's sake, help me," Frank spat out through gritted teeth.

"Is it your hand Frank? Is it your hand?" Bridget was bend-ing over Frank's crouching form.

"He's caught his johnson in his zipper," I said.

"God …"

"Just the skin. It hurts even more unzipping because of the way the skin is caught up in the teeth."

"You sound like you're talking from experience."

"The suffering of men, women have no idea."

"Do you think," Frank gasped, "you could discuss this later? Can one of you—I can't bring myself to—please ..."

"What?" Bridget said, slow on the uptake.

"He wants us to castrate him. That's your speciality, Bridget."

"Ha—bloody—ha," Frank said, groaning.

"We'll have to undo his zipper for him," I said to Bridget. We looked at each other for a moment.

"Straighten up, Frank," I said. "As best you can. Hang on, can't see from here." I got down on one knee in front of him. Bridget followed suit. I tried to ignore the thing just above my eye level and reached for the fastener.

"Frank, could you kind of hold it steady," I said, peering underneath to where the teeth were embedded in a flabby lump of foreskin already turning angry purple at the edges. Bridget, looking away, fumbled for the fastener and caught the underside of Frank's penis with a long, lacquered scarlet nail.

"Ayee," Frank cried.

I was vaguely aware of the elevator decelerating. I found the fastener and gave it a quick yank.

"Oh God, thank you, thank you," Frank groaned, as the elevator came to a juddering halt, its doors snapping open behind us.

TWO

I'd only done my yoga practice twice since I arrived in Montreal. The second time Cissie Parker had given new meaning to the resting posture known as the corpse position.

Six hours after Bridget, Frank, and I had our zipper incident in the elevator, I started to do my salutes to the sun again, simple stretching and bending exercises. I kept well away from the window.

I was pushing thirty when I first heard about astanga vinyasa yoga. For years before that my idea of healthy exercise had been going to put my pay check in the bank. I tended to agree with Samuel Pepys, who said that, "fport is a naufeous obfeffion of the fimple-minded." (I like a man who calls a fpade a fpade.)

Julie, my girlfriend at the time, took me to dinner at the Islington house of Clara, a friend of hers who was a travel editor on one of the nationals. Clara held forth about tantric yoga, the sex one.

"The man puts his erect penis inside a woman. For two hours neither person moves. Then they both come and the orgasm lasts half an hour." Clara looked round the table. I smiled nervously. For me the two hours finished it before it even got started. I was more your split-second-of-bliss kind of guy. Premature ejaculation—taking the waiting out of wanting.

Clara went on to say how the other approach in tantric yoga is to make love avoiding orgasm.

"Oh, I've been doing that for years with Nick," Julie blurted out. A little unkindly I thought.

I should have seen that was a "For Whom the Bell Doesn't Just Toll But Does A Bloody Carillon" moment. But I was listening to Clara talking about a place in Crete where you could go and do a different form of yoga. Astanga vinyasa. It was mostly single people who went there. You practiced intensively, you ate healthily, and—if your body could still function—maybe fooled around a bit.

Two weeks later, on my thirtieth birthday, Julie and I broke up. We'd been together three years, the longest I'd ever been with anybody. She left me for a younger man. Sure he was bright, good looking, and earning ten times what I earned, but he was nine months younger, too. So I went to Crete. I had the most wonderful fortnight of my life, didn't fool around,—my body wouldn't function—and got hooked.

And here I was in a hotel room in Montreal, contorting my body into ridiculous postures for the good of my health. But, frankly, I wasn't in the mood. I kept remembering the elevator. Bridget and I down on our knees in front of Frank. The elevator doors opening. About thirty people waiting to get in, including Rowan Atkinson, Bruce Hills, Bob Newhart, Charles Joffe.

"It's that man again," an indignant voice said. I looked at the familiar turquoise dress. "How disgusting."

As I staggered to my feet I saw Lenny Finnegan's grinning mug.

"Nick, we gotta sit down and discuss your sex life sometime," he said as he snaked his hand around inside the elevator and pressed the button to close the doors.

As the doors closed and the elevator started its ascent, Bridget said, "What happened?"

"Loud Lenny rescued us."

We hustled Frank to his bedroom. His hand was in bad shape. I didn't check anything else. We wondered whether we should get a doctor but since Frank had passed out on one of the beds we covered him with blankets from the other bed and left him there.

When we got to my room the list of occupants of rooms on the eighteenth floor had been pushed under my door. 1814, the room four floors above me, was a hotel hospitality room, whatever that meant. Bridget was all for phoning Gerard to find out but I was whacked and I didn't want to call any more attention to us that night.

Now I gave up on my yoga practice and called Bridget. The phone rang for a long time. When it was picked up I heard a rattling as if someone was trying to get it the right way round.

"Fuck off," Bridget said and put the phone down. She wasn't at her best in the morning. I checked my watch. It was probably too early for Frank as well but I rang him anyway. More fumbling on the line.

"Hello," Frank croaked.

"Frank, it's Nick. I thought we should all go for breakfast together after last night. Present, you know, a united front."

I could hear his heavy breathing but he said nothing for a moment or two.

"Frank?"

"Last night?" he said. There was a strange noise on the other end of the line. Frank was crying.

"Frank?"

"What happened last night, Nicholas? One of my hands won't work and my cock - my cock looks like someone tried to bite it off. Where did we go? Did we go to Madame Leila's?"

"Madame Leila's?"

"The torture cham—nevermind." He was quiet for a few

moments. "I have no recollection of last night. Doubtless I will remember it in nightmare flashes in the course of the day." He was quiet again. "I think I may need a doctor before breakfast. My hand looks quite poorly."

On the way to the hotel doctor I said, "Are you going to show him your cock?"

"I don't show my cock willy-nilly, you know," Frank huffed. "Despite appearances."

"Willy-nilly. Right. I meant where you said you'd been bitten. It was your zipper by the way. You got it caught."

"I curse the day they were invented. There used to be nothing quite so lubricious as fumbling with a lad's fly buttons."

After the doctor had bathed and bandaged Frank's hand—and charged him $89 for the privilege—we went up to the mezzanine breakfast room. Halfway up the stairs we heard a familiar voice raised in anger.

"So it's okay for a naked man to explode a firework out of his ass in the restaurant at breakfast but it's not okay for an old man to leave his fly open by accident in the middle of the night?"

An indignant male voice replied, "It's a certain standard of behavior we expect of journalists. You are after all guests here—"

"Bollocks. We're here to give this festival publicity in the U.K. - as we have very successfully in recent years. It's *quid pro quo*, buster. Nobody gives a damn about one little incident, and what's it got to do with you anyway?"

"I'm handling the public relations for this hotel whilst I'm here," the male voice said stiffly.

At the top of the stairs Frank and I came to Bridget, in a low cut T-shirt, appallingly tight jeans, and high-heeled, red slingbacks, face to face with a stocky, bearded man in blue tinted spectacles. She spotted us.

"Here are the other two now. Nick, Frank, come and meet

Steve Hewitt, the new publicity director for the hotel. He's threatening to throw us out."

"I never said that." The man took off his spectacles and gestured with them. "I was trying to point out that the hotel has passed on its concern to me."

"It has, has it?" I said. "Steve, I'm Nick. We've spoken." I turned to Bridget. "Did I hear you say Chris Lynam did his firework trick at breakfast?"

"Allegedly," Bridget said. "It was the climax of the Nasty Show last night. Everybody was talking about it, so rumor has it Chris came into breakfast and did it again. Malcolm Hardee—deshabille, natch—apparently lit the blue touch paper."

"If it's true, that's not the kind of behavior we expect from artists here either," Hewitt said huffily, twisting his glasses in his hands.

Frank had been listening intently. Now he said in his most gentlemanly voice, "My dear chap. All my fault. Most terribly sorry." He waggled his bandaged hand. "Impeded as I was, I was unable to zip up my fly and these dear friends were selflessly attempting to assist me. Unfortunately, their timing was a little off."

"I should say." Hewitt sighed. "Well, it's okay, I suppose, Frank. I had to pass the message on but now that I have I hope we can all forget it and enjoy the festival."

Frank and I nodded. Bridget gave Hewitt her gimlet stare. She forgets nothing and forgives less.

"Okay then, goodbye for now." Hewitt nodded and walked away. He had gone a few yards when he turned and called. "And of course if there's anything I can do for you …"

"Yeah, you can fuck off," Bridget muttered. We smiled and waved him away. "What a joke. A little nobody like that—"

"He's not a nobody," Frank said, a disgustingly complacent smile stuck on his blotchy face. "He's the man I heard on the eighteenth floor two nights ago."

That afternoon all the Brits had been invited to the British consul's house for drinks. Bridget and I decided we had to keep Frank relatively sober, at least until we got there, so we went down to the old French quarter for a proper lunch.

"So what have we got?" Bridget said. "Cissie Parker falls to her death in a hotel she's not staying at, full of drugs she doesn't use anymore? She falls out of a window somewhere above Nick's room. So room 14 on any floor would fit. Frank heard a raging row on the eighteenth floor in a room near a telephone with a room service tray outside. Checking the list we got from dear Gerard there are four rooms that fit those two criteria. They include eighteen fourteen.

"1814 is registered as a hospitality suite for the hotel, to be used as and when by hotel management. Steve Hewitt, as the publicity man for the hotel, is part of that management. Ergo, Frank heard Steve Hewitt in room 1814."

"Whilst two doors along in 1810 is Phil Peter's room."

"Was it Hewitt or Peters?" I said.

"Hewitt, I told you," Frank said.

"My money is on that creep, Phil Peters," Bridget said. "But okay, we've got to establish whether Hewitt knew Cissie Parker—and well enough to argue with her, then kill her. We've got to check on his drug use, too. Then we've got to see what Phil Peters was doing."

"Are you two serious about following this thing through?" I said. "I mean, you're not just joking?"

"Of course I'm serious," Bridget said indignantly, a tabloid look coming on to her face. "A young woman with all her life ahead of her killed by some male pervert."

"I hate to appear ignorant in such a fundamental way," Frank said. "But who is this Cissie Parker anyway?"

"Pretty girl who scammed a job on pop TV because she was such a loudmouth. You must have heard that trademark back-of-the-classroom raucous laugh. Druggie, drinker, D-list celeb. Occasionally said something quite funny. Interviewed some cult film director for a four in the morning movie show when he came over. Probably shagged him. Next thing you know she's got a bit part in his next movie, which could either be fifteen minutes of cult fame or a stepping stone to something else. Then she turns up doing a comedy set in a couple of L.A. clubs. The clubs close down soon after but I think that can be put down to coincidence. Learns to hold her own, decides to try to make it as a stand-up. Gets a gig here. Dies. And not just on stage. Actually she hadn't performed here at all."

"Did you do an obituary, Nicholas?"

"I did. The obituaries editor called just before I came out to ask me to make the opening paragraph sexier."

"Sexier? An obituary?"

"Yeah, well, it's competing with other parts of the paper, you know. Quote." I squeezed Bridget's hand. "But you're just going to give our information to the police aren't you?"

"Somewhere along the line, sure. But if we can crack this— what a story! Anyway, you got anything better to do on these long afternoons?"

I shrugged. "Guess not. What dirt did you dig in your drink with her the other night? What about this wild child thing?"

"Oh, she slagged around all right. Underage clubber. She liked older men, much older men. But she told me she was in love, was hoping to confirm a committed relationship soon."

"Did she seem suicidal?"

"Not in the least. Enthusiastic, egotistical, ambitious, competitive. She was going to upstage all the other women comedians at the festival. Pretty much all she talked about was the future."

I wondered how to ask tactfully.

"Maybe she was a depressive, subject to mood swings," I said. "Do you think you would know for certain in a half hour chat she was telling the whole truth?"

"I would have known," Bridget said tersely.

"Nicholas has a point, darling. Perhaps this committed relationship went awry." Frank looked somber. "They do you know."

"I would have known," Bridget said, closing the conversation down.

She reached across for the ashtray, knocked over the bottle. I grabbed for it—my reflexes are good when it comes to alcohol—but before I could right it great red gouts of wine had spilled into Frank's lap.

"White wine," Bridget said. "That's the thing to get out red wine stains. We need a bottle of white wine quickly. What time's this do? Make that two bottles."

When we finally took a cab to the consul's house—a mock-Gothic pile on the heights behind the park—Frank had a large pink wet patch across his crotch and upper thighs. He stank of alcohol.

"Keep your jacket buttoned and you'll be okay," Bridget said.

It was a hot, humid day and perspiration was running freely down my face and neck. Frank was sweating pure alcohol. He kept mopping his sunburned, peeling head with a disintegrating tissue, leaving lumps of white paper dotted across his pate.

Bridget had made a big effort for the do. Worldly wise as she was, she had a blind spot when it came to the upper classes, imagining every encounter with them was going to be like a cocktail party at the Mitfords. She was wearing a flouncy scarlet number with lace at the wrists and collar. She still had the fishnet stockings and the scarlet platforms of course. And from somewhere she'd got a black pillbox hat. With a veil yet. She looked like a deranged bridesmaid or as if she'd stopped off in a red light district on the way to Ascot.

The window of the taxi was open. In the draught, tendrils of Bridget's hair were coming loose and as I followed behind her into the house I could see that the whole edifice hidden under the hat was about to topple.

"Bridget," I said just as she picked up speed and abandoned Frank and me, tripping up the path to the front door where Angus Deayton and Rowan Atkinson were waiting to go in.

"Hello, sweeties," she said, pushing in between them. I waited for Frank, who with his bandaged hand was fiddling with a tape recorder out on the pavement. He saw me looking.

"You never know what incriminating things I may uncover, Nicholas. This calls for the hard-nosed stuff, the real journalism on which I cut my teeth. Watch and wonder."

The consul's wife was just inside the door alongside a butler with a tray of champagne glasses. "Ah, more journalists," she said nervously. "I've just met a lady from, well anyway I'm sure you know her."

"I'm sure we do," Frank said, taking a glass with his injured hand. "Frank Wyatt, ma'am." He dropped the glass on the terracotta floor.

As the glass shattered and wine and sharp splinters exploded round our ankles the butler was quicker than the consul's wife at jumping back. Which was unfortunate since in doing so he jerked the tray and the glasses started to tip. He, the consul's wife, and Frank all reached to save them but a moment later the glasses slithered off the tray and cascaded to the floor.

At the tremendous noise and the consul's wife's histrionic cry everybody rushed from the three rooms onto which the foyer opened to see what had happened. Foremost among them were Phil Peters and Steve Hewitt.

I thought I carried it of with remarkable elan. I leaned against the wall and raised my intact glass to my lips.

"I'm so sorry, so very sorry," Frank declaimed to the hostess, waving his bandaged hand. "My fault entirely."

"Not at all, not at all," she declaimed back, though without enthusiasm. She was staring at the wet pink patch across his trousers. He followed her look and quickly buttoned up his jacket. She smiled reluctantly. "Accidents do happen and I keep meaning to carpet this hallway. John, another glass for the gentleman." She turned to the other guests. "Sorry ladies and gentlemen, a little domestic mishap. Do carry on."

The guests dispersed, some of them throwing Frank and me disapproving glances. I noticed Bridget ignoring the furore to fawn over the consul.

Frank came up to me and I levered myself off the wall. We'd only gone a pace or two when the picture I'd inadvertently been leaning against slipped down the wall and landed with a by now familiar crash of glass on the floor. I didn't look back.

The place was full of British comedy stars, the TV production gang, managers, and agents all intent on avoiding Frank and me.

"I need a bloody drink," Frank said, leading me instinctively into the small room where the makeshift bar was.

The room was empty except for a Channel 4 exec and Steve Hewitt. When the Channel 4 man saw us he made rapid excuses and with a nod and a quick smile left the room.

"This is my chance," Frank said in a stage whisper. Steve looked down his nose at us as we approached.

"Guess you're not used to this climate," he said, none too cordially. "You're kind of red in the face, fellas. Or maybe that's embarrassment."

"Ha-ha, probably," Frank simpered, with a sickeningly ingratiating smile. "So how's your new job working out? Must be long hours."

"Sure is. Matter of fact if you'll excuse me I must—"

"No, no, wait a moment. I think maybe we got off on the wrong foot. I'd like to put things straight. Drink?" Frank waved towards the table.

"No thanks," Steve said. He sniffed. "You know that wine the butler spilt on you—you should sponge it off."

Frank checked that his jacket was still fastened.

"Aye, I will. So where are you from, Steve. I may call you Steve may I?"

"Sure, er—Frank. I'm from Alberta actually. And I know the jokes, before you say anything."

"Alberta, eh? Must have been quite a wrench for your family moving all the way here. You are married are you? Or maybe just a long-term girlfriend?"

"I really must see—"

"Or have you left her back in Alberta? Are you just here for the duration of the festival then you'll be heading back I expect. Probably staying in the hotel. You are, aren't you? In fact I think I saw you on my floor. The eighteenth."

Steve looked at Frank oddly.

"No. I'm single and I'm here in Montreal to stay. Now, please excuse me. I have to talk to some people."

He brushed past me and headed for the door.

"I watched, Frank. And wondered."

He looked at me.

"I almost had him. Did you see how shifty he got? A couple of minutes more and that would have been it."

Addison Creswell and Jonathan Thoday, the yin and yang of British comedy management, walked into the room. Between them they had most of the major post-alternative names in comedy under contract. Every year some hapless journalist was instructed by an unimaginative editor to do a piece about their non-existent rivalry. This year it was Frank's turn.

"Frank," I said. "Addison and Jonathan. Go get 'em."

I sauntered into the larger room in time to see Bridget, her hair rapidly unravelling and pillbox awry, trap Phil Peters in the corner. This I had to hear. The consul came over to me first.

"Thanks for inviting us," I said, for want of anything better to say.

"Had I known you were going to make such an entrance I shouldn't have," he said, looking at me sternly through steel-framed bifocals. He was in what I assumed to be diplomatic service casuals, open-neck striped shirt and suit trousers. To show he was aware he was hosting a party for arties he was wearing a "jazzy" cravat.

I was about to go into my instinctive grovelling mode and say I was an innocent bystander when he broke a smile.

"Hated those damned glasses ever since we got here. My wife is already planning which new ones to buy. Of course, your name will be mud in the diplomatic pouch. Uncouth gentlemen of the press, etc."

I smiled with relief. Sometimes, after a few days at the festival you don't know if someone is joking since, paradoxically, your sensitivity dulls rather than sharpens the more gags you hear. You need to go on a good diet of serious dramas and documentaries to get back to normal.

I started to excuse myself and looked round for Bridget again. I saw that Frank, flushed of face and unsteady on his feet, had cornered Steve Hewitt. Hewitt looked furious. Then I heard a forceful voice.

"Fuck off, Bridget. Just fucking fuck off for fuck's sake."

The voice—it belonged to Phil Peters—was loud enough to stop all conversation in the room. Well, all but one. In the sudden silence everyone heard Steve Hewitt yell at Frank, "How fucking dare you, you drunken fucking fuck?"

The consul's mouth dropped open. I leaned conspiratorially towards him.

"One's the product of a comprehensive education. The other's from Alberta."

Phil Peters rushed out of the room before Bridget could respond. Steve Hewitt also headed towards the exit. Everybody in the room looked at Bridget or Frank. I went over to Frank whilst Bridget, unfazed, sashayed across to the consul.

"Sorry, your consulship. You never know when temperamental artists are going to go apeshi—hit the roof."

Frank swayed, a befuddled look in his eyes. Bridget curtseyed to the consul and backed to my side.

"Would you say we were making progress, girls?" I said in my politest voice.

By that evening everyone in the hotel seemed to know that Bridget had more or less accused Phil Peters and Frank accused Steve Hewitt of complicity in Cissie Parker's death. In consequence the British contingent and the festival organizers had rapidly closed ranks against them.

Until then, scarcely anyone had referred to Cissie's demise. Not many people seemed to know her and though everyone expressed sadness that she had died the waters had, so to say, quickly closed over her.

"How has word got around so fast?" Bridget said as we huddled in a corner of the bar, ignored by all.

"A few people overheard me question Steve about his whereabouts that night," Frank said. "They kind of eavesdropped."

"By the volume you were both speaking at, most of Quebec state probably eavesdropped," I said. "What did you actually say to Phil, Bridget, to get him so mad?"

"I said he'd got her loaded that night and he was responsible for killing her."

"That was subtle. Ever heard of softly, softly catchee monkee?"

"I got pissed off by his self-pitying misery. I know it was wrong but sometimes you've got to be true to your instincts, right?"

"Wrong, it would appear. So where do you go next, you two?'

"I try to find out where Steve was all that evening and get some background on him."

"I do the same with Phil, though I have all the background I need. I'll also go over to the apartments where Cissie was staying and check out her movements. I might even try to get in to search her apartment."

"That is the real stuff," I said in genuine admiration. "But you can't both be right about who was involved in her death. One of you is going to be disappointed."

"Which of us do you think is correct?"

"I don't know that either of you are. I'll wait to hear."

On the way out of the bar I bumped into Amanda. She looked embarrassed to see me. I assumed she'd heard about the altercation at the consul's house, too, and was tarring me with Bridget and Frank's brush. I leaned towards her.

"Hey, how did it go the other night?"

She looked down her nose at me.

"What do you mean?" she said frostily.

"You know," I said, too stupid to know when to quit. "Did it have a bend in it?"

She frowned, looked away, called out, "Hey, Tommy, well done." She looked quickly at me. "Excuse me, Nick. I must go."

And she was gone.

I went back to my room to shower and change. As I was drying myself I wandered to the window and looked across at the apartments on the other side of the road. I remembered there had been a silhouette of somebody in a window looking out when I was doing my yoga. That person must have seen Cissie fall—and where she fell from. Looking across to the apartments now I hadn't the faintest idea which window it was.

I wasn't sure what to think about Cissie Parker's death. Did I really care? I'd seen this woman plummet past my window, but did that mean I owed her anything?

Frank and Bridget were going to stay inside the gala auditorium tonight, which was unusually tactful of them. I was going to spend the evening down at Club Soda, try to cut back on the boozing. Well, for one evening.

The driver glared at me when I climbed in the bus. Lenny was sitting up in back with his legs sprawled out.

"Hey, Nick. Figure you got off light, buddy. Am I a friend to you or not?"

"Thanks for the other night, man," I said, plonking myself down on the seat in front of him.

"Nick, you're a piece of work. I like you. I know you're not sure about me—hey it's okay. A lot of people think I'm a big phoney. By the time they find out I'm not it's too late." He laughed. "And if I am a phoney, at least I'm consistent."

"About the other night. It was all quite innocent—" I burst out laughing at the expression of disbelief on Lenny's face. "Bastard."

A couple more people climbed in and we set off.

"Did you know Cissie Parker?" I said to Lenny.

"Can't say I did, though I wish I had. She looked good. What about you, she was a Brit after all."

"Knew of her vaguely."

"She was pretty sexy in her film debut. You seen it?"

"You mean she could actually act?"

"I said she was sexy, that's all. Actually, I tell you who must have known her. Bradley Stokes."

"How come?"

"He's in the film with her. They have a couple of scenes together. I bet he schtupped her. He's a hound."

"That so?" I pondered for a moment. "Is Stokes staying in the hotel?"

"One of the penthouse suites."

"The penthouses?"

"Yeah. The hotel has four up on the roof. I wanted to stay in one. Pay for it myself."

"Business must be booming."

"Nah. I inherited some dough. I don't do this for the money, I do it 'cos I like it."

"Who is staying in the other penthouses?"

"Billy Cash, Phyllis Diller—I don't know about the fourth. Some big shot."

I left Lenny in the bus when I got out at Club Soda. Once inside it took only a moment's glance at the audience to see that I'd misread the program. It was gay night, with Lea Delaria hosting. Given that comedy is notorious for political incorrectness, misogyny, and homophobia, this was a brave night. Except that I may well have been the only straight person there.

I got to the bar as some guy was confessing to experimenting with heterosexuality in college. "I was really drunk and I slept with a straight guy," he said deadpan.

I stood in my usual spot and downed a few beers. Frank Maya came on and taught the audience how to say "FABulous."

I noticed a tall woman in a baseball bat, scuzzy sneakers, faded jeans, and a cotton tank top in serious need of an iron shuffle in and stand pigeon-toed against the wall. She had a press tag round her neck and a camera slung over her shoulder. She didn't come over to the bar nor did she seem to pay too much attention to the acts. Instead she leaned against the wall, arms across her body, tapping one foot, and keeping her eyes down under the neb of the cap. I knew I'd seen her before but I couldn't immediately recall where.

I bought a couple of beers and wandered over.

"I've never been able to master that trick—sleeping standing up," I said, offering her one of the beers. She looked up and grinned. She had a gap between her two front teeth. She had a pretty face with big eyes and freckles on her nose. With the grin she looked like a kid, although she must have been in her thirties and not in the best of shape. When the smile went she looked wan, her skin pale and dry. Her clothes were grubby and she gave off a slight sour odor. She had a good figure, basically, but her jeans were getting too tight. She accepted the beer and told me her name was Ruthie.

"You need any photos?" she said, indicating my tag. "Of the acts."

"Maybe. Who are you doing?"

"Well, I was doing the Brits for *Global Village* but Vera and I had a falling out."

When she said that I remembered where I'd seen her. Outside the VIP tent having a slanging match with the unlit candle, old Doom and Gloom.

"What about?" I said.

"Well, basically she didn't like me at all. She was trying to tell me how to take the photos. And every idea I came up with she scorned."

"Scorned, huh?"

"Yeah," she said, grinning again. "Scorned."

"That'll get you every time. I hope you showed her the door."

"Showed her the door? What's that?"

"Gave her the bum's rush? Told her to go forth and multiply?"

"Right. You bet. I called the picture desk and said either I get to take the pictures my way or I quit."

"And …"

"They fired me. And now she's trying to get me banned on the grounds that I'm not attached to a magazine anymore. So I'm keeping out of the way. Long as I got this—" she touched the press pass hanging round her neck "—I'm okay. Though I may have to start wearing disguises."

She laughed and swigged her beer from the bottle.

"Some PR called Hewitt says he might have some work for me but it probably means I'll have to fuck him," she said matter-of-factly. "I'm not sure I want to get into that. I hear he likes hurting women."

"Where'd you hear that?" I said casually.

"Friend of mine had a thing with him in Toronto. He beat up on her."

"Do you know if he knew Cissie Parker?"

"That girl who died? I don't know. But I knew her."

"You knew Cissie?"

"Well, I met her. The night before she died. There was a party down on St. Vincent by the Vieux Port in one of the old warehouses. I'd been allowed in to take photographs for the Montreal press. Cissie came up as she was leaving and said I'd been taking quite a lot of her. I didn't know if I had or not. Anyway, she was asking about my job and stuff, being really friendly and interested and saying how she was hoping to make it big—"

"Did you know who she was?"

"Only by her name-tag. I knew she wasn't famous because the well-known ones don't wear them."

"Then what happened?"

"She asked if she could buy the photographs off me. I said the newspaper might want to use them. She said that's why she wanted to buy them off me. A performer who didn't want publicity? She ummed and ahed and came up with some shit about trying to control her image and unflattering candid photos."

I was trying to remain calm.

"What do you think the real reason was?"

"I think I'd photographed her with someone she didn't want to be seen with."

"Did you give her the photographs?"

"How could I? Even if I'd wanted to, they were all mixed in with my other shots. She was virtually demanding the rolls of film. In a very nice way, of course. She offered me quite a lot of money, too. If I'd known what was going to happen with the 'Woman in Black' I would have agreed."

"So who was she with?" I asked very quietly. We'd moved to the bar by now and I signalled for two more beers.

"I should know? I live and work in Montreal. I've got a two-year-old daughter. The work I usually do is flower shows and office testimonials. I never watch TV, never go to the movies. I don't know who any of these people are."

"Bit of a handicap in your line of work I would have thought."

"That's why I shoot everything then, if I'm doing it for the Montreal papers, dump the films on the picture editor's desk, let him get the contacts done, and choose what he wants himself."

"How did you leave it with her?"

"We made a deal. I said she could have any the picture desk didn't want to use, negs and all. She said maybe I could do some exclusive shots of her performing. Maybe she'd use them as her own publicity shots or I could sell them. I gave her my card and she said she'd be in touch."

"And then what happened?"

She looked at me oddly.

"Then? Then I was mugged."

"What?"

"Right outside my home on St. Laurent. My apartment's above a row of shops. A big guy was waiting for me with a knife in the shop doorway next to my door. He held the knife to my throat, took my bags, then told me to open my door. I thought he was going to rape me. I lied and said my little daughter was inside with my husband. But he made me open the door then walk up the stairs—I'm on the first floor and the staircase starts right inside the door. I was terrified. I couldn't hear him behind me. Then I heard the front door close. Halfway up I made a bolt for the kitchen to get a knife. But he hadn't followed. I don't know if he'd changed his mind or if he never intended to come in but I was alone in the apartment."

"Jesus. And where were your husband and daughter?"

"I don't have a husband and my daughter was staying over at my mother's."

"So they got your camera and the shots of Cissie Parker."

"They got my cameras." She indicated the one she had now put on the bar. "This is my spare. It's old and I think there's something wrong with the shutter release but it's all I've got."

"And your film?"

"I'd already posted the rolls through the door at the newspaper office on the way home so they could run them in next day's paper."

"And did they?"

"Yes, though none of Cissie Parker. I don't think they know what she looks like. I've got to go in tomorrow to identify her so they can do a spread."

"Listen." I moved closer. Mr. Personable. "Could I have a look at those contacts? A couple of other journalists and I have got some reservations about her death. How did she seem?"

"You mean did she seem like she was going to kill herself the next day? Well no, but then drugs can do that to you."

"You speaking from experience?

"Past experience."

She bit her lip and looked sidelong at me.

"I'll let you see the photos if I can stay with you tonight."

I must have looked surprised for she quickly said, "I'll sleep on the floor. I just don't want to be in my apartment right now."

"Sure," I said slowly. "Okay. What did the police say?"

"About the theft? Tough shit. My assailant? He shoulda' raped you, you fucking dyke."

She looked at me and gave me a cagey smile. Another wrong number.

"The police, er, know you?"

"Yeah, they know me. I took some photographs of them breaking up a gay party down in a warehouse on the harbor a few weeks ago. People just having a good time, dancing and drinking. No drugs that I saw. The local gendarmerie came down in riot gear and baton-charged us. I managed to get shots of them beating men and women whilst they were on the ground. I sold them to the local papers and they splashed them over four pages. The cops weren't expecting any publicity so they were kind of peeved. I got stopped in the street a couple of times by patrol cars and harassed. One time at three in the morning they took me to the station to do a drug test on me. They're bastards. Matter of fact I thought the guy in the doorway was an off-duty cop. I wasn't going to call them but I needed to for the insurance claim."

Lea Delaria came back onstage.

I looked at Ruthie. She was grinning at me.

"Your baby's with your mother?" She nodded. "Only I'm getting kinda tired. Do you mind if we go soon?"

She picked her camera off the bar.

"Let's go now."

As we were walking out of the club she took my arm.

"I'm not gay you know. I just happen to have lots of friends who are."

"Me too," I murmured. Feeling her body so close stirred my imagination.

"I'll sleep on the floor," I said.

"I insist," she said.

As it turned out, neither of us did.

THREE

I woke late the next morning. Alone. That bad, huh? I was under no illusions about my talents as a lover. Julie once patted my hand and said to her friends, "Poor Nick, he tries so hard." Another time I overheard her tell someone, "Sex isn't everything—at least not the way Nick does it."

I was an old fashioned guy. Bridget and most of the female comedians referred to sex as shagging, a term I hadn't used since my fifth year at Oldham comprehensive. I still talked about making love. And "with" somebody not "to" them. Some putz.

Ruthie had left a note and her business card on top of the TV. "Thanks for the bed (and the bedding). Meet me at four at the Comedy Museum for the pix. Any problems call. Love, Ruthie xx." I checked my watch. Wallop. Ten o' clock already.

I called Frank. No reply. I called Bridget. No reply. I called the festival press office and put in a request for interviews with Bradley Stokes (again) and Billy Cash. I'd concluded the rumors Hewitt had started about Carrey and Martin were unfounded.

The red light on my phone was flashing. There were two messages. One was from the paper that had commissioned me. It was mid-afternoon in London. They could wait. The other was from Bridget. She and Frank were meeting at La Reine Catherine on the waterfront at one sharp. "BE there."

I took the elevator down to the basement health club. A few guys were lifting weights. Now, I don't want to reinforce stereotypes when I talk about weightlifters. They're not necessarily narcissistic Neanderthals, I just feel that, despite inflation, a penny for their thoughts is still a fair price.

Women in Lycra wearing headphones were using the two jogging machines. A couple of guys went by heading for the squash courts. I'd always regarded squash as one of God's better jokes—two people expending a great deal of energy belting a piece of rubber against a wall for half an hour. Grown men and women do this—the kind who confuse age with maturity.

The tall, willowy Anita Wise, in street clothes, was talking to an agent who was dressed for a workout.

"You're going to use the gym?" he said.

"No," Anita said, in her slightly breathless voice. "I don't like to work out in public. I've got one of those bodies that cracks all the time. Whatever I move—my neck, my elbow, you name it—it cracks."

The agent was nodding at her but I could sense a punchline approaching.

"On the plus side," she said, "when things are slow I work as an exotic dancer for the blind."

The guy nodded solemnly. Anita gave a nervous little laugh. I looked through at the pool. It was, as usual, empty. I could never figure this. Maybe people preferred lounging outside beside the other pool. It was in use again though the joke going around was that there was strictly no diving. The indoor pool was plain and narrow—three broad people doing breaststroke would have trouble getting by each other—but it was a good length. There was a sauna and jacuzzi alongside, but that was it. I usually had it to myself.

When I came out of the changing rooms a woman in a low-backed swimsuit, goggles, nose clips, and swimming hat was doing a powerful crawl down the middle of the pool. I slid in at one side and began my breaststroke. I detest guys doing the crawl in pools. They are so macho and bullying, bulldozing everyone else as they plough their labored way up and down the pool. Me, I'm terrified of accidentally touching another person and have them think I molested them so I creep along the side.

I put my goggles on and did a few lengths. The woman shifted over slightly to one side. After ten lengths I went into backstroke. I can usually tell where I am and keep in a straight-ish line. The other swimmer had also switched to backstroke. We collided and both went under, arms flailing.

I collected myself first, since I could stand at the bottom, and concentrated on getting the water out of my sinuses as quickly as possible. She came to the surface, coughing and sputtering, tugging off her nose clips, the goggles, and even the cap. It was Amanda.

We apologized to each other rather stiffly and I started to wade away when she reached out and touched my shoulder.

"Nick, do you want to have a drink somewhere afterwards?"

I turned, surprised.

"Sure," I said as her face crumpled and she burst into tears.

"Was that the wrong answer?" I asked before wading back and putting my arms around her. She was a good height for me. She laid her head against my neck, put her arms around my back, and sobbed and sobbed.

To keep my balance I had to keep going up on tiptoe. I was conscious of her breasts pressing against my chest, her hips pressed against the tops of my thighs. We broke the embrace a few moments later. She gave me a knowing look, slightly under-cut by the fact she had thin strings of clear slime hanging from her nose over her top lip.

Actually, I found this quite intoxicating. I reached across with a wet finger and gently brushed her top lip free. She looked at me, said "What?" then tried to restrain me, giving a little shriek. She turned away and busied herself with two hands as she walked towards the shallow end.

"Better?" she asked turning her face to me.

"Perfect," I said, unable to stop a glance at her now uncovered breasts and belly. She caught my look and repeated it down my chest and abdomen.

She looked me in the eye. "I don't really want to swim anymore."

"Me neither," I said quickly. "Are you a jacuzzi sort of girl?"

"I've never much cared for communal bathing. I always wonder if all those suds are soap."

She took ten minutes longer than me in the changing rooms. But then, unlike me, she didn't smell of chlorine anymore. She smelt of Chanel 19, one of my favorite perfumes. She'd also put her makeup on carefully.

"A gift," she said, holding her hand out solemnly.

I held out my hand and she dropped into it a soggy tissue, a mischievous smile on her face.

"Something to remember me by—*mucus mutandis*."

"*Mucus mutandis*? I prefer the Beatles classic 'While My Catarrh Gently Weeps.'"

"Not bad. You should be a comedian."

"So should you."

"Watch where you're treading, buster. Giant ego at large."

"You got time for a walk to your coffee?"

"I have all day." She looked at me in a way I hoped was significant.

"Ah. I don't. Got a lunch appointment then I've got to be at the Comedy Museum by four."

She laughed, "I wasn't asking for your itinerary."

I flushed.

"I know. There's a nice street of cafes a couple of blocks away. Tables on the pavement in tree shade, that kind of thing."

We didn't say much as we walked. I didn't ask why she'd cried and she wasn't ready to tell me. At least not until we sat and ordered tisanes and hot croissants.

"I'm sorry I was so pompous last night."

"I'm sorry I was so crude. I didn't intend any offence."

"I know. I was feeling sensitive about it. It didn't work out as I had imagined."

"Did you go to bed with him?"

"No. I went to bed with her." She frowned. "Juliette."

"Ah. How was it?"

"Horrible. Not because it was another woman. It's never appealed but I've nothing, you know, against it. I thought it would be nice and if not nice then gentle."

"But it wasn't."

"I feel abused. I told her I was new to this but she didn't care."

Neither of us spoke for a moment.

"Is she likely to want a second, ah, bite of your cherry?"

Amanda giggled and wagged her finger at me.

"Well, she's not getting one. I've never understood people who like rough sex or hurting people. Sadism—biting the hand that feels you …"

We both grinned at her joke.

"When will you hear about your spot on the show?"

"She said she'd let me know." Amanda looked off down the street, her face suddenly hard. Tough business full of tough people. She seemed too nice for it.

"Is Juliette discreet?"

"Who knows?" Amanda said.

"So you didn't get to see Cash's penthouse suite?"

"Oh, I did. She took me up there. I thought I was meeting

Cash right until the moment she moved on me in the lounge."
She shuddered.

"Why didn't you stop her?"

"I figured I'd got this far I had to go through with it." Amanda
suddenly reached a hand out and gripped mine. "Christ, you
don't think Cash was watching, do you? I assumed he was out
for the night. Maybe he took a video to show to his friends. Do
you think he gets off watching Juliette with straight women?"

From what Hewitt had told me, Cash had lived a fairly wild
life.

"It's possible. I don't know the guy. But I can't imagine
watching Juliette have sex is much of a turn-on."

"Maybe you're right."

"So what's the view like from up there?"

"The view?"

"Yeah. Can you see the pool, for example?"

She frowned.

"Peculiar questions journalists ask. Actually, no you can't.
He's on the other side of the hotel looking west. Why?"

"Just curious."

I walked Amanda back to the hotel and we parted with a hug
and a soft kiss on the lips. She held my gaze as she kissed me.

"Where are you performing next?"

"Club Soda tomorrow night. A bilingual show called 'Lost
In the Translation.'"

"I'll come down, if I may." She nodded.

Now don't get me wrong here. I'm no Lothario. I know I'd
slept with Ruthie the night before but that had been a compan-
ionable fuck, with nothing deeper on either side. Amanda now
… be still my beating heart. This could get heavy.

Frank and Bridget were already in the restaurant when I arrived.

It was another sunny day and my sunglasses were sliding down my nose.

"Hey, shagger!" Bridget called loudly across the restaurant. I blushed as the other diners looked across at me.

"Hey, team," I said, plonking myself down and turning my glass right-side up.

"So how was your night?" Bridget leered.

"How come you know everything?" I said.

"Evidence of witnesses, knowledge of you and a tabloid mentality trapped in the body of a broadsheet writer. How was she?"

"Who?"

"The photographer *Global Village* fired. See—I do know everything."

"We had a very pleasant evening and she may have evidence of use to our investigation."

"Shagging in the line of duty." Frank said. "How selfless, Nicholas."

I helped myself to the wine and took my first sip of the day.

"Where are we at?"

Frank and Bridget smirked at each other.

"That smarmy PR Steve Hewitt was definitely in room 1814 the night Cissie Parker died," Frank said. "Your friend Gerard confirmed he signed a room service bill for wine and sandwiches at around three in the morning."

"So what do you think? They had some wine and then food, then he beat her up and dumped her out of the window?"

"I've had dates like that," Bridget said.

"Did anyone see him with Cissie that evening?"

"We don't know," Frank said. "Nobody will talk to us."

"Have you given up on the comedian—what's his name— Phil Peters?"

"Not likely. I checked in the apartment block where Cissie

was staying. The one right across from the hotel. The concierge remembers Phil Peters coming and going several times in the past few days."

"With Cissie?"

"No, but presumably on his way to and from her."

"And on the night in question?"

"The bloke can't remember and no one else is talking. Even the Brits who hate the little shit close ranks as soon as we even hint at anything," Bridget said sourly. "I can't find out anything about him except from him, and he isn't talking to me either, you'll be surprised to hear."

"Well, I've got a lot of news for you." I told them the story Ruthie had told me the night before.

"You think the mugging was linked to the photographs rather than to this other police harassment thing?" Frank said thoughtfully.

"It would fit our scenario of someone else's involvement in Cissie's death. But I would think it might let Phil Peters off the hook. It wasn't him doing the mugging and where's he going to hire the muscle in a strange city?"

"I think the mugging is coincidence," Bridget said. "But when can we see the photographs?"

"I'm collecting them from her straight after this lunch. Let's meet tonight."

I reached the Comedy Museum dead on four but it was closed. According to the sign on the door it had been closed all day. I stood watching the traffic on Lawrence Boulevard, Montreal's main north-south thoroughfare. A taxi pulled up but it was just a couple of geeks heading off towards Sherbooke. It was still hot and humid. Rivulets of sweat trickled from my hairline and dripped off my ears.

The museum, devoted to all kinds of humor through the ages, was housed in a nineteenth century industrial building, the old Ekers brewery. At ten after four I walked its length looking for another entrance. There were double doors about twenty yards down but they were locked. I went back to the main entrance and peered through the glass. I tried the door. It opened.

Cue sinister music. The late afternoon sunlight streaming through the windows provided the only light in the foyer. It was deserted and very quiet.

"Ruthie!" I called half-heartedly. Silence.

I walked up an incline on to a bridge over a sunken court-yard. It was at the base of a three-storey light well, an atrium that acted as the focal point of the museum. The courtyard was the site of the Humour Hall of Fame, its walls hung with photographs of comedians who had been honored by admission to it.

The last time I'd been here it was to see Leo Bassi, the Italian clown who looks like a bank manager, give an extremely dull lecture entitled "What is Comedy?" That was shortly before he organized a slapstick fight on Rue St. Denis in which the mayor of Montreal was savagely beaten about the head with custard pies.

The exhibition rooms on this floor were lit only by dull red emergency exit and fire warning lights. There was a central stair-well that linked with each floor. I figured Ruthie must be in the admin offices, maybe doing a photo shoot.

I walked up one flight of stairs and across to the elevators. I heard the elevator bell, then I was startled to see a punchinello and a clown walk out of the elevator. The punchinello was hump-backed, grimacing, wearing a hook-nosed face mask, and carrying a stout club. The clown was in oversized shoes, pancake makeup, and a red mophead wig.

They stopped when they saw me and looked at each other. I smiled and moved to go past them into the elevator. Punch hit me over the head with his big club.

"Ouch!" I yelled, ducking instinctively. It had hurt, even if the club was only hollow plastic. "Ha-ha—"

Coco the Clown shot his oversized foot out and tripped me. I managed to stop myself from falling and turned to face them.

"Come on guys, leave it alone," I said as calmly as I could. Punch took another swing at my head. I ducked and caught sight of Coco's face. He looked kind of angry. I realized these guys were for real.

I abhor all violence. I don't mean I'm a pacifist, I mean I'm a coward. Always have been. Partly it's a morbid hatred of physical contact, specifically contact with knuckles and feet. I haven't the first clue how to fight. At school I used to use what Woody Allen once described as the old Navajo Indian trick of grovelling and pleading.

However, the yoga and a little tsai chi that I do means I can adopt martial-looking postures. Sometimes they're enough to scare people off. Other times I get the shit beaten out of me.

I looked at Coco and Punch and dropped into a tsai chi pose called something like "stroking the bird's tail," which I usually think of as washing the duck. They paused. Then I did a very high kick, courtesy of my uthitha hasta padangusthasana yoga practice. James Coburn carries it off in *Pat Garrett and Billy the Kid,* but I was worried I just looked like a Tiller Girl.

It stopped them long enough for me to turn and run for the elevator. I jabbed the first button my finger touched and the doors started to close. Coco jammed his foot between them but I leaned forward and pressed the flat of my hand against his bright red conk. He fell back, the doors closed, and I was on my way into the bowels of the comedy museum.

A French accented voice came over the loudspeaker fixed in the wall of the elevator. "As a comedian I want to make you laugh. As a Frenchman I don't care." I remembered this from my last visit. Throughout the museum you are bombarded with one liners and hysterical laughter. A German voice, "My first joke. Take my wife—I command you."

When the elevator stopped and the doors opened I walked gingerly through a history of comedy, from Neanderthal man (a clip from the film *Quest For Fire)* through the Greek civilization (papier mache columns and animatronic orators) to the *commedia dell arte*. The room had been created as a Canadian version of an Italian market place. Shingle roofs, cobbled courtyard, small stage. No Punchinello. Yet.

"Ruthie," I called. All around were crowd noises—rhubarb in Canadian Italian. Then more one-liners. I recognized a snatch of the great Max Miller's rapid fire patter: "'Ere missis, I don't care what I say, do I? I don't! I don't! Honest I don't!"

I was halfway through the room, heading for a narrow passage, when Punch appeared again. I didn't know if Ruthie had set me up or if she was in some kind of danger too, but I had no time to think about it now. Punch came toward me very quickly, the club raised above his head. I didn't get this, what damage could he do with a rubber club? Then I saw the writing on it— The Toronto Sluggers—and ducked just as the baseball bat whistled past my head and gouged a hole in the wall beside me.

As Punch struggled to free the bat, I dodged past him down the corridor, eyes peeled for Coco the Clown. I slipped on an extremely large banana skin and slid, ass first, into the next room. I lay there looking round me. Hysterical laughter ricocheted out of hidden speakers. Ha-bloody-ha.

I stood up and looked round to see Punch hopping nimbly after me. A sign on the wall said "Interactive Slapstick." I hate slapstick. I hoped Punch would slip on the banana skin but he leaped across it and came for me. He was a fit bloke.

Most of the space was taken up with a half-built house. I ran into it and trod on a loose board. I ducked when I saw a plastic bucket at the far end of the board arc into the air toward me. It passed over my head and I looked back to see it land with spectacular precision over Punch's head, drenching him from head to toe in some kind of bright yellow goo.

There were two doorways ahead of me. I ran at the nearest and ricocheted back again. It was a *trompe l'oeil* doorway. The hysterical laughter was unrelenting.

Punch pulled off the bucket and hurled it into the corner. I dashed toward the second doorway. This one had a door and it was ajar. I thought to look up. Another bucket was balanced on the top of the door and the lip of the doorframe. I edged through without moving it. Fooled you, I thought smugly just as a custard pie hit me in the face.

I staggered to my left, blinded for a moment. I got the goo out of my eyes in time to see Punch burst through the door. The second bucket landed over his head.

We were in a kitchen. A mechanical figure dressed to look like a matronly cook was making pies a few yards away on a long table. She picked a pie up and hurled it at the doorway. It hit the outside of Punch's bucket.

I grabbed a bottle from the kitchen table and walloped the bucket over Punch's head with it. Had this been a slapstick film the bucket would have been metal and Punch would have passed out listening to the bells of Notre Dame. As it was the bucket was plastic, the bottle made of sugar glass. It disintegrated in my hands. I kicked him in the balls instead.

Dodging custard pies the cook had speeded up, swivelling from side to side as she threw, I dashed toward the back door. A stepladder stood in the entrance to the door. Was I stupid enough to go under a stepladder? I edged to the left and Coco the Clown belted me in the ear.

I fell against the ladder and went sprawling with it to the ground. I heard Coco shout and turned my head in time to see a sack of flour explode over his head. I scrambled away to the center of the room where a builder was carrying a plank of wood across his shoulders. I knew this gag. "Hey," I called and the builder swung round toward me, catching Coco full in the face with the plank. I laughed despite my perilous position but Coco stayed standing. The plank was made of sponge.

Coco was joined by Punch and they both headed my way, one covered in flour, the other in bright yellow slop. Punch was cursing, boy was he pissed. I noticed Coco had swapped his boots for sneakers. I hate sneakers outside of a gym, don't you?

There was a long ladder to my left leading on to the roof of the faux house. I took it two rungs at a time and spotted the trick rung in time to avoid it. I hit the roof in seconds. Coco was on the ladder. He hit the trick rung just as Punch got to the bottom of the ladder. All the rungs retracted and Coco slid back down, landing on Punch. Some days some people should just stay home in bed.

I made a crouching run across the roof towards an exit sign. The roof opened beneath me just as I reached the sign and I plunged down on to a brass bed in a turn of the century boudoir. The bed was more like a trampoline. As I bounced up almost to the ceiling I saw two dummies bounce out of the bed to the sound of a loud alley-oop from a nearby speaker.

It took me a couple more bounces to come to a halt. I dashed to the door, grabbed the knob. It came off in my hands. I hit the door with the flat of my hand, looked around for another means of escape. The window looked out on to a rose garden. The window and rose garden were painted on to a paper screen. I walked through the screen leaving a pleasing silhouette behind. I had an idea. I nipped back to the boudoir and checked the window on the other side. Same thing. I walked through that one too. Confusion to the enemy. I rushed at the third wall, hit it, and bounced back. Oh well. Two out of three ain't bad.

It was almost pitch dark behind the scenes. I climbed under

some tubular steel scaffolding and came out beside a staircase with three landings. A notice stated the staircase had been constructed in remembrance of the Quebecois comic Max Linder.

I'd turned the first landing before it sank in. In *Max Linder Takes a Bath*, Linder was caught on the staircase from hell. As I took the next step the whole thing started to lurch from side to side. I grabbed for the banister. It came away in my hand. I was swaying there, holding a three-foot length of banister when the tread I was on gave way.

One leg sank through. Somebody grabbed hold of my foot and twisted. Hard. I yelped, kicked out, and with a mighty effort pulled my leg free. I took the stairs to the next landing three at a time. Coco had started up the stairs behind me. Punch was waiting for me on the third landing. When he saw me hesitate below him he started to come down. The stairs flipped and the staircase between landings two and three turned into a slide. He came down flat on his back, legs spread. When he reached me I kicked him in the balls again. It just wasn't his day.

I hauled myself up by the banister to the next landing and took an exit back into the main display rooms. I was in the cafe-cum-lecture theater.

I was worried about Ruthie. If she hadn't set me up—and I couldn't imagine it—she might already have been injured. These guys were playing for keeps. If I was to survive this I needed a weapon. I scrabbled through the props someone had been using for a lecture or demonstration on circus sideshows. I picked up a sword swallower's sword. Years ago I was a very keen fencer. I was pretty good, largely because my terror at being hit made me very fast.

I heard footsteps behind me. Punch and his baseball bat. I went *en garde*. My problem was that if I tried to parry the sword would shatter but if I thrust at him I might kill him. Then again, he was trying to brain me.

I let him move to within about six feet of me then I took a quick step forward and lunged. It was a strong lunge, straight off my back leg, the sword a stiff extension of my outstretched arm. And it was fast. I hit him solidly between his right shoulder and his neck.

I knew I'd missed bone but I was expecting some resistance. There was none. The blade went straight in. And in. I almost overbalanced as I reached the full extent of my lunge. I'd just pushed eight inches of steel through him as easily as putting a knife through butter.

He looked startled, which I could understand. I was even more startled when he carried on moving toward me, pushing another six inches of sword into him. I twigged a moment before he did. My faith in sword swallowers shattered. A bloody retractable sword. I pulled back and kicked him in the balls.

"Johnny, we gotta get outa here," I heard a voice call from the cinema on the other side of the cafe. I dashed into the next room, which was filled with about fifty bright yellow waterproof coats with hoods on coat hangers suspended from the ceiling. How should I know why? A screen on the wall was showing an early silent of a storm at sea.

"Johnny?" The voice was nearer. I fumbled in my pocket for the packet of matches I'd picked up in Bridget's cafe. Striking one I lit the rest and reached up, wafting them beneath a fire sensor in the low ceiling.

"Charlie, what the fuck?" I heard the voice from the cafe, then the fire alarm went off and the sprinklers came on full force.

I hid at the far end of the room, snuggled in beneath a waterproof coat, the water sluicing down all around. I didn't hear my pursuers again, but after a time I heard other voices coming nearer. I left my hiding place and threaded my way between the hanging coats. I noticed one at the far end looked bulkier than the others. I walked slowly across to it.

Ruthie was draped across the steel hanger at the end of one of the steel chains, a waterproof over her shoulders, her baseball cap pulled down over her face. Her head was tipped forward, her legs trailed on the floor. She looked very dead.

The police kept me four hours. I must say the museum staff, whilst being tremendously pissed off with me, were great. A French-speaking deputy manager came down the nick with me.

I thought at first I was a witness but then I realized they had it in mind to finger me for Ruthie's death. I refused to say any-more until they'd got hold of the consul for me. I wasn't entirely sure what consuls did but it seemed the right thing to do.

I was wrong. He was on his way to some posh do in a monkey suit and medals. He didn't appreciate being bothered. I'm sure I heard him ask in rapid French about the death penalty in Quebec.

Okay, so my story was a little fragile. I was found in the Comedy Museum on a day it was closed, with a dead woman. I claimed to have been chased by Coco the Clown and a Punch with a bad hump. Thousands of dollars worth of damage had been done to the museum both in the slapstick room and because of the sprinklers, which I admitted setting off. I had also admit-ted I spent the previous night with the girl, whom of course the police knew and loathed.

I was pretty shaken up. I'd never seen a dead person before. Especially someone I'd known so intimately a few hours before. I kept thinking about Ruthie's little daughter.

I told the consul our theories about Cissie Parker's death. He wasn't interested.

"You're journalists—you would look for a sensational story."

"I write about the arts for God's sake. I'm not exactly a new-shound."

"Her death was either suicide or accidental death," he said curtly. "Frankly the woman wasn't worth a damn. Using that amount of drugs when she was pregnant."

I could see the consul make an almost physical attempt to take his words back.

"She was pregnant?" I said.

"Apparently," he said tersely.

"How far along?" I said.

"That's irrelevant to your present situation unless it transpires you had something to do with it."

"Please. How far?"

"Six weeks. I suppose there's no point asking you to keep that to yourself."

" I'm hardly going to broadcast it. But that makes it even more likely that we're right. There was no reason for Cissie to kill herself and no reason for her to go back to taking drugs, especially if she was pregnant."

"Perhaps she didn't want the baby."

"So she threw herself off a tall building? They have such things as abortions, even in Quebec."

"Perhaps she didn't know she was pregnant."

"Possible. Look, maybe we should present you with a formal report. Then you can get something under way. You do look after the rights of the British here I presume?"

"She wasn't British. She had taken out American citizenship." The consul looked down his nose at me. "As I understand it the authorities are happy it was a case of misadventure. They don't—and I don't—want three members of the British press ferreting around for sleazy stories, making up God knows what."

"We don't make things up. You're mixing us up with proper journalists."

"Nevertheless. Now I've persuaded the authorities to let you go, but it is on the understanding that you don't concern your-self with the Cissie Parker case or indeed this case anymore."

"What about Ruthie? Who killed her?"

"You tell me. There's no evidence that anyone but you and she were in the Comedy Museum."

"So how did I kill her? I forget."

"You broke her neck."

I looked at the ground in front of me. I might be joking but this was no laughing matter. I could see Ruthie's gap-toothed grin.

"So how come they're letting me go?"

"There's a scintilla of doubt about your guilt."

"A scintilla," I said flatly. "Nice one. Of what does this scin-tilla consist?"

"They found a clown's and a punchinello's costume aban-doned near the back exit. A witness saw two gentlemen rush into the street in a great hurry at the time you were discovered in the museum."

"Bastards! So they knew all the time I was telling the truth."

"There's some confirmation for your story. *They* will explore the possibilities. They emphasize this. You should get on with your job."

"I will. But it leaves me so much free time."

I got back to the hotel around nine. I didn't feel like talking to anyone so I went straight to my room, cracked a half bottle of wine from the room bar, and ordered a room service club sand-wich. I selected a film on the video channel and sat cross-legged on the bed until the food arrived. Then I hunkered down in bed, drinking, eating, and not really watching the film. Cost ten bucks too. Things must be serious.

Ruthie's card and her handwritten note were on the bedside table. I didn't know what I felt about her death. I didn't care for her deeply, I hadn't known her long enough. But she had touched me. She had been giving and gentle and sad. And I felt sorry for her. My fatal flaw.

Ruthie probably had a drug problem. Was she also a fantasist or was she telling the truth about the police harassment? I decided to check the back issues of the local papers the next day and pick up the story. I also wanted to check with the newspaper about the photos she had of Cissie Parker. She didn't have them on her when the police examined her body.

Could Punch and Coco have been off-duty policemen out to get her? But why attack me? If they were linked with Cissie Parker's death in some way, who had hired them? I couldn't see Phil Peters, an English comic a long way from home, having the contacts. Steve Hewitt was new in town but he might know the right people. Or it might be somebody totally different.

When I'd finished the food and wine and the movie was over I lay back and tried to sleep. I couldn't. I was feeling mawkish and self-pitying. I cried. Only after another half bottle did I go into a deep sleep.

I was woken by a loud hammering on the door. Blearily, I looked at my wristwatch. It was already nine in the morning. I let Bridget and Frank in.

"You haven't been to bed, right?" I said, looking at the state of the pair of them. They both looked as if they'd been poured into their clothes and forgotten to say when.

"You must have a very low opinion of us," Bridget said, settling down on my bed, scanning the empty wine bottles and food plate. "Only one glass. You getting a fixation with yourself, Nick?"

"It happens that you're right, Nicholas," Frank said, having clearly drunk himself sober. "It was some cable show's breakfast party—and you were not in attendance."

I got back under the blankets, casually tidying away Ruthie's note and card into the bedside table drawer. Frank wandered over to the window. Cable show breakfasts traditionally started at three in the morning. For Los Angeles people who are in bed by nine it was easy, they had their six hours sleep then got up again. The rest of us were still usually up from the night before and a little the worse for wear. In my case, usually a lot the worse for wear.

"We came hammering on your door at three in the morning to get you but you weren't answering," Bridget said.

"Early night."

"You all right, old chap?" Frank came over from the window, where he'd clearly been reconstructing the fall of Cissie Parker, complete with whistling noise as she went past, and a quick ker-plump as she hit the pool. He touched my shoulder. "You seem a bit peeky."

"Was nobody talking about what happened in the Comedy Museum yesterday? Was Steve Hewitt not around?"

"Steve Hewitt was noticeable by his absence," Bridget said as she raided the mini-bar for a bottle of wine. "What happened at the Comedy Museum?"

"It's only nine o'clock," I protested as she passed me a glass of what proved to be very palatable Chardonnay. I told them what had happened to Ruthie and my own experience in the Comedy Museum. They sat down either side of me on the bed and each squeezed a hand.

"Poor love," Frank said.

"I'm going to the newspaper office to check this stuff about Ruthie and the police—the party bust she's supposed to have witnessed and photographed."

The phone rang. Bridget was nearest so she took it, though I knew if it was Amanda I'd get shit for hours. Bridget put the phone down.

"Why do you want to interview Phyllis Diller?" she said.

"To get a look at the penthouses."

"You don't like your room?"

"I was thinking of a third option for Cissie's death."

"What—she was smoking crack with Phyllis and fell off the roof?" Bridget cackled. I hadn't really heard a cackle until then. Cackles and chortles all on one trip. Life wasn't so bad.

"There are four penthouses. We can discount Billy Cash's because it faces the wrong way. Diller has another one. Bradley Stokes has the third. Now he knew Cissie. He's in a film with her."

"She killed herself for Bradley Stokes?" Bridget laughed again, less cackle, more withering contempt.

"Or he killed her. Maybe he had a thing for her and she wasn't playing. We all know about Fatty Arbuckle." Bradley Stokes was about seventeen stone, one of those comics who'd carved a niche for themselves by being comforting. A shoulder to cry on in mawkish sitcoms. Discomfited by animals and kids in family movies. A John Goodman, John Candy kind of guy.

"Worth having a look," Frank said, nodding sagely. "Who is in the fourth penthouse? Gerard could tell us."

"Bollocks," Bridget said. "What about the floors between eighteen and the penthouses? Why aren't they as likely as the penthouses? We need to get Gerard working on who's in the fourteen room on each floor."

"What time's my interview, Bridget?"

"Five this afternoon. You'll just be back from the rapids."

"The rapids? Today?"

I groaned. Montreal was founded at the confluence of two rivers that combine to form the St. Lawrence Waterway. Where the two rivers meet there is a hazardous series of rocks and rapids. A number of boat companies down on the harbor run regular trips out in flat-bottomed boats for groups of fifty or so to ride the rapids. It's a rough ride—a very rough ride—but there was a tradition at the festival that all the VIPs did the trip at least once.

"I don't think I'm up to the rapids this year."

"Sure you are," Bridget said. "Frank's never done it and he's feeling a little twitchy so you've got to help him out."

"I really don't know."

"You're doing it. Eleven in the foyer. And don't give me any morning shit. We're going to nail the people who did this, but who knows who else may be on the boat, eh? You've time to scoot down to the newspaper first."

Frank grinned. I noticed for the first time the gap between his front teeth.

"Okay," I said. "Oh, two more things. According to Ruthie, Steve Hewitt likes beating up women. And according to the consul, Cissie Parker was pregnant."

I got back to the hotel with minutes to spare. Around forty people were milling in the hallway. Billy Cash's agent, Juliette Smith, was talking to her big guy with the dork knob. Amanda was over on the other side of the foyer. When she waved I noticed Juliette and the dork knob both giving me a hard look. Frank's murder suspect, Steve Hewitt, was there talking to Lenny Finnegan. Bridget's preferred suspect, Phil Peters, and a small English contingent were puffing away on what they clearly thought were the last cigarettes of condemned men.

Bridget and Frank were sitting on the stairs by themselves. Rule one for the rapids ride is that you wear your oldest clothes. Bridget and Frank had taken this to extremes. Bridget was wearing ripped jeans that probably dated back to an early Glastonbury Festival and a crumpled T-shirt with golden glitter on it. Frank was wearing what I suspect were his old Scout shorts. His flabby legs were white and hairless. He was also wearing what looked remarkably like a green and blue wincyette pajama jacket.

Frank was hissing at Bridget, "Of course it must be Hewitt. He set those thugs on little Ruthie. Poor kid, I could have had a daughter her age."

"Genetic engineering hasn't developed that far and you didn't even know her."

"I can still empathize."

When I joined them on the stairs, Frank took my hand and squeezed it. He looked at me, his own eyes filled with tears.

"I know, Frank, I know." I smiled cheerily. "Nice shirt."

"Thank you, dear boy. It's my pajama jacket actually but I didn't think anyone would notice."

"No, no. It looks great."

"How did you get on at the newspaper office?"

"Picture editor is doing a late shift today so I can't find out about the photos until this afternoon. But I checked Ruthie's story out about the gay thing. She was telling the truth."

Five minutes later we went off in four buses down to the quayside. It was a bright, windy day. Down on the harbor the cocky guy in charge of the boat made us sit around on benches whilst he went through a long spiel about the cruise we were about to take. He cracked a few labored jokes—a big mistake given the company he was keeping. I kept glancing over at Amanda but she was sitting with two or three of the American comedians. I caught sight of Steve Hewitt glaring at Frank.

The guy from the boat company finally allowed us to go to change into our waterproofs. In a crude changing room the men stripped down to their Calvin Kleins—Frank kept his shorts on—and put on waterproof trousers, thick army surplus pullovers still soaked from their last use and waterproof jackets with elastic wrists and hoods. We each had a life jacket and rubber shoes, which felt as if they'd been cut from car tires.

We went outside to join the others. Bridget already looked like a drowned rat, although she was quite relaxed. She had done this once before. Frank looked like he didn't mind if he never did it.

"I can't swim actually, Nicholas."

"I've seen *Deliverance*. If we get into trouble, swimming won't save you."

"Nicholas, thanks for that."

Steve Hewitt was counting us on board and the officious guy was getting us settled. "I need my fags," Frank said as we were about to climb on board. He scurried back to the changing rooms.

"That's the last we'll see of him," Bridget said as we sat on the third row at the far side of the boat. I looked down into the water. Another four people squeezed on to our bench. Amanda turned and winked at me from the front row. Bridget caught it and gave me an arch look.

Frank stumbled back on board, a cigarette clamped between his teeth. Hewitt directed him to the back of the boat.

We had a four-mile trip out on the waterway until we hit the rapids. The boat was wide and low in the water. The skipper steered from a cockpit at the top of an eight-foot tower at the back, with a crew member fore and aft. We sat in our rows on the hard benches gripping long wooden bars that ran in front of us. I slipped my watch and some tissues into the waterproof bag in front of me. We'd been warned to take off all jewelery and even spectacles since the water would yank everything right away from us.

A photographer had snapped each of us as we got on the boat. As we passed under a high bridge we saw him standing on it. We were instructed to wave for another photograph.

It took a half an hour to reach the rapids. The St. Lawrence was about a quarter of a mile wide and relatively free of water transport. The sun was hot but the cold wet pullover next to my skin made me chilly.

Bridget and I didn't say much. Conversation around us was of business deals and bookings. I swear I saw business cards passing to and fro.

"I was on here one year when one of the British acts panicked and demanded to be taken back. The pilot wouldn't do it. This guy was almost having a fit but they took him anyway. Nearly killed him."

"Thanks, Bridget, that's just what I want to hear."

"You've done it before. You know what to expect. You have done it before haven't you?"

"I think now is a good time to tell you the truth. No."

"Oh sweetie, have you got a treat in store."

Our pilot had warned us that however well covered we were we would be soaked when the first wave hit us. It was an understatement. We skirted the rapids whilst watching another boat dip and slither through them. Then our pilot turned our boat and we plunged suddenly down. Water, hissing and pounding, rose up all around us as we bucked. I gripped the rail tightly. Bridget screamed. A wall of water some ten feet high broke over us from the right.

I hadn't expected the sheer force of it. It boxed my ears so hard they rang, lifted me right out of my seat and crushed me against the side of the boat. When the boat broke free, there was water three feet deep around our legs. My sinuses were in agony from the water forcing itself up my nose and down through my eye sockets. I could hear nothing but a loud roar.

Bridget pressed against me and shouted something. The boat raced through the boiling water past swirling and sucking whirlpools. I clung to the bar in front of me when the boat took a left turn and slid down into another great hole in the river. Another wall of water rose up on my left and lurched towards the boat.

I scarcely had time to regret that I was sitting at the side of the boat when the wave hit me like a wall of concrete. I thought it had taken my head off as again my feet left the deck and I was carried a good three feet across the bench, pushing Bridget along with me.

Everybody was screaming and hollering as the water sluiced round our feet and another wave came over the front of the boat, pounding us from above. I saw a couple of men looking shaken and scared.

Then we were back in a trough, the boat bucking, water breaking over us with phenomenal power and noise. The boat dropped down, sprang up, then swung into another wave that hit us head on. Only when we turned out of this did I catch sight of a life jacket swaying and bobbing in the water. As it was flung by the water this way and that I realized there was somebody in it. I grabbed Bridget and directed her attention to it. She yelled something at me but I still couldn't hear.

The person in the life jacket was at the mercy of the rapids, twisting and rolling, arms flung out, dragged under the water then tossed back out. Our pilot had seen the person, too. The boat aqua-planed as we pursued the body. It seemed weightless as the water carried it towards an outcrop of black rocks. It flopped on to them like a rag doll.

"Whoever it is can't be alive!" Bridget yelled. She was trying to look around, a task made difficult by the amount of wet clothes that were weighing her down. "Is it somebody from this boat or the other one?"

The crew had long poles with hooks on the end. They were trying to snag the body. It seemed to take an age. I was half-standing, gripping the bar in front of me, looking round the boat. Bridget was doing the same. A sort of numbness came over me as Bridget shouted what I had been wondering.

"Where's Frank?"

FOUR

"It's a funny word, *defenestrate*. Why a special word for throwing yourself out of a window? I mean how often do you get to use it? I looked it up in the dictionary once. First used in 1620. Was there a rash of people jumping out of windows around then?" I took another swig of my wine. "I've always wanted to use it and I thought Cissie's obituary provided the excuse. But then I realized I didn't know how. Is it 'Cissie Parker defenestrated,' 'Cissie Parker defenestrated herself,' or 'Cissie Parker was defenestrated'?"

Bridget looked at me with unfocused eyes but said nothing. She was holding her glass to her lips with both hands.

"And if you can defenestrate you must be able to fenestrate, mustn't you?" she finally said. "Throw yourself back in through a window? It could be some Einsteinian time relativity thing."

"*Refenestrate*. Fenestrate just means putting a window in."

"Wonder if there's a special word for throwing yourself out of a boat and drowning."

Bridget drained her glass. Her face was puffed and blotchy with crying and drinking. There were three empty bottles on the table next to a nearly empty fourth. The ashtray was overflowing with cigarillo and cigarette stubs.

"It was an accident, Bridget. He didn't do it deliberately."

"Knowing Frank, he'd have buggered it up—no pun

intended—if he had meant it. The old sod was so inept." She rubbed her eyes. "*Inept.* There's another word for you. If you can be inept you must be able to be 'ept' surely. That must give you hope, Nick."

I smiled glumly, looked back out of the window in my room. The sun was just disappearing behind the apartment block opposite. Bridget prised herself out of her chair and made her way to the bathroom. A few moments later I heard the sound of her throwing up. Sobbing and throwing up.

The skipper had radioed for help and a police cutter had joined us at the rapids within minutes. The cops had managed to get the body out of the water. As they hauled it on to their vessel I saw a flash of Frank's pajama sleeve above a pale wrist.

Back at the dock they'd questioned the crew and the few people sitting at the back of the boat. Bridget and I had formally identified Frank's body before it was taken away by the police. To be honest, he looked better dead than he had alive. He had a big bruise on his temple but his face was less ruddy, his expression less anguished than usual. I think Frank had been a very unhappy man.

"I'm going to stay to talk to the skipper," Bridget said. She shivered. There was a stiff wind blowing across the water and our clothes were sodden. I was feeling numb, inside and out.

"Let's get changed first."

In the changing room I rubbed myself down roughly with a towel. When I came back out the police had gone. Bridget was already sitting with the skipper, a tanned young guy with stringy blond hair and clear blue eyes. He looked wretched.

"Nick, this is John."

"Hi, John," I said, sitting on the other side of him.

"I'm real sorry about your friend," he said, looking at his feet. "I was just telling Bridget here, nothing like this has ever happened before."

"The police are assuming it was an accident," Bridget said.

"It couldn't have been anything else," John said.

"Did you see him fall out of the boat, John?"

He shook his head.

"First I saw, he was in the water. I'd seen him right at the outset because he'd been sitting on his own on one of the benches at the back of the boat. He was taking a nip from a hip flask. Tom, one of the crew, advised him to grip on to the bar in front once we got to the rapids." He wrung his hands. "Guess he didn't grip tight enough. But even then he shouldn't have gone in."

"How come?"

"The boats have got that yard wide walkway running all the way round them. It's really hard to fall out, especially with the water pushing in on you."

"So how'd he come to be in the water?" Bridget said quietly.

"Only way I can figure it—and forgive me for saying this about your friend—was that maybe he'd drunk a little too much and stood up for a better look or something. I try to keep my eyes open for stuff like that but when you're steering the boat round those rocks your attention has to be pretty focused."

Bridget looked across to the boat. "Was he sitting alone?"

"When I first noticed him he was. Don't know about later. There were two rows at the back with only a couple of people on each. It doesn't matter as long as you keep hold of the bar."

We thanked John and took a cab back to the hotel. As we made our way up to my room a few people came over to commiserate—a word, a pat on the back, a touch on the arm. In my room Bridget headed straight for the bar. Her tears didn't come until the third bottle.

"Poor old Frank," she sniffed. "Not even old. He was fifty-one. Maybe that is old for gays these days. He always drank too much but he was a bloody good sub. Hated the magazine. He only stayed for the money so he could take early retirement."

"What happened between his partner and him?"

"The usual story—thrown over for a younger boy. Neither was faithful, they liked to go and pick up younger men. But Alec fell in love with this guy. It was rotten because suddenly Frank's whole future, the future on which he'd been banking for years, was up in the air. I must phone Alec. He's an old tart but he did love Frank. He'll be devastated."

"Are there relatives we should ring?"

"His mother. But she's never forgiven him for squashing her cat."

"Come again?"

"He went to see her one day, having passed the pint of no return, and sat down like a sack of potatoes on the sofa without looking behind him. Heard this little 'ouf' of surprise. You can imagine the cat opening a sleepy eye to see what was blocking the sun and seeing a vast darkness descending—forever. What upset his mother was not that he'd squashed her little darling flat as a cartoon cat into the Dralon but that he didn't let on. He sat there for at least ten minutes holding a normal conversation with her. When he eventually levered himself up he made a fuss about her parrot to distract her—claimed he told her he'd had a cockatoo himself—then fled for it. She never mentioned it but their relationship was never the same after that."

Our laughter had a touch of hysteria in it. When we had calmed down I said, "What about the magazine?"

"I'll tell them tomorrow morning. I'll offer to do an obituary. There's nobody on the staff he'd want to do it. And it is my fault."

"Come again?"

"I should have remembered you need to hang on to the bar. You'd never been on the rapids before so how were you to know? But I knew. I should have thought that with his bad hand, how could Frank hold on tight?"

Bridget taking the blame was nonsense of course but I could do little to comfort her. Whilst she was in the bathroom I wondered if there was any way Frank's death might not have been an accident. Three deaths in four days and you start to get a little twitchy. But I couldn't see Steve Hewitt offing him just because Frank had embarrassed him with his wild assertions. Unless, of course, there was truth in them.

Bridget came out of the bathroom and crawled into my bed. She curled up into a tight ball and was asleep in moments. I was wide awake. Drink does that to me sometimes. It was six and I'd cancelled my interview with Phyllis Diller but I was reminded of the picture editor.

I looked across at Bridget. She'd be asleep for hours. I slipped out of the back exit of the hotel and picked up a taxi straightaway. In the air-conditioned room I'd forgotten how hot Montreal was, even at this time of day. Within five minutes I was sweating again. The taxi dropped me at the newspaper offices.

When I left, an envelope in my hand, I took a taxi down to the wharf. Bridget had polished off most of the booze in my room so I was relatively sober. Or at least at that level of drunkenness where I looked forward to a quiet drink and some time to think. I stopped at a cafe at the bottom of Rue Lachaise and ordered a beer at a table outside. A group of English students were sitting at the next table, noisily discussing their exploits travelling in North America.

I spent most of my early twenties travelling. In the long summer breaks from university and after for a couple of years, following what was left of the hippy trail, reduced by then to mounds of coke cans and used toilet paper. I was going in the steps of my father, strangely enough, an unreconstructed old hippy who'd taken me to the Isle of Wight Festival when I was five and a string of other festivals thereafter until I was old enough to get into punk and disgust him totally. By then I was pretty disgusted with him, too.

I came back to England from my travels wanting to be a writer. It didn't take me long to realize I had nothing to say. I said it anyway. I was renting a studio flat in Hammersmith and working on the "Great Novel." It was the mid-eighties and there was a boom in magazine publishing. I wrote a few articles about my travels and sent them, unsolicited, to these new mags. Some were used. I was asked to do other stuff. My career as a freelance journalist began.

I switched to newspapers, fondly imagining that if I could get one piece in a national newspaper a week I'd be living the good life. I would do journalism for one day and work on the novel for the other six. The problem was the newspapers paid such lousy money I needed to sell three pieces a week to make a decent living. I couldn't find that many features to write.

As it went on I got increasingly cynical about it. I regarded myself as a great prose stylist but I got work mostly because I could turn things round very fast. It started with a London daily. The news editor phoned the morning after the Oscars one year and asked me to do a piece about how Hollywood hated Warren Beatty.

"I don't think it does," I said.

"We'll pay you five hundred pounds."

"Then again, it might. When do you need it?"

"Soon."

"How soon?"

"An hour."

I did it. It was rubbish. They used it. A reputation was born. One of the nationals phoned.

"Hey, I hear you're quick at turning things round. I need eight hundred words on trash television in two hours."

I did it. It was rubbish. They used it. I did more for them. And for other nationals. I got hooked on the speed. If I had two weeks to do a piece I'd either leave it to the last minute or not do it at all. A frantic two hours, forcing my brain to work faster, trying for almost stream of consciousness elegance, was awful but exhilarating.

I sipped the beer I'd ordered and took the contact sheets out of the envelope. The picture editor, a good-looking young French guy, had really liked Ruthie and had been happy to help. As a *quid pro quo* I'd agreed to let his paper know early on if we came up with anything.

I looked at the contact sheets and prints. Ruthie hadn't been a great photographer but at least they were in focus. They were unflattering in the way flash photographs from parties always are, freezing mobile faces into eye-popping, leering expressions. There were around a dozen ten by eights of Cissie Parker.

One showed her with her arms round Juliette, who looked uncomfortable. In the background was Juliette's colleague with the dork knob. Two were of Cissie laughing with Bradley Stokes. Nothing I could read into their body language. There was one of her listening intently to—here we go—the PR, Steve Hewitt. One of her planting a big smacker on the cheek of a very happy-looking Phil Peters. A few others of her with small groups of people. And then one curious one of her looking startled as if Ruthie had surprised her doing something she shouldn't be doing.

I looked more closely at this one. The flash had been very bright on Cissie, bleaching her, whilst almost missing the man she was sitting with. His face was turned away from the camera—deliberately?—and with dark hair and dark clothes he almost merged with the dark background. Cissie's white hand gripped his arm.

I looked back at the photos of Cissie with Phil Peters and Steve Hewitt. Both were wearing dark clothes, both had dark hair. Steve Hewitt was too short to be the mystery man but Phil Peters, as far as I could judge, looked to be about the right size.

I didn't know much about Phil. I'd seen him on TV and at the Comedy Store, doing his stuff, but he was one of those interchangeable stand-ups—good but not great, not distinctive enough. He was a bit of a coke fiend and a womanizer. I think Bridget had had a thing with him, which he'd broken off. A brave man. There are women scorned and then there's Bridget. I'd already been wondering if that was why she was so determined to link him to Cissie Parker's death.

It was nine o'clock. Did I want to go back to my room? Bridget would still be passed out. I had an urge to see Amanda. She was doing her Club Soda gig on Parc Avenue tonight. I'd raise a glass for Frank there.

I was unsteady on my feet when I got up from the table. I got the cab to go via the hotel so I could drop the photographs off at reception to collect later. Ten minutes after, I jumped the long queue outside Club Soda, flashing my tag at the doorman to get straight in. Well, yes, I do love doing that.

I was surprised to see Amanda standing with Juliette Smith and a couple of other people near the bar. I was even more surprised when she rushed over to me and gave me a big hug.

"I'm so sorry about your friend Frank," she said. "What a terrible thing. Are you okay?"

I nodded.

"Come over and meet the others." She took my hand and led me towards Juliette.

"I thought you'd be in the toilet throwing up with nerves," I said.

"I'm not on for another hour—lots of time for that yet," she said brightly. A little too brightly. She seemed very hyper. Because of the gig or because Juliette was here?

"You know what Lea says about the classic stand-up profile?" Amanda said. "The insecure egomaniac. I think I'm a piece of dung the whole world revolves around."

We reached Juliette, who thrust her hand out at me.

"Hello, I'm Juliette Smith." She had one of those very limp, I-don't-really-want-to-be-doing-this handshakes. She introduced me to an agent and a manager whose names I instantly forgot.

"Steve Hewitt tells me you want to interview my clients Bradley Stokes and Billy Cash."

"You manage Bradley Stokes too? I didn't realize."

"Are these magazine pieces?"

I nodded.

"Cover stories?"

"Can't guarantee that but they will be major features, three thousand word jobs."

"Tell you the truth, Nick. Billy's not doing any interviews right now. He's come down with some darn bug and he's feeling fifty kinds of shitty." She leaned conspiratorially into me, wafting expensive perfume. "Off the record we're not sure he's going to be well enough to do his gigs, which he's incredibly upset about."

"Sorry to hear that. Another time maybe. What about Stokes?"

"Bradley is possible. How long you in town for?"

"Another four or five days."

"I'll talk to him. Billy, you know, is going to your Edinburgh Festival with his one man show."

"I didn't know."

"Sure. So you could talk to him there. Things will be a lot easier then. Actually, Bradley may be going over too, to promote his new film at the film festival. We're waiting for confirmation from the distributors."

All the time we'd been talking Juliette had fixed me with an unblinking stare. She was an attractive woman in a hard-bitten sort of way. Long black hair, a wide mouth. She had had a good figure once upon a time but now she was very plump. I couldn't help thinking of her with Amanda. I looked over at Amanda. She was watching us closely. I grinned and Juliette followed my look.

"You'd better be getting ready, hadn't you, dear?" Juliette said. Amanda gave a quick smile.

"Guess so. See you all later."

Juliette and I watched Amanda thread her way through the tables to the side of the stage and through the door to the dressing rooms. Juliette gave me an appraising look.

"Talented woman. But sometimes talent isn't enough. The right place at the right time. Or a friend in the right place."

"Absolutely," I said.

Juliette continued to look at me. I didn't attempt to meet her eyes. After a few more moments I thought I heard her sigh.

"I was sorry to hear about your friend," she said.

"Which one?" I said, looking past her to where the guy with the dork knob was easing his way along the crowded bar towards us.

"Your colleague. Frank, was it? Terrible thing to happen."

"Yeah. It was. Third death this week."

"Will you be making that a feature of your festival report?"

"I hadn't planned to."

"Good. You know, Nick, I heard stories about wild accusations your friend and another journalist were throwing around about the woman who fell to her death. Those kind of accusations can do nothing but harm. Harm to the reputations of serious journalists, harm to the individuals who are on the receiving end of these charges, harm to this festival, and harm to the comedy industry in general."

"But what if there's some truth in the accusations?"

"Are you saying that you know for certain that young woman's death was more than a drug-induced accident?"

"I don't know yet. It's possible."

"Well, until you do know, don't you think it's highly irresponsible to be making wild assertions? That kind of behavior isn't going to make you any friends here." She looked at me meaningfully. "And we all need friends."

She half turned as dork knob arrived.

"This is John Rolfe, my assistant. John say hello to Nick Madrid."

Rolfe nodded and held out his hand. He was a helluva big guy, with the impassively handsome face of a Steven Seagal. He had a firm handshake but didn't go in for the test-of-strength bullshit you often get. He watched as Juliette leaned close to me again.

"There are people here who can be very good friends to you." She tapped me lightly on my chest. "Or very bad enemies."

I stepped back a pace. "Including you?"

She looked at me for a moment then bestowed one of her rare smiles on me. "Let's watch the show."

It was billed as a bilingual comedy evening, with English speaking performers doing their acts in French and vice-versa. But the first act quickly figured out that most of the audience were Anglophone. She spoke in French for a couple of minutes, cleared her throat noisily, apologized for the frog in it, then continued in English.

I discovered later there were few francophones in the audience because, ironically, the title of the show—Lost In the Translation—didn't translate.

It was a curious night. Amanda did a good set. She got the local audience on her side by showing she'd done some local research. She made jokes about the language laws and about the Quebecois making money out of the contraband cigarette trade before going on to her standard set.

I'd moved away from Juliette to the bar but I watched her watch Amanda. There was a proprietorial look on her face. I glanced at Rolfe and was unnerved to catch him, in turn, staring at me.

Whilst Quebec's most popular comedian, Marie-Lise Pilote, was doing her best-known character, La Mechante, the nosy neighborhood snoop, I pondered Juliette's words. Had she been giving me words of wisdom? Or threatening me? Was she warning me off investigating Cissie Parker's death because Bradley Stokes was involved? I glanced across at Rolfe. John Rolfe. In the Comedy Museum, Coco the Clown had called Punch *Johnny.* I shivered suddenly, as if someone had walked over my grave. Or Ruthie's grave.

Amanda reappeared at Juliette's side. She smiled over at me. When Pilote finished with her trademark line, "*Eh, que je suis mechante,*" Juliette turned to Amanda and spoke to her for a few moments. Amanda snatched quick glances across at me as she listened. She nodded meekly at Juliette. When Juliette turned to speak to Rolfe, Amanda slipped away to me.

"Eh, but I am so bad!" she said, mimicking Pilote's catchphrase.

"You were great," I said.

"And you are a man of great taste. I kept wondering if I had enough punch lines. You know some guy from *The Tonight Show* was telling me that to go over well a comic should aim for twenty-five punch lines in six minutes. On the Showtime channel, programs now have minute by minute ratings."

"Terrifying. And did you get good advice from Juliette?"

"She had a couple of things to say about the act, sure. Looks like I'm going to be on the show, so what I did wasn't in vain."

I nodded, looked back at the stage. I couldn't quite figure Amanda's mood this evening. But then I hardly knew her. I focused on the stage. Judy Toll was getting some big laughs. "What do you call that insensitive bit of skin behind the penis? Oh yeah. The guy."

Amanda smirked.

"When I first started doing stand-up all the women comics did were jokes about menstruation or gynaecology," she said. "I really resent women's hygiene products that makes the user look like she's smuggling a canoe in her knickers—that kind of stuff. Things are moving on these days, thank God."

We watched the act until Amanda leaned against me and put her mouth to my ear. "Listen, Nick. I'm in the mood to party. I've got some toot back in my apartment. Want to come back with me?"

I actually hesitated. I was feeling shitty about Ruthie and Frank. Amanda's breath tickled all the way down my spine. But maybe I needed to let myself go, to release some of that pent-up emotion. Then again, maybe I was just justifying my rampant lust for this woman.

"So what are we waiting for?"

We slipped out without saying goodbye to Juliette. I felt a momentary guilt about Bridget. But hell, I could maybe call her from Amanda's. In the taxi Amanda twined herself around me, kissing me hungrily, her tongue probing my mouth. When we reached the apartment block across from the hotel we rushed to the elevator. Amanda was not exactly backward at coming forward. She unzipped my fly and put her hand inside, pressing her body against me.

We fell into her apartment and straight into her bedroom. She scrabbled backwards on to her bed, her eyes slitted, a lascivious look on her face, her breath coming in pants. My pants were already round my ankles. She pulled her blouse over her head and popped her tiny bra off, her breasts quivering. She looked at the bulge in my shorts.

"I see you're smuggling a big canoe," she said huskily.

I didn't like to slow the momentum, but I had some urgent business to attend to.

"Won't be a second. Wait there."

I dashed to the bathroom, cursing the beer I'd drunk that caused this interruption. I was very excited so I was either going to pee in my eye or it was going to be one of those stand-on-your-head-to-use-the-toilet jobs. I tried to calm down a little. There was an envelope on the vanity with two or three photos peeping out. I flipped through them to take my mind off what I intended to do with Amanda.

They were some of the pictures the photographer had taken on the boat trip to the rapids. The top couple were of Amanda in waterproof gear getting into the launch at the dock. There was another of her in the boat. The final picture was the one the photographer had taken of the boat as we passed under the bridge on the way out to the rapids, all of us waving and grinning idiotically. Bridget and I looked particularly imbecilic. I looked for Frank. A couple of faces were obscured by waving hands, especially near the back, but eventually I spotted him, red-faced and pop-eyed, waving merrily. He was on a bench right at the back. With someone else, face obscured by a hood, sitting beside him.

Amanda didn't take it too well. It seemed mad to me but it was incomprehensible to her. I mean no couple was ever more ready to consummate their passion than we two. But my feelings about Ruthie and Frank had resurfaced and I needed to talk to Bridget about the significance of the photograph.

Amanda drew a ragged breath and sat up in bed.

"Nick, don't do this to me," she said, her voice unsteady. "Not right now." She lowered her voice and gave me a look of sheer lust. "I really, really want you."

I stood by the bed, my stupid erection still blowing in the breeze. I wanted her, but I couldn't.

"I can't believe I'm saying this, love, but when I'm think-ing that maybe Frank was murdered too, it would feel really bad doing this."

"I guarantee it would feel really good."

"This is just really unfortunate timing. I wish I hadn't peaked at the photographs but I did. Another time."

"I don't make the offer twice," she said angrily. "If not now, forget it."

"Amanda, come on, you've heard of *coitus interruptus*. This is an extreme—"

"If you're not going to fuck me, go fuck yourself —which I hear you're pretty good at."

She turned her back on me. Great back too.

"Sorry," I mumbled. There was no way to leave the room with dignity. I picked up my trousers and shoes and walked into the sitting room. I took a while to fasten my zipper since my erection was too dumb to know it wasn't needed anymore. That reminded me of Frank, too. I felt I deserved to feel noble, turn-ing Amanda down out of loyalty to Frank. I mean, it's not every day I get beautiful women offering me their bodies. Not any day usually. But I didn't feel noble. I felt like a total jerk.

Bridget was sitting in the dark watching a movie when I got back to my room. I climbed on the bed and gave her a hug. She'd sobered up but her face was a wreck and her breath stank of stale alcohol. Even so, looking down at her stripped to her underwear, I felt a twinge of desire. Men, eh? However, we'd long ago decided that having sex would mess up a beautiful friendship.

I showed Bridget the contact sheets, then the photograph I'd taken from Amanda's bathroom.

"Shit. So he wasn't on his own on the boat. Who is that?"

"Well, if you look for our suspects I can't see either Phil Peters or Steve Hewitt in the photo. But then there are some other obscured faces further up the boat."

"Hewitt was being Mister PR-in-Charge and shepherding people aboard. He must have been the last one to take a seat. He must have gone to the back."

"But there are other people here whose faces we can't see. He could be any of them. Did Phil Peters get on with the other Brits? There's somebody next to him whose face has got a waving arm stuck in front of it."

Bridget dropped the picture on the bed. "We're going to have to ask around and find out who was sitting next to whom."

"Why don't we just tell the police?"

"We will, we will. But I'd like to offer them something on a plate."

Bridget yawned.

"Can I stay here tonight?"

"Sure. I'll behave."

"The last thing I'm interested in is sex. But I could do with a cuddle and if that's too much for your libido to handle it's a big enough bed to keep a healthy distance."

Bridget woke me with a cup of coffee. She was already show-ered and dressed and looked better for her sleep. She kissed me on the forehead. "You're a nice person to snuggle up to," she said. "Maybe I've been too rigorous in my rule-making the past few years."

It was already eleven.

"What's the plan, boss?"

"I've phoned Frank's magazine. They're arranging to have the body shipped back. I said I'd check when the police are going to release it. I'm going to write his obituary this morning. This afternoon there's a big party at the Water Amusement Park. I know, I know. Bad taste or what? But it's been arranged for weeks. It's over on an island across the Lachaise Bridge. Flumes and stuff. Probably a rapids ride. Everybody will be there so I think we need to get along, check out the seating."

"But subtly, Bridget. None of your crashing in and see what happens."

"You have my word, sweetie."

I wasn't in the mood for yoga so when Bridget had gone I tried to get through to Amanda. I looked across at the apartments in the vain hope of catching sight of her in her window as I got her voicemail. I left my name and an apology, asked her to call me before lunch.

I spent the next hour writing up my notes for my color piece. I wasn't sure how much longer I'd be staying and I'd got enough material. Hell, I'd known journalists in the past arrive on Monday and file their copy Tuesday for Saturday's paper because the production schedule demanded it. They still managed to talk with great authority about a festival they had been at for approximately twelve hours.

Amanda didn't phone back. I took a stroll down to Rue St. Denis for a quiet lunch in one of the cheap pizza places there. It was a hot day and a few street performers were out doing their schtick. I sat under an umbrella on the terrace of a crowded cafe, chugging at a cold beer and toying with my calzone.

I'd picked up some leaflets and press releases at the press desk in the foyer of the hotel. One was from the Institute of Humor in New York promoting a workshop: "Humor and Laughter as an Empowering Tool." This doctor had developed the Ha Ha technique, with four steps critical to laughing problems away: hurt, anger, humor, and acceptance. According to the leaflet, this "revolution of the spirit" began with the recognition that a wise and loving child dwells within each of us.

Not within this bloke. I hadn't been much of a child even in childhood. Oh, not poverty or abuse—unless you count having to listen to hour upon hour of Frank Zappa, Captain Beefheart, and the Grateful Dead. My mom died when I was three and my dad brought me up on his own. But he was always into drugs and as I got older he got a habit. The real thing. Tried to stay off by having a beer or two. Pretty soon he was hooked on alcohol, too. I was looking after both of us from the age of about seven. He must have been the only grown man to have a ten year old telling him to turn his music down.

He had a heart attack when I was eighteen. All he had to leave me was his record collection. All the Emerson, Lake & Palmer records a person could wish for. Thanks, Dad. Weird to think that he must have been the same age as Frank. Two such different people. I thought about Ruthie's little girl. What kind of life she was going to have?

To be honest, I favored the cops for doing Ruthie after her run-in with them over the gay thing. I was having doubts about Bridget and Frank's hypotheses. Steve Hewitt may have been a bit of a tight ass and was obviously abusing some woman that night, but I couldn't imagine him knocking off Cissie. Phil Peters had a reputation for having a quick temper, and for being a doper, for that matter. But that didn't make him a murderer. Maybe Cissie's death *had* been an accident or suicide. Frank's, too. Maybe we'd all been getting too paranoid. Maybe.

Bridget and I reached the water park a half hour after the party had started. The place was heaving. Most men were dressed but a lot of pretty women were stripped down to bathing suits, tucking in their stomachs and thrusting out their breasts. They were giving each other the once over as they competed for the attention of the men.

"I didn't think there were so many people at the festival," Bridget said.

"This is Montreal's finest too," I said, catching sight of

Amanda engaged in a giggly conversation with Juliette's man John Rolfe. I watched her for a few minutes whilst Bridget got beers. Amanda was wearing a pair of tight leather trousers. Very tight leather trousers. I don't know what they were doing to her but they were crippling me. I turned my back on her when Bridget rejoined me.

The park was noisy with the rush and splash of water and people's shrieks. There were a series of paddling and swimming pools with more women draped around them. We walked across to the main attraction: a wall some hundred feet high and fifty feet wide with a sheet of water falling down it. It was a giant slide, except that it was a sheer vertical drop down the wall until it curved at its base. I watched in awe as people sitting on the top of the wall pushed themselves off, slid down the wall in the flow of water, hit the curved base, and shot along a kind of landing strip for thirty yards, carried along by the water. It looked like instant death to me. Bridget looked up at it.

"Are you going to do it, Nick?"

"You jest," I snorted. "I'm not into this risking your life for a thrill business. I take enough chances eating my own cooking."

We wandered around for ten minutes or so. People we knew acknowledged us briefly but all seemed disinclined to engage in conversation with us.

"I feel like a leper," Bridget said.

Loud Lenny Finnegan caught sight of me and waved me over. He was standing with Phil Peters.

"Perfect," Bridget said, dropping her empty beer bottle into a bin and stalking towards her number one suspect.

Peters had his back to us when we approached. He turned to follow Lenny's glance and did a double take when he saw Bridget bearing down on him.

"Bridget, hi," he said coolly. He nodded at me.

"You know Nick?" Lenny said. "I don't think I'm giving

away any secrets when I say he's a man of unusual sexual pro-clivities. Whoosh, another fifty-dollar word. *Proclivities.* See ma, that college education hasn't been wasted."

"Before you start on me, Bridget, I'm really sorry about your friend, Frank. That was a terrible thing."

"Yeah it was, Phil," Bridget said, looking steely. "You wouldn't look at a photograph for me, would you?"

"Bridget, if this is to do with Cissie Parker we're just going to fall out again."

Peters wasn't a particularly big guy but he was famous for flattening a hapless journalist at a private party three years after the journalist had written a stinking review of one of his shows. In the grudge bearing stakes, that was almost up to Bridget's standards. The two of them together must have been quite a combination.

"You've caused me a great deal of upset not to mention total embarrassment," he said. "It's only 'cos we go way back I'm not suing you, though everybody says I've got a clear case."

"Hey, if you guys have got private business to attend to—" Lenny started to move away. Peters laughed.

"Private? Nothing stays private when Bridget's on the scent."

"Bloody right," Bridget said. "I think you were involved in Cissie's death. If I'm wrong, I'll apologize. If I'm wrong."

"Then we've got nothing to talk about."

"I'd like you to look at this photograph. You too, Lenny. Please."

Peters took the photograph from Bridget, shaking his head. "Bridget you've always had your head up your ass about me and Cissie, just because she was around when we had our scene. But you're way off beam. What's this?"

"It's the boat trip to the rapids," Bridget said. "I know you were on the boat but I can't see you in the picture. Wondered if you'd mind telling me which one is you."

Peters studied the photograph for a moment, Lenny looking over his shoulder. Peters looked up. "Wait a minute. Wait a minute. Bridget, are you—what, you think I dumped Frank over the side? You really are fucking nuts."

Peters was suddenly very angry. He glared at Bridget who glared right back.

"We don't think that," I said. I pointed at the photograph. "We're just trying to place everybody so we can work out who that guy is sitting next to Frank. We're not even saying Frank's death wasn't an accident. We just want to talk to this guy. Please, Phil."

Peters glared at me too. Then he exhaled.

"The hell with it," he said, stabbing at the middle of the picture with a chewed down fingernail. "That must be me, on the row in front of Frank. I was sitting next to that guy from Fox— the one with the fancy business cards? I've got a very soggy one back in my room. Check with him if you don't believe me. He'll confirm I didn't turn round and throw Frank off the boat."

"Any idea who this guy next to Frank is?"

"None." He handed the photograph back to Bridget. "Can I go now?"

"A minute more?" I pulled out the contact sheets. "You were at this party with Cissie."

"Here you go—" Peters began to get riled again.

"No, no. It's just there's a photograph here and we can't figure out who Cissie is standing with. I thought maybe you could recognize him. He's a big guy all in black."

"Well, that narrows it down to three quarters of the men at the party," Peters said. "It could even be you, Lenny."

"Yeah, right," Lenny said with a grin.

"But really you want me to confirm it wasn't me, that's it isn't it, Bridget?" Peters looked across to where Bridget had been standing. She had disappeared. Peters looked at me. "Nick, you seem like a sensible guy. You've got to get Bridget off my case about Cissie Parker. She's getting ridiculous and I don't particularly want her spreading this stuff about me and drugs. That's all in the past."

"So did Bridget know Cissie?"

"Not exactly. Bridget loathed Cissie because she thought I was shagging her whilst I was with Bridget. I wasn't—though I would have liked to. It caused problems for us. It's probably why we split up. Cissie and I got together later. I had a real soft spot for her. I'd never do anything to harm her."

"Bridget thought maybe it was an accident. That you and Cissie had been doing drugs together."

"Cissie was clean and I promised her—and her fucking mother for that matter—that I'd never tempt her with anything like that again. The last thing I wanted to do was fuck up her life."

"Cissie's mother?"

"Yeah. Jilly Dougan."

"What, THE Jilly Dougan? The journalist?"

"That's the one."

"But that wasn't in any of the cuts."

"She kept it pretty quiet. They had a falling out when Cissie was fourteen. That's a story in itself. Listen, Lenny and I got to meet some people. Sorry I can't help you with this photograph. If Cissie's death wasn't an accident, don't you think I'd be the first to want to know about it? But I've got no reason to think it wasn't. She could be pretty wild when she was high. She got hold of some drugs from somewhere—not from me—and went weird. And that's all she wrote."

I ambled down to the water wall looking for Bridget. I looked up and saw her on the balcony at the top of the wall, waving the photograph from the rapids ride in the air, giving Steve Hewitt some serious shit. A group of four or five people in swimming gear were watching with awed fascination.

The water was making too much noise for me to hear what they were saying but I could make out Hewitt's expression. Bridget had him on the ropes. Wild-eyed, he darted glances at the people around him then suddenly lunged towards Bridget. Whether he was going for her or for the photograph I couldn't say for sure. Bridget stepped back and Hewitt seemed to over-balance.

What followed happened very quickly. Hewitt went head first down the wall, outside the flow of water. He fell remark-ably quickly and landed with scarcely a sound in the gushing water on the slipway. As his body was whipped round and car-ried along to the end of the slipway I saw a distinctive pink stain spreading in the water around him. He came to a halt where the water ran out, arms outstretched, his neck twisted at a horrible angle, blood pumping from a huge hole in his head.

Bridget and I flew home with Frank's body the next evening. Hewitt was dead, of course. Bridget didn't know whether Hewitt had been trying to attack her or get the photograph. Hewitt probably didn't know either. He'd just snapped. In his room the cops found not so much a confession as a spoken explanation on a dictaphone of how Frank had died. Hewitt had been building up to telling the police.

According to his account, he had been sitting next to Frank. They had rowed some more about Frank's accusations. Hewitt had lost his temper and lunged angrily at Frank. Frank had half risen to his feet, both hands off the bar, to ward Hewitt off and then a huge wave had hit the boat. Hewitt was sent skidding along the bench. When he recovered, Frank was nowhere to be seen.

It sounded reasonable, although we would never know for sure. What was missing was a confession about Cissie Parker or

Ruthie's death. I kept the set of prints but handed Cissie's contacts over to the police. Although they couldn't trace the movements of either Hewitt or Cissie on that evening, for the sake of their crime clear-up rate they were inclined to believe Hewitt had killed her too. They were less convinced about Ruthie's death but as I was no longer a suspect they allowed me to leave the country.

There were very few goodbyes. I wasn't able to speak to Amanda, although she may have attempted to contact me the day we left. The phone message service at the hotel had a message for me from a woman who hadn't left a name saying it was imperative I speak to her and that she would call me back. She didn't, at least not before I had to take a cab out to the airport.

EDINBURGH

FIVE

Nature abhors a vacuum, except in Groucho's. In Groucho's, she loves them. In the Soho media club they sit pertly on low sofas blowing cigarette smoke at me. Good-looking, ambitious young men with sideburns and narrow lapels. Women in skimpy black skirts and clumpy shoes who write columns in mainstream men's magazines about the pleasures of giving blowjobs or the use of sex aids.

Whenever I go there the journalists around the room are split between those who don't have their own columns (me) and those who do (just about everybody else). On this occasion I was supposed to be meeting Bridget, but she was late. I sat in a corner occasionally flapping away the smoke that engulfed me. When my phone rang, as usual everyone in the bar grabbed for their bags or pockets.

"Sorry, sweetie," Bridget said. "These fucking lawyers are going through my piece line by line. I'll probably still be here tomorrow morning. See you in the Assembly Rooms bar around midnight Sunday."

Bridget and I had scarcely seen each other since we'd come back from Montreal. We'd attended Frank's funeral, of course, and we'd spoken on the phone a lot as we wrote up our triple murder stories. They were running in rival papers this Sunday.

Mine had been heavily lawyered, too, since the police were dragging their feet completing their investigations linking Steve Hewitt to more than Frank's death. Until they caught up we had to be careful what we said.

I'd decided to give my fee to an AIDS charity in memory of Frank. Then I got my credit card statement. Maybe I'd do something else in memory of Frank. I mean, I felt bad he was dead but there was no point being a damned fool about it.

Bridget and I were both going up to the Edinburgh Festival. She was doing some stuff on the Fringe, which this year was bigger than ever, with around 10,000 performers and 1,200 shows. They were the kind of statistics you got in the press pack. The press office had fun expressing figures in colorful ways. For example, if the Fringe groups formed a human tower by standing on each other's shoulders they would exceed the height of the world's tallest building by fourteen kilometers. Well, yes, I do find that interesting.

I was covering both the Film and Book festivals. Steve Martin had never materialized in Montreal but he was definitely going to Edinburgh to talk about his new film. Bradley Stokes was expected to promote his new movie, too. It was going to be old home week in the Assembly Rooms, one of the big three Fringe venues. Billy Cash and Lenny Finnegan were both doing one-man shows there.

"Jilly Dougan's just come in," the woman with the fag next to me said. "She's had her book launch upstairs."

"A book?" the man next to her said, following her gaze. "I didn't know she could write."

"She's a journalist."

"That's what I mean."

"She and a bunch of other old dates from the sixties have written about life in their fabulous fifties."

"Riveting. Jilly Dougan and her 'Fabulous Fifties.' Sounds

like a doowap group." The man smiled a sneery smile. "What's the book like?"

"Bit New Age. When they dry out, alcoholics always turn cranky one way or the other. It's either God or wearing hemp."

Dougan was holding court to a couple of younger women when I went across to her. She looked rough close up. The heavy makeup couldn't disguise the web of purple veins from years of boozing. Her face was lined and haggard with big pouches under the eyes. She was wearing one of her trademark hats, some huge velvet concoction, and a silk blouse with a very low neck, her large breasts pushed up by a wonderbra. Her neck had gone. She eyed me when I came up to the table and I saw that her eyes still had it. Life and mischief and cunning.

I asked if at some time I could have a quiet word with her.

"Make it now."

I looked at the other two women.

"Joan and Liz. They're my minders. From the publishers. Don't worry about them. They know me better than I know myself."

"It's about Cissie," I said, sliding into the seat opposite her.

She looked at me.

"I was in Montreal when she died."

She didn't respond and I thought for a horrible moment she didn't know her daughter was dead. Then her eyes filled with tears.

"You must be Nick Madrid. Bridget told me about you."

"You know Bridget?"

"We go way back. She interviewed me for her piece." Damn. Why hadn't I thought to do that?

"It was a well-kept secret that Cissie was your daughter. Did you see her much?"

"Not really. She blamed me for a lot of things. My sister Ellie brought her up you know. I wasn't exactly the mothering sort. She didn't know I was her mother until she was fourteen. She freaked."

"You had a falling out?"

Dougan grinned, spidery lines cracking her makeup. "Big-mouth, Jilly. I was skint so I wrote an article about her conception and the fact that I didn't know who the father was. She saw a copy of it. Bad enough that her dissipated aunt was actually her mother but the manner of her conception was hard for her to handle."

"You wrote it in an article before you told her?" I must have looked shocked.

"Told you I was a lousy mother. I've always lived my life in public. Found it easier to tell a newspaper readership of millions what I could never reveal to a lover or a friend. Or a daughter."

"Why didn't you know who the father was?" Joan asked hesitantly.

Jilly leaned over and patted the woman's hand.

"Orgy, darling, orgy. In the sixties I was a researcher on a TV pop show. Met all the big rock stars. Most of them wanted to lay me. And that was fine by me. I loved sex." She took a sip from a steaming beaker of coffee. "Do you know, it's twenty-five years since the last Isle of Wight Festival. The best festival ever."

"I was there," I said, wondering why she was going off at a tangent.

"You're not old enough, darling."

"I was five. It's time to stand up and be counted—my dad was a hippy."

My dad and I were even in the film they made, although it was twenty-five years before the BBC screened it. Watching it, my hair stood on end to see my dad suddenly sitting there on film, a handsome young man of twenty-five with long hair and a Jesus beard. And I'm wandering around ass naked except for a jumper. They filmed him mixing up some shitty food with a lot of bacon in it over a little camping stove, saying to me the usual cocaine paranoia shit about how the sky can suddenly cave in on you so you mustn't trust anyone. I'm five, right? And he's talking to the camera and saying that sure he's given me marijuana and even acid. He lied about the acid but he omitted the cocaine. And seeing the footage on the TV I was thinking a) that's my dad and b) why didn't someone arrest the crazy bastard for exposing his child to harmful drugs.

"Do you remember much of it?" Dougan said.

"I remember on the boat over these French hippies terrified me. They looked so rough and one of them pulled a knife. But my dad muddled through with them in his stoned way. Then at the site we were so far back the stage was just brass instruments glinting in the lights. He told me years later about Joni Mitchell almost in tears saying "Give us some respect, man." And Ricky Farr really pissed off when the audience booed Kris Kristofferson off the stage."

Dougan sighed, her embonpoint heaving impressively. "That was so stupid. I was at the side of the stage. Kris started singing a song called 'Blame It On the Stones' and the audience were too thick to understand the title and the chorus were ironic. Those bloody French anarchists. The French aren't big on irony. They don't care for double entendres either—funny that isn't it? Kris kept saying to his band, 'I think they're going to shoot us.' Not before I fuck your brains out, I wanted to shout."

The two women laughed nervously.

"I had a backstage pass—for services rendered to a roadie—and I had a hit list of rock stars whose knickers I wanted to get into. Some hope. I really fancied Kris. I didn't go for his music but Janis Joplin, who I interviewed when she was passing through, said he was a great lay. But I couldn't get near him. Or Leonard Cohen or Roger Daltrey or Jim Morrison, who was looking, frankly, a bit porky. I was lined up with Jimi Hendrix, who was only going to be around for a few hours. But he was busy with that woman who used to go round making plaster of Paris casts of rock stars' dicks."

"What?" Joan said, giggling.

"She had this thing about making casts of rock stars' erect penises. Would coat them in plaster of Paris. Judging by some of the musicians I slept with, it was probably the only way to keep them stiff. They're not great lovers, you know. Use up too much energy on stage. Then there's the booze and the drugs.

"Anyway, I never got to Hendrix, which really pissed me off. Competition was fierce. Some of the female performers were in the mood for a little loving. One of those famous singer songwriters had a big reputation as a sword-swallower. Frankly I began to worry I was going to have to fuck another roadie.

"But I was enjoying just hanging out backstage, too. It was chaos there. Lots of security guards with dogs to protect all the cash. Cash from the gates and cash to pay the bands. Everyone wanted payment in cash, they'd done festivals before and knew about not getting paid at all. I heard Tiny Tim trilling in that weird voice of his 'Can't tune the ukulele without cash.' But what a scene. Of course there were plenty of drugs around so I was getting into that. And that's when I met Mick Gaven."

"Mick Gaven?" I said.

"He's pretty big in America as a record producer these days. Then, he played boogie woogie piano in this band of Texas rockers. Seriously bottom of the bill. They did the graveyard shift on the second night to 600,000 sleeping people. But what did they care? They were just there to have fun. Good looking boys, too. Mick invited me and another girl I'd hooked up with to join them for a party."

"An orgy ensued?"

"I should say so. I had 'em all."

"All four of them?" Jane said, saucer-eyed.

"Seven. They had a rhythm section."

Her three listeners tried not to look disapproving. All I knew about orgies was that everything you touched seemed to have batteries in them.

"Seven," I murmured.

"Well, it was a three day festival, darling," Dougan said, pleased to have shocked us. "Besides, as I said, rock musicians are usually so lousy in bed you need that many to make it worthwhile. And actually I may be exaggerating. I think that technically I only did do it with four of them. One couldn't get it up, another preferred the other side of the ballroom, if you get my meaning. And I passed on one who strapped on a huge dildo. He went off in a huff."

"And that's when you conceived Cissie?" I said. "But you don't know which one the father was?"

"Well, actually I sort of do know. By a process of elimination I worked out it was Mick Gaven."

"I'm curious to know how you eliminated the others."

She didn't blink. "One was only interested in the tradesman's entrance, another only wanted my tender kisses. One was very particular about using a condom. Very particular. So that left Mick. Besides, we spent a couple of nights together in Amsterdam after that."

"And that's what you wrote in the article."

"That's it. Cissie freaked. Then she went wild. Children of high-profile people like me are going to go one of two ways anyway. Cissie became a party girl like her mom. Eventually I told her that Mick had been sending me money for her from time to time. He's loaded. He got religion and makes a fortune producing popular Christian music. We'd never got into a heavy thing about paternity but he did send money. When I told her, Cissie went to stay with him. That was the last time I saw her."

"That being—"

"Three years ago." Dougan couldn't hold her bright smile. Bravado only takes you so far. She looked vaguely around the room. Her face seemed to sag. When she looked back she reached across the table and took my hand. I waited for the further revelation she seemed to be building up to. She looked into my eyes.

"God, I'd kill for a brandy," she said glumly.

Depending on your point of view, four hours on a train in the company of a bunch of writers, with a free supply of all the British Rail sandwiches you can eat, may or may not count as a good time. But if you're freelance you don't turn down a free first class return ticket when it's offered. The Edinburgh Book Festival had two first class carriages, stacked with free food and booze, reserved for London's literary folk on a Scotland-bound Intercity 225 leaving Kings Cross at ten the following morning.

The trip was intended to be a party. My ticket even had a plus guest on it. But I was travelling alone. Sad, eh? I had thought of inviting Bridget to travel with me but putting her in a sealed carriage with a bunch of literary types was like giving the fox a den in the henhouse. Fortunately, she preferred flying.

I've always found it best to keep booze away from writers. The history of drunkenness in literature teaches us that it's the poets you have to watch, but children's authors can be pretty tricky, too. I envisaged that the combination of free drink and artistic temperament meant friendships springing up by Peterborough could be legendary feuds by York.

The trip was, however, sadly uneventful. People table-hopped along the aisles. A couple of film crews for those cable channels that no one ever watches shot footage with the look of people in whom hope was battling with experience. PRs ferried journalists to and from the handful of celebrity authors. As the bottles of wine and whisky circulated things got a little raucous but, as an attractive American woman pointed out to a group at the table next to mine, there was no shagging in the aisles. I thought for a moment she was interested in me—she kept looking over, a half smile on her face—but I think I'd just dropped food down my chin. Her attention was soon monopolized by an editor famous for being the most campy womanizer in publishing.

The Film Festival accommodation office had got me a flat in New Town. New Town is actually an old part of the city, a beautiful area of exceptionally well-preserved Georgian terraces, villas, and town houses. It was called the New Town when it was planned at the end of the eighteenth century to distinguish it from, you guessed it, the Old Town. The Old Town is the cluster of medieval streets and alleys, tenements, and closes that developed in a ramshackle way to the east of Edinburgh Castle, set high on its rocky perch in the center of the city.

I would normally have stayed with Bridget but she was shacking up with a couple of other journalists from her newspaper. We needed a bit of a break from each other after the intensity of Montreal.

The train was on time into Waverley Station. A tall, strapping man in his fifties was standing on the platform in a kilt and sporran, as if to assure us we were indeed in Scotland. I immediately assumed he was a laird, whatever one of those was, but I overheard someone else saying he played the bagpipes on street corners for loose change. When I looked closer I saw that although he had a dirk tucked down one stocking, the effect was spoiled by the quarter bottle of whiskey tucked down the other.

I know Edinburgh has a high rate of drug use and AIDS cases, that it has slums and no-go areas, but whenever I'm there I can't see beyond the beautiful old buildings in the center of the city. I took a cab to New Town, ogling the city en route. We crossed Waverley Bridge onto Princes Street and drove past the huge Gothic memorial to Sir Walter Scott. I don't think of Scott when I think of Edinburgh. I think of James Hogg and *The Private Memoirs and Confessions of A Justified Sinner*, his nineteenth century Gothic novel about a religious nut lured into committing horrific murders around

Edinburgh by the Devil in the guise of his friend.

I've had friends like that.

I was staying in one of the tall mansions in Cathay Place, which I only later discovered was the most desirable address in Edinburgh. The apartment was on the first floor up two flights of flagged stairs. Its usual occupant was waiting for me. A middle-class, horsey-looking woman. She thrust out her hand as I stood on the doorstep. "Hilly," she said.

"How are you, Hilly?" I said, putting down my luggage to shake her hand.

"Oh, you know," she said, breaking into a toothy grin, "a bit up and down."

I smiled. "Hilly by name and nature."

"That's me," she said.

She was a big-boned woman who hunched her shoulders, perhaps out of embarrassment at being so tall or at having large breasts. I found her quite attractive. She led me through to the kitchen, pointed at a cat's litter tray. "That's for Kevin."

"Kevin?"

"Didn't the accommodation people say you'd have to feed my cat?"

"Of course."

"Clarence, my other pet, lives out in the back garden. The downstairs people will feed him. He plays with their dog. I'm looking after Lionel for a friend of mine whilst she's in Africa but you don't need to bother with him. The cleaner will feed him, if he'll eat. He's been terribly off his food. Moping for my friend, I suppose. Bless him."

"Poor Lionel," I agreed, wondering what he was.

"You only need to empty the litter tray every couple of days. There are some dustbin sacks in the cupboard."

"Fine," I said, waiting for her to go. "Will Lionel be using the litter tray too?"

"Lionel? Ha ha. Lionel using the litter tray. That's very funny."

I smiled uncertainly. "What exactly is—" I started when the phone rang. Hilly bustled off to answer it.

I waited a couple of minutes then wandered around the apartment. It was enormous. The sitting room ceiling was some fifteen feet high. The room was cluttered with two large sofas, chests, tables, standard lamps, and a piano, a baby grand. A set of long bay windows looked out over the wooded valley of the River Leith below and across to the north of Edinburgh.

I was standing by a coffee table piled high with books when Hilly rejoined me.

"*Goat Medicine?*" I said, looking at the book on top of the pile.

"I'm a vet," Hilly said, blushing. She blushed again when she led me through to the bedroom. "This is the boudoir. Hope it's not too chintzy for you." I looked at the whore's drawers on the windows and the row of soft toys. I shook my head and looked at the large double bed.

"I've put fresh sheets on," she said, laughing nervously. There was a moment's silence, then she marched over to a cupboard.

"This is where you can usually find Kevin, sleeping on my clean linen."

I went over and stood beside her, reaching out my hand to stroke the tubby ginger cat. It hissed and swiped at my hand, drawing blood.

"Kevin! He's a bit nervous with strangers at first. Are you all right?"

I sucked at the beads of blood on my hand.

"No problem," I said, fixing Kevin with a beady stare that said, remember sucker, for the next two weeks your ass is mine.

Hilly and I stood awkwardly side by side.

"Well," she said, after another silence. "I'd better leave you to it. I'm staying with friends in Elgin. The number's on the pad by the phone if you need anything. Oh, watch out with the main door downstairs. The lock's a bit temperamental. You've got to push and then kind of twist down."

When she'd gone I had a root around. Living in someone else's flat always brings out the voyeur in me, especially if it's a woman's. Not that I go looking for their underwear to try on or anything. Unless it looks really slinky.

Here there was a bookcase full of books on medicine for large animals and reptiles. The bathroom cupboard had a range of cosmetics and shampoos and what looked like a thick yellow condom shaped at the top into a cat's head, complete with smiling mouth and whiskers. The secret life of vets indeed. I couldn't find any trace of the mysterious Lionel, although one cupboard door in the corridor was locked.

Later that evening I went into Charlotte Square to the Book Festival. Edinburgh was undergoing an untypical heatwave and the tents in which the festival took place had their doors open to let in air on the sweating hordes within. I listened from the doorway as Joanna Trollope and Michael Dobbs, looking slightly indignant, defended TV adaptations of their works.

I went into the spiegeltent, a wonderful 1920s Austrian beer tent, and sat with my beer in one of the wood and glass booths around the outer rim. It was lit by soft yellow light. I loved this place and the thought that in the twenties it had been parked in some Austrian village halfway up a mountain for a dance or a wedding party.

Sipping my beer, I looked through the Fringe brochure. Irvine Welsh was still hip and omnipresent. Six different versions of *Macbeth*. A musical history of Edinburgh's Royal Mile and musicals about the lives of Robert Burns and Rasputin. Not my thing really. Oscar, the Hypnotising Dog, now that was more like it.

Half a dozen men were milling around on the small stage, fiddling with microphone stands and amplifiers. Around the center of the tent were fifteen slender pillars inlaid with mirrors. I found that by looking at the mirror in the pillar nearest to me I could see the reflection of one of the people in the next booth. The woman whose face I could see seemed to be looking at me, too. I smiled. She smiled.

A few moments later she came into my booth and sat down beside me. It was the woman who had talked about shagging in the aisles on the train. My pulse rate increased.

"I saw you in the bar every night but you never said hello," she said, flashing me a big smile.

"The Assembly Rooms bar? I've just arrived."

"Not here," she said.

"The Glue and Toupee?"

The Glue and Toupee was the regulars' name for my local in London, an actors' pub where ham was always on the menu.

"In Montreal."

The band started up and a woman sitting a few yards away started getting into it—legs bobbing, fingers snapping, head shaking. I wouldn't have minded but it wasn't exactly the birth of the cool. Just a bunch of middle management types in candy striped waistcoats, beer guts, and straw hats playing Dixieland. The woman clapped out of time.

"You were at the Comedy Festival?" I looked at her more closely. Cropped black hair, nice smile, intelligent eyes. "I think I remember you," I lied.

"Naw, I was only around for a few days." She looked down. "I had to skip the rest of it."

"Well, I'm not sure you missed much. It was rather different this year."

"Yeah, I know. That's why I wanted to talk to you, but you'd gone by the time I phoned back."

I recalled that somebody had called but not left a message as I was leaving Montreal for the airport.

"That was you?"

"The very same."

"But what are you? How did you find me here?"

"Oh, I'm a journalist. For an agency based in New York. They send me here every year. I didn't expect to see you—I thought I'd get you in London."

"What did you need to talk to me about?"

The band struck up another dire tune from the good old days of Dixie.

"They should be on a paddle steamer on the Mississippi," I said, grimacing.

"Preferably one that's sinking. Why don't we go outside?"

We sat on the grass. She caught me looking at her exposed thighs and pulled her skirt demurely down over her raised knees.

"I'm Mary Kelly, by the way."

"Nick—"

"Ach, I know who you are, right enough. I'm sorry about your friend Frank. Listen, I read your piece. You think this Canadian PR, Steve Hewitt, killed Frank and the photographer Ruthie to prevent anyone discovering that he had also murdered Cissie Parker. And your friend Frank thought Steve Hewitt had killed Cissie Parker because he heard Hewitt giving a woman in room 1814—a room in a direct line above yours—a hard time. And he assumed that woman to be Cissie Parker."

"Maybe," I said cautiously.

She snorted. "For sure."

"Okay. Yes."

"But Steve Hewitt wasn't giving Cissie Parker a hard time. It wasn't Cissie Parker in his room."

"How can you be so sure?"

She looked me in the eye and took a deep breath.

"Because I was in his room. I was the one Steve Hewitt was beating up."

Bridget was squatting by a table in the Assembly Rooms bar when I walked in. She was talking to journalist Carol Sarler, producer David Johnson, and performers Simon Fanshawe and Graham Norton. When she saw me standing on the three steps leading down into the bar, she jerked to her feet, waved, and yelled, "Shagger!"

A hundred heads turned my way. I blushed and tried to saunter down to the bar, nodding at familiar faces. Bridget squeezed Norton's shoulder and tottered forward a few yards. Drunk or yet another pair of terrible shoes? I looked at her feet. She was wearing the highest pair of platforms I'd ever seen. They did great things for her legs. Shame she couldn't walk.

We pecked each other's cheeks. "Nice piece," we both said.

"So now we can party?"

"Maybe. We need to have a word."

"Okay. I'm getting a drink. Get you one?"

I looked around for somewhere to sit whilst Bridget was at the bar. The place was packed, mostly with journalists. As usual there was an excess of smokers.

There was a chair free at a gay comedian's table. She had a reputation as a toughie. She was reputed once to have thrown Addison Creswell over the bar in this very room. After allegedly headbutting a policeman the night before, she had this morning been charged in court with breach of the peace and contravening the Scottish Police Act. She was sitting with a Praetorian Guard of tough looking young women with cropped hair. I thought I'd stand.

I nodded at a comic I knew who was by the bar with his wife. A guy who looked a little the worse for wear was swaying slightly in front of him.

"You missed Ray Davies," Bridget said accusingly as she

handed me my beer. "You must have been the only journalist who didn't go. You coming to the Shock Boys?"

"Sure," I said absently, sipping my beer.

"So what'd you want to talk about?"

"Bridget I just met the woman that Frank heard Steve Hewitt beating up in his hotel room."

Bridget looked over the rim of her glass—she was drinking some horrible pink concoction.

"How come?"

"She read my article and came looking for me."

"Shit," Bridget said.

We suddenly heard raised voices and looked round in time to see the man who had been the worse for wear go crashing over crowded tables, sending drinks flying. He was being pursued by the comic, who I believe used to be a boxer, who was yelling something about insulting his wife. The comic cornered the drunk but a couple of blokes held him back. One of them, a comedian who this year looked like a wild-eyed prophet with a John the Baptist beard was shouting, "You're too talented for this."

The situation was calmed down. I was standing by one of the Assembly Room administrators. I saw him lean over to press office supremo Liz Smith. "We'd better try to keep this out of the press," he shouted in her ear. Liz looked round the room at the thirty or forty journalists all reaching for their notebooks. She nodded dutifully.

"I've got tickets for the Shock Boys," Bridget said. "Are you going to come?"

"Sure. But what are we going to do?"

"Go after that shit Peters. I said it was him."

I shook my head.

"I don't know about that, Bridget. I had a chat with him the afternoon you—the afternoon Hewitt—"

"The afternoon I hounded Hewitt to his death. Is that what

you were going to say? Don't forget he killed Frank. There was no doubt about that." Her eyes blazed. "He got his just desserts."

"I've got no argument with that. I'm just not sure about Phil, that's all."

"Phil? Since when did we get so chummy?"

"It doesn't hold together. I think we should look further afield."

"Which field?"

"Any field. What about Bradley Stokes? Juliette Smith was up to something very peculiar in Montreal. Maybe she was protecting Stokes. Remember he and Cissie made a movie together."

"You think it's Bradley Stokes?"

"I don't know. I just don't think it's Phil Peters."

"Well if it's Bradley Stokes we'd best leave well alone."

"What do you mean?"

"You don't tangle with the big Hollywood players when your career involves feeding off them."

"So we drop it? But I thought you were the one who was so keen to find out who killed Cissie."

Bridget gave me a tight-lipped look.

"What about those photos of Cissie at the party? Did Phil identify the mystery man?"

I shook my head.

"Probably because it was him. Don't look at me like that, you supercilious bastard. You don't want to believe he's guilty because you've got chummy with him."

"I'm just surprised you want to drop it."

"Look," she said fiercely. "I've got a good lifestyle that I don't particularly want to lose. We've got no evidence against Bradley Stokes at all and no chance of getting it here. We start sniffing around him and not only will his lawyers sue us back into the Stone Age, we might as well kiss goodbye to any more work interviewing Hollywood stars because the doors will slam shut.

And I like going to Los Angeles three or four times a year. I like staying in nice hotels and hanging out in nice bars and restaurants. Don't you?"

I realized she was acting angry because she was feeling defensive but even so I was stunned by the vitriol in her voice. Before I could think of anything to say in reply, she said, "Your new mate Phil Peters has just walked in. Why don't you go over and suck his dick."

I watched Bridget turn and totter away, ostentatiously ignore Peters, who was standing by the door looking around, and sweep out of the room. It would have looked more impressive if she'd got some sort of ambulatory skill in those shoes but it was a toss-up which she'd do first—get out of the room or fall flat on her face. Peters glanced at her retreating back. He saw me and raised an eyebrow. I gestured him over.

"Nick, how are you? Read your piece in the paper. Good story."

"Yeah, but I was wrong. Hewitt didn't off Cissie or the photographer."

Peters looked at me intently. He had very piercing blue eyes.

"So you're back on me again?"

"No. Look, do you have time for a chat? I wanted to talk to you about that party that Cissie went to and those photographs that Ruthie took of her. I'm sure there are clues there. You could be a real help."

He looked at me for a moment, glanced around the bar.

"Sure," he said. "Let me buy you a drink."

We elbowed our way to the bar and he bought me a pint.

"So can you remember who Cissie was hanging out with at the party?"

"Not really. Come on, you know what parties are like. I was busy trying to get my end away."

"Did she arrive with anybody?"

"Pass."

"There were two photographs of her with Bradley Stokes. Did you see them together?"

"What, the Hitman? Sure. They were together for a while."

"D'you think they were an item that night?"

"Have you seen the size of Stokes? Popular guy, I know, but I don't think Cissie had a thing about shagging elephants."

"Maybe it depended on the length of the trunk. Or maybe she had a thing about hanging out with famous people."

Peters scowled, looked into his beer for a minute or so.

"Possibly. She didn't take sex too seriously—I mean she took it very seriously but she wasn't exactly discriminating. Maybe she was curious about fat men. Robbie Coltrane turns a lot of women on. She was pretty touchy-feely with Stokes. But then she was like that with most people." He took a big swallow of his drink. "She never mentioned him to me. But maybe. I don't know."

"Did you see Cissie very much in Montreal?"

Peters shook his head.

"Hardly at all."

I shot a glance at him. I remembered that, according to Bridget, Peters had been seen regularly coming and going from the apartment building Cissie was staying at in Montreal.

"Did you know she was pregnant? Do you know who the father was?"

Peters shook his head and looked back across the room. He put his hand on my arm and directed my look with a jerk of his head. Juliette and her heavy John Rolfe had just walked in with Loud Lenny Finnegan and a guy I didn't recognize.

"I saw Lenny with her at the party," Peters said, still watching the quartet as they made their slow way down the room. "They seemed to be having an intense discussion."

"Lenny?" I remembered talking to Lenny about Cissie—was it in the bus or the VIP tent? Hadn't he distinctly told me he didn't know her? I thought back to the photograph of Cissie with her hand on the arm of the man in dark clothes whose face was obscured. "Could it have been Lenny in that photo I showed you of the guy in black?"

"I dunno. Maybe. Christ, Nick, every man at the Comedy Festival wore black, you know that."

He turned away from me as Lenny Finnegan reached the bar.

"Phil—Nick! How you guys doin'? Say, I knew Edinburgh was known as the Athens of the north but I didn't know it was because of all the transvestites. The town is full of all these guys in skirts. What gives?"

We smiled politely. Everyone comes up with the same kilt joke sooner or later. Juliette, Rolfe, and the other man crowded in behind Lenny.

"Nick, isn't it?" Juliette said to me. "Nice to see you again. You remember John. And do you know Billy Cash?"

She indicated the fourth member of their party, a big, grizzled guy with long gray hair, a lined face, and too much gold jewelry. More rock 'n' roll than comedy. So this was Billy Cash. The "Next Big Thing" in comedy movies. The guy Amanda had been willing to sleep with to get on his cable show, *Prize Cash*.

He glanced at me without interest.

"Billy, Nick is a journalist who'll be interviewing you whilst you're here."

There was a flicker of something in his dead eyes and he offered me a firm handshake.

"Nick," he growled in a smoke damaged voice. He dropped my hand.

"Nick, why don't you call the hotel in the morning and we'll sort out the details," Juliette said briskly. "Maybe you two could have lunch the day after tomorrow when you've had a chance to see the show."

"Sure," I said. Then, I don't know why, I asked, "Did you read my piece about Montreal?"

"Why, yes, as a matter of fact I did," she said, eying me coolly. "I thought you trod a fine line rather skilfully. You must be pleased with yourself."

I shook my head.

"I realized I only told half the story. I don't think Hewitt was involved in Cissie's death. I'm going to have to start looking again."

"Looking where?" she said, icily.

"Dunno. I've got these photographs from the launch party …"

Cash had been looking around the room as I was talking to Juliette. At my words he switched his attention back.

"Somebody die?" he said in his gravelly voice.

"That young English performer fell out of a window at the hotel in Montreal," Juliette said. "I mentioned it to you at the time."

Cash nodded slowly. "Sure," he said, looking round again. "There anywhere more *congenial* we could have our drink? This is one sad fucking place."

"Sure," Juliette nodded. "You coming Lenny?"

"Think I might hang out here for a little while," Lenny said, his eyes fixed on a foxy girl with long blonde hair sitting at a table by herself. Juliette followed his look. She smiled thinly.

"Yeah, she's keen to get on, Lenny. Real keen. I get the business cards, she gets the blowjobs."

"Tsk, tsk, Juliette. Live and let live, y'know."

"Look forward to seeing you again, Mick." Cash nodded at me.

"Sure," I said, not bothering to correct him. "Day after tomorrow."

Lenny bought Peters and me another beer and got himself a pint of Guinness. "Jeez, I love porter," he said. "There are some Irish bars in Seattle I have to be dragged from."

I watched Lenny for a minute from behind my beer. Had he deliberately lied to me about Cissie? Could he be the mysterious man in the photo? He was an affable man but he was big and there was something about him made you think he could turn very nasty if the occasion demanded it. Face it, any successful comedian has got to be ruthless to get where they've got. I had a stray thought of Amanda, wondered for a moment what she was doing, where she was right now.

"My article about Cissie Parker's death appeared today," I said.

Lenny turned his attention back from the girl sitting on her own.

"That so? But you don't figure Hewitt for the man no more. He didn't do your gay friend, Frank, and that photographer chick either?"

"Frank, but I don't think the others."

"So where's that leave you? That crazy dame, Bridget, gunning for Phil here again? I mean, I've seen the guy in action." He punched Phil cheerfully on the arm. "He's a ladykiller all right but he ain't no murderer, you get my meaning."

"What did you make of her the night of the party?" Phil said. "You were talking to her for a while."

My man! The very question I was wondering how to ask.

"Cissie Parker? Did I talk to Cissie Parker?" Lenny looked puzzled. "Shit, I have no recollection of that."

"Sure did," Phil said. "I saw you."

If Lenny was lying, I have to hand it to him he was a very cool customer. He didn't seem embarrassed, or flummoxed. He looked mildly at Phil as he apparently thought about this. Then he grinned.

"Fact is, I was pretty much out of it that evening. I've seen her picture. She was blonde, she was pretty, she was just the way I like 'em. I could have tried to hit on her without having a clue who she was. Was she talking to me or was I doing all the talking?"

"How the bloody hell can I be expected to remember that?" Phil said in exasperation. Then, "Actually, though, wait a minute. Yeah, you were giving it plenty of mouth. I remember her looking across and kind of raising an eyebrow at me. Guess you must have been exaggerating your talents, as always."

"Just telling it like it is, buddy. I like the ladies to know what they can look forward to."

"So you were just chatting her up?" I said.

"I don't even remember," Lenny said, his attention drawn back to the woman sitting alone. He picked up his glass. "But if you'll excuse me gentlemen, I can't abide to see that young woman sitting so alone across there."

I watched him wander across to the woman, then turned my attention back to Peters.

"Do you believe him?" he said.

"I don't know. But even if I don't, I'm no cop. What am I supposed to do about it?"

"You're asking me? I'm one of your suspects remember."

"No, no, not mine. I'm curious about Bradley Stokes "

"The Hitman? How come?"

I laughed. "Circumstantial stuff. He had a penthouse suite at the hotel. Phyllis Diller and Billy Cash were in the others. I think we can discount Phyllis and Cash's suite was at the wrong side of the hotel. Charismatic bloke in person, by the way. Ha. Anyway, Cissie could have fallen from Stokes' window."

Peters frowned. "I don't really know anything about Stokes. I've heard he's a bit of a hound, but I wouldn't have thought him a Fatty Arbuckle. What with all the tabloid interest in his divorce, he's got to be careful. He's got too much to lose. You know, perhaps it was just an accident as the police first said."

"What about Ruthie, the photographer? That was no accident."

"But didn't you say she was being threatened by the police? Maybe her death was coincidental."

"Hell of a big coincidence."

He nodded slowly. A hard look came on his face. "Well, if Cissie was murdered I'm as keen as you are to find out who did it."

"So can I ask you a couple of questions without you blowing your top?"

He sighed.

"Like what?"

"Where were you the night she was killed?"

He seemed to be looking for something in my face. Finally he said, "From what I've heard you may not want to know."

"Trust me. I do."

But he was right.

I was pretty drunk when I finally left the Assembly Rooms a couple of hours later. It was two in the morning but I had to push through a crowd milling around on the pavement. I thought of finding a pub for a few more drinks—all the pubs in the city stay open until three in the morning—but instead I meandered across the road, misjudging the speed of a black cab that had to brake to avoid running me over.

It was a warm night and I was sweating by the time I hove into Cathay Place. I had considered calling in on Bridget to get things sorted out and give her Phil's alibi but I doubted she'd be alone. Edinburgh was one big shaggathon for her.

I could hear a bird singing in the garden in the center of the square. I stopped for a moment to hear it more clearly. I didn't know a lot about birds but I knew enough to know that more than just nightingales sang at night. I heard soft footfalls some distance behind me. As they entered the square, they abruptly stopped.

I looked around. The street I had come down looked deserted, although it would have been easy for someone to conceal themselves in the shadows. I listened to the bird for a couple more minutes, listening too for any resumption of the footsteps. Nobody else came into the square.

In the apartment I went straight to the kitchen to drink a liter of water before bed. As I stepped in I glanced at the litter tray and recoiled in horror.

In it was a pile about a foot high. It looked like one of those towers ants in Africa make. I looked round the kitchen warily. Surely no cat did that on a can of Whiskas a day?

I went looking for Hilly's cat, Kevin. He was still in the cupboard shedding hairs over the clean linen. I looked at him. I wondered at the thought of producing your own body weight in poop. I mean, I'd seen some amazing and repellent sights in public loos. But that's to be expected. Nobody uses a public loo unless they're desperate because of the state they're in and they're in the state they're in because only desperate people use them.

I reached out to stroke Kevin's head, impressed, despite myself, that he had the defecatory powers of an elephant. His paw shot out but I was too quick for him. Just.

Could it be Lionel? Who indeed was Lionel? Some Mrs. Haversham figure locked in the airing cupboard? I went to the locked door and peered through the keyhole. Blackness. I went looking for the key and found it hanging on a hook behind the fridge. I unlocked the door.

It took me a moment to find the light switch but when I did I could see that the locked room was the apartment's dining room. The furniture had been pushed to one end to make room for an enormous glass cabinet some twelve feet long by four feet high. In it, coiled around a short tree trunk, was a large snake. A very large snake. I mean we're talking boa constrictor or python here. How should I know the difference?

I moved to get a closer look, but not too much closer. I couldn't make much of it. I couldn't even locate its head. I waited for it to move but its thick coils didn't so much as quiver. After a couple of minutes I withdrew, closing the door behind me. I got into Hilly's large bed and lay looking at the ceiling. Terrific. I'd rented an apartment in *The Jungle Book*.

I dozed off contemplating snakes but I didn't dream of them. Instead, I have to confess, I dreamed off Hilly, my temporary landlady, her big-boned body beside me in the bed. And then on top of me. Her heavy weight on my chest. I woke with heart-lurching suddenness and jerked upright. Kevin yowled, hurtled off my chest, and skidded out of the room as soon as his paws touched the ground. I lay back again and tried to steady my breathing.

I was contemplating getting some water from the kitchen when I heard, somewhere in the distance, the sound of glass shattering. A lot of glass. Shit. That could only mean one thing. Lionel wakes. I slipped out of bed and tiptoed to the door of the bedroom. I could hear movement in the dining room, then a ferocious rattling of the door handle. Startled, I shrank back. I didn't think snakes went much on manual dexterity—not having hands, for one thing—so I hadn't bothered to relock the door.

As I watched, the door abruptly opened and I feared I had made a terrible mistake. But I was relieved to see not a snake but a man emerge from the room. My first thought was thank God for that as he glanced at me then set off down the corridor to the front door. My second thought was what the hell was he doing in my apartment?

"Hey!" I shouted, without thinking. He stopped, turned, peered back to where I stood in the bedroom doorway. He looked a tough customer—stocky, close-cropped hair, angular face, broad shoulders. As he contemplated me I became uncomfortably aware that for such occasions I really should start wearing pajamas.

He didn't move, I certainly didn't move. Only the snake moved. I saw its head appear for a moment at the entrance to the dining room. He saw it too. Suddenly he was off, hauling open the front door and charging through it. I started off gingerly down the corridor, made a kind of running jump past the dining room door, hoping the snake wouldn't be able to lassoo me or more specifically anything dangling from me in mid-air.

It couldn't. I dashed out of the flat, closing the door behind me so Lionel couldn't go on a New Town rampage. I chased my intruder down the stairs. Well, chased is perhaps too strong a word. I followed him, the less quixotic part of me praying he wouldn't suddenly turn to defend himself. I heard him clattering across the foyer and slowed down to give him time to fiddle with the front door latch. It took him forever. He looked back over his shoulder. God, he looked fierce. I pretended to stumble on the last step. Delicate business. I didn't want to fall so he'd come back and jump up and down on my head but I didn't want him to feel trapped. He was taking an age to get the door open. "Lean against it and twist down," I wanted to shout as he yanked at the latch.

Eventually he managed it and dashed out into the night. I poked my head round the door and shook my fist after him for the sake of any passersby then made my slow way back up the stairs. I kept thinking of the Paul Merton joke: "I disturbed a burglar last night. I told him God didn't exist." I was smiling when I got to my door to find I'd locked myself out.

I groaned. The thought of knocking on a neighbor's door at four in the morning without so much as a sporran to hide behind didn't exactly thrill me. Besides which, if no one had come to the door after the racket the burglar had made on the stairs, no one was likely to come forward when I knocked on their door. Good old Edinburgh hospitality. Someone once told me the difference between folk in Glasgow and folk in Edinburgh. In Glasgow when you call they say: Come away in and have your tea. In Edinburgh they say: You'll have had your tea.

Still, I had to try. I crouched before the door upstairs and hammered on it. No response. I did the same with the one below. Utter silence. I scurried down the basement steps. I was getting cold. There was a door out into the garden. Maybe I could climb into my flat the same way my intruder had.

I stepped out into the garden, the grass pleasantly soft and cool beneath my feet. I took another step and the garden was suddenly flooded with light, thanks to an infrared device on the wall above me. I froze then gave a yelp when I realized I was not alone. There was a camel standing directly in front of me. It looked like I'd just interrupted its reverie of hot sun, desert sand, and a significant other dromedary.

"You must be Clarence," I said, then it spat in my eye.

The inside of a camel's mouth is a syphilitic green mess of warts and strange extrusions. Its phlegmy spit issues with remarkable force and surprising accuracy up to a distance of ten yards. I was about four yards away. The large ball of green slime clung to my eye socket for a moment then began a slow slide down my face.

When alarmed, dromedaries either spit or break wind. Clarence, I soon discovered, had done both. I inhaled sharply in horror. Given Clarence's noxiously plosive anus, this was a *big* mistake. Gagging, I reeled, lost my footing and fell backwards into a pile of dromedary droppings. Actually, droppings is too genteel a term to describe what I fell into. Nor are roses what I came up smelling of.

I'm sure Clarence sneered as he wandered away across the garden. I spent five minutes rolling around in what appeared to be a clean part of the lawn, wiping off my back what a dromedary does naturally. I tiptoed over to the extension tacked on at the back of the ground floor flat. There was a drainpipe running up the side. A climbing rose, studded with thorns, wrapped around it. I looked down at my unprotected body. Perhaps not.

I found the ladder my burglar had used and got back into the apartment without difficulty, if you discount crushing my testicles on the windowsill as I crawled back into the dining room. The snake's glass box was lying on its side on the floor, the lid in pieces. I steered well clear of it as I tiptoed barefoot out into the corridor.

I put the door on the latch in case I had to make a quick getaway then went in search of Lionel. I couldn't find him at first. I couldn't even find the cat. Armed with a long-handled brush I went from room to room, turning on all the lights as I progressed. Eventually I found Lionel lounging under the piano. I guessed I'd found Kevin, too. At least I assumed that's what that lump partway down Lionel's body—about halfway through his digestive process—was.

Strictly speaking I suppose snakes can't smile. Tell that to Lionel. He looked, if you'll pardon the unfortunate simile, like the cat who'd swallowed the canary.

"Oh, Lionel," I said under my breath.

I thought of chastising him. But how? With a dog or a cat you maybe boot it up the arse. I was sure Lionel had an arse but I'd be damned if I knew where it was. Clutching my brush, I got down on my hands and knees and started to get under the piano. I'm not sure what I intended but "Action This Day" has always been my motto. Well, almost always. I was down on all fours, mouthing what I imagined to be soothing snake noises, my naked, poop-streaked bum sticking up in the air, when the policeman walked in.

SIX

"Hilly, it's Nick. The bloke renting your apartment. Me? I'm fine. Kevin, that's something else again. But the good news is, Lionel has his appetite back."

She took it rather well in the circumstances. The circumstances being her dining room had been trashed, her cat eaten, and she had a fourteen foot snake curled up in her sitting room. She need never know about the dromedary doo-doo on her linen sheets, since they were in the wash. Because I was tired, that's why, and forgot to shower.

I'd just been interrogated by a policeman, who for some reason found my story hard to believe. One who upset me with totally unnecessary and gratuitously offensive remarks. I know bestiality is a criminal offence but I was not attempting to have sex with a snake when he found me. Nor had I been trying to arouse the camel by rolling around naked before it, despite what my ground floor neighbors said when they phoned the police. And calling me wasp willy was just plain cruel: he'd be a wasp willy too if he'd been through what I'd been through.

Hilly admitted it had been foolish of her to try to keep the snake in an apartment when her friend let it roam through a couple of rooms in her house. I didn't want to think about what kind of friends she had. She said she'd get it moved temporarily to the zoo in the local Zoological Gardens. "It's best known for its penguins," she said, "but I think it'll manage." I had a sudden vision of Lionel munching his way through a line of seafowl.

We arranged to rendezvous at the flat at eleven. It was only nine now. I hadn't got to bed much before dawn and my head was spinning. Had it been an ordinary burglar or someone after the photographs I'd mentioned in the bar? Someone who had followed me home to do me harm?

I made a jug of strong coffee—Hilly knew her beans—and went back into the bedroom to sit on a chaise longue by the window. I was gazing gloomily down into the square when a taxi pulled up and Bridget got out. She looked up at the facade of the house and I waved down at her. Unaccountably she was soberly dressed in a trouser suit and deck shoes.

"We'll have to go in the bedroom," I said when she entered the flat. She gave me an arch look.

"Really?"

"You won't believe it if I tell you why."

She plumped down on the chaise longue and looked for a moment at the book I had left open on the floor beside it.

"*Goat Medicine?* Nick, I had no idea."

I blushed. "It was just lying around the place."

"Must run in the family. When you said your granddad was a pigeon fancier I told you there was a law against it."

There was silence for a moment.

"You're looking very ... quiet," I said. She shrugged. Gave me a hard look.

"Nick, don't try to investigate Bradley Stokes. You'd be way out of your depth. You could get hurt. It'd be professional suicide."

I looked at her and shook my head.

"I'm sure you're right. I'm no hero. And I haven't a clue how to be an investigative journalist. But this is all so fishy. And, Bridget, Phil Peters has got an alibi for where he was when Cissie died."

"Witness?"

I nodded.

"So what are you looking so miserable about? That means you were right doesn't it?"

I smiled.

"His alibi is Amanda Colgate. You know, the comedian with the long legs, the Louise Brooks bob … my heart."

She looked at me for a moment.

"Oops."

I nodded.

"She was with him all night. And other nights."

"Are you inclined to check if he's telling the truth?"

"He spelled it out. You know you'd heard he was coming and going from the apartments across from the hotel? Well, Cissie Parker was staying there, of course. But so was Amanda. It was Amanda he was visiting. On the night in question—God, that tripped off the tongue—on that night, he told me he fell asleep wrapped around her, he woke up wrapped around her."

I must have looked a little like the way I felt.

"So where does that leave us, apart from you looking like someone just pushed your house down on top of you."

"I'm all right," I said stiffly. "I was just surprised. Phil was very nice about it."

"Bully for him. So what about your Bradley Stokes' theory?"

"I still think it could run. But there are other possibilities." I filled her in on my conversation with Phil and told her about Loud Lenny's memory loss.

"Lenny Finnegan? Now that's interesting. He was dogging you pretty closely in Montreal wasn't he?"

"I can be quite good company," I said tersely.

"So they tell me." She reached across to pat my hand. "Darling, I adore you. But if I were a murderer and you were trying to solve a couple of murders, I'd stick close to you to find out what you knew. Maybe that's what Lenny was doing."

"All I know is that somebody here in Edinburgh was involved in what happened in Montreal. This place was broken into last night."

"Did they get anything?"

"A shock. I think they may have been after the photographs Ruthie took of Cissie at that party."

"What kind of shock?"

The doorbell rang. It was Hilly. She looked extremely wary.

"I called in at my ground-floor neighbors on the way up," she said hesitantly. "You didn't tell me about you and Clarence."

Bridget looked from her to me.

"Clarence?"

"My dromedary," Hilly said.

"Of course," Bridget said. "I was just telling Nick it must run in the family. His granddad was a pigeon fancier, you know. If I'm not mistaken, a lover of horseflesh too, the filthy devil."

Hilly looked bemused. I ignored Bridget.

"I'd locked myself out of the apartment trying to make sure Lionel didn't escape," I said to her by way of explanation.

"Lionel?" Bridget said.

"Her friend's python," I said.

"Boa constrictor," Hilly said.

"What's the difference?" Bridget and I said together.

"Pythons are from Africa or India, boa constrictors are from Brazil. Lionel was from Brazil."

Bridget nodded and looked from Hilly to me again.

"You had a boa constrictor loose here?"

"Have," I said. "It's shut in the sitting room."

"Of course," Bridget said again. "Isn't that, er, dangerous?"

"He's probably sleeping off his dinner," said Hilly. "Kevin will keep him going for a while."

I forestalled Bridget's next question.

"Kevin is Hilly's cat. Was Hilly's cat."

"Was?"

"Lionel ate him."

Bridget let out a whoop of laughter. I looked nervously at Hilly. She was looking at Bridget, shocked, but as Bridget's unrestrained laughter continued she too started laughing and within a few moments we were all cackling helplessly.

Hilly waited for the people from the zoo whilst Bridget and I went on our way. I caught a cab to the Film Festival launch. In a few days, when the festival was properly under way, traffic in the city would grind to a halt and catching cabs would be pointless.

The launch was taking place at the festival headquarters on Lothian Road. The bar had been converted for the duration of the festival into a special film cafe. Areas of the room were partitioned off by large glass tanks raised on shelves containing exotic fish of various kinds.

I said hello to a couple of journalists I vaguely knew and surveyed the room. Edinburgh isn't like Cannes, you don't get many stars turning up to promote films. The room was full of producers, directors, and distribution people. I got talking to a director from Iceland—probably the only director from Iceland—about a comedy he'd just made there. He told me it reflected the fact that a good proportion of the people are suicidally depressed in winter, merely suicidal come spring, and alcoholic all year round. It sounded a laugh a minute.

As we talked I saw Juliette come into the party. Unusually, she was on her own. She saw me and nodded. I excused myself and went over to her.

"Lunch at the Forum with Billy, tomorrow, Tuesday, at twelve thirty," she said. "There'll be a couple of tickets on the door for you for the first show tonight. You haven't seen Billy perform before, have you? I think you'll enjoy it."

"Thanks," I said. "What about Bradley Stokes? The Hitman. Can I talk to him?"

"Is this still for a magazine cover?"

"I never said it was a cover. No, this will be for a daily. Big piece though."

"And nothing about his divorce?"

"His divorce wasn't uppermost in my mind, no."

"He flies in tomorrow. I'll arrange something for Wednesday. An hour enough?"

I nodded, turned to leave, and walked straight into Juliette's heavy, John Rolfe. It was like walking into a wall. I bounced back, missed my footing on a raised step and lost my balance. Before I fell I saw Rolfe reach out to grab me. At least, I think he was trying to grab me. Then I hit the edge of a shelf and went sprawling.

The taxi driver charged me double for bringing me home. The back of his cab wasn't too wet although I noticed a couple of dead fish lodged down the back of the seat. Those aquaria really should have been secured more firmly. As I told the Film Festival staff who were, frankly, unsympathetic. They presumed I was drunk.

"How can you presume such a thing?" I asked indignantly.

"We know you," they replied. Fair enough.

I squelched across to the entrance door of the house, trying to ignore the curtains twitching on the ground floor. I took a long soak in the bath, working my way half way through a bottle of rioja. Not wise, but I'm that kind of guy. Live quite fast, die relatively young, and leave a moderately nice looking corpse.

Bridget was busy that evening so I called Mary Kelly, the American journalist who had given me such a shock about Steve Hewitt, Frank's multiple murder candidate. I invited her to see Billy Cash with me.

We met in the spiegeltent. She looked very sexy in a sleeveless, short, black dress, her legs bare, her short hair made spiky.

She greeted me with a peck on the cheek and insisted on buying the drinks.

We sat in a booth. It was too early for the live music but Bill Evans was doing pleasing things in the background. I asked her about herself. Twenty-something Arkansas farm girl, studied journalism at college, worked on a Hicktown gazette somewhere in Texas until she got her break with a local sex 'n' rock 'n' roll scandal. Broke the story, sold it on to the New York papers, one of them gave her a freelance contract and since then she'd been New York based.

"If you don't mind my asking, how did you meet Steve Hewitt?"

"When I got to Montreal. It was one of those mistakes. My first time covering the festival, I was feeling fragile at the end of a long relationship, he was nice to me."

"Clearly not that nice."

"Until that night he'd been very helpful, very gentlemanly."

"So." I hesitated. "What happened that night?"

I tried not to look as she re-crossed her legs then tugged ineffectually at her skirt.

"He got angry when I wouldn't sleep with him," she said after a moment. "Turned really weird. Scared me to death."

"Did he hit you?"

She looked down. "He lashed out at me, yes."

"So why didn't you report him to the festival?"

"You know how it can be. I wasn't sure if it was my fault in some way. Didn't know if I'd been leading him on. These situations can be very complex. Plus I felt embarrassed. My first time at the festival and here I was fucking up."

'Yeah, it's a tough call."

"When finally I decided I would report him, well, that was the day he died. But you know, angry as he got with me, I didn't see him as a killer."

"Me neither. I don't believe he killed Cissie Parker, the first victim. And I don't believe he killed the second victim, Ruthie, the photographer. But he did kill my friend, Frank."

"I understood that may have been an accident."

I grimaced.

"Maybe."

"So have you anybody else in the frame?"

I hesitated.

"Oh, I'm sorry," she said. "I didn't mean to pry."

"It's okay." I told her my suspicions about Bradley Stokes.

"Bradley Stokes. Really?"

"You don't sound wild about the idea."

"I haven't heard your evidence. Listen, I'm going to tell you something I was hoping to make use of myself. I overheard Cissie at the party you mentioned."

"You were there? I thought tickets were like gold dust."

"I told you Steve Hewitt was nice to me."

"Who was Cissie with?"

"Don't know. I was sitting by one side of a partition; she was sitting by the other side with somebody I didn't see. I heard her say very distinctly to that person: 'Don't you see how this changes everything for both of us?'"

I looked at Mary's triumphant face.

"That's it?"

She looked impatient. "Well, yes. What did you want—a name and address?"

"Would've been nice. How did she say it? Was she up? Down? Excited?"

"Kind of excited, kind of insistent, kind of wired."

"I wonder what she was talking about. Her pregnancy?"

"You know her pregnancy must be the key to it, don't you? Has a father come forward?"

"Not to my knowledge. Do you think maybe the guy she

was talking to was the father?"

"Hey, you're the Sherlock Holmes in this partnership, buddy. I'm just a probationer."

"I've got some photographs of Cissie with various people at the party. In one she's with a man we can't identify."

"Let me look. I'll see if I can."

"It's back at my apartment. Maybe you could come back after the gig."

She gave me a knowing look and I reddened.

"Well, now, Mr. Madrid. Let's see how the evening pans out first, shall we?"

I swear Bridget has antennae. The Assembly Rooms bar was packed when Mary and I got there after the show. Bridget was sitting with her back to us, but almost the moment we walked in she looked over her shoulder and clocked Mary. She gave me what can only be described as an old-fashioned look. When I went to the bar she sidled up to me. Which was nice, since, although I knew the word, I'd never seen a sidle in action before.

"You at it again?" she said.

"That's Mary Kelly. The woman who was with Steve Hewitt on that celebrated night. Want to meet her?"

Bridget shook her head and smirked.

"You're a calculating bugger," she said.

"Why?"

"Because you're thinking if she was willing to nob Hewitt she's bound to nob you."

I was shocked. Bridget had become a mind reader.

"But she didn't have sex with him," I whispered to her as I left the bar. "That was the problem."

"I was going to," Mary said, matter-of-factly. "He'd been nice to me, I was horny, I figured why not? But when he came out of the bathroom dressed in a crotchless g string and a won-derbra, lipstick daubing his mouth and moustache, I'm thinking is this a comedy festival or what?"

As I was laughing a man came and planted himself in front of us. Medium height, scruffy charcoal suit, once white shirt, and ratty tie of an indeterminate color. He looked the very defini-tion of shiftiness.

"Nick Madrid?" he said out of the corner of his mouth, darting glances all around. I nodded cautiously. "Got something for you. Information."

"Who are you?"

"Never mind that," he said. He glanced at Mary. "Do you want to fuck off for a minute, dear?"

Mary's hand shot out and caught him a resounding whack across his mouth. She'd moved so quickly that whilst some people turned at the sound no one actually saw it happen. The seedy man rocked back on his heels.

"Then again, why don't you stay?" he said sourly. "Mr. Madrid, I got something you want to buy."

"I don't think so," I said.

"That's 'cos you haven't heard me out."

"That's because you're taking so long about it."

"Do I look familiar to you?" he persisted.

"Only as a type," I said. "Why? Do I know you?"

"Not exactly. But if I say I saw you doing your yoga on a certain morning in Montreal, perhaps you can guess who I am." Suddenly a look of alarm came on to the man's features. I fol-lowed his glance. Two hard looking men were wading through the bar towards us, their eyes fixed on our new acquaintance.

"Meet me outside the Castle gates in two hours. Midnight sharp. Be there." And before I could say anything he was gone. A few moments later the two men were alongside us. As he passed, one of them gave me a harsh look.

As they hurried from the bar, Juliette's heavy, John Rolfe, walked in. He nodded stiffly to me. When he glanced at Mary she rather demurely lowered her eyes.

After a moment she said, "What was all that about?"

"If that scruffy git is who I think he is, then he saw Cissie fall." I told Mary about the silhouette I'd seen in a window of the building opposite the hotel just before Cissie's death.

"Who were the tough guys?"

"Search me. Do you want to come with me at midnight?"

She looked surprised.

"Sure."

Bridget was looking across at me with a puzzled look on her face.

"Hang on a sec," I said to Mary, making my way over to Bridget. I told her about my silhouette taking on bodily substance.

"Do you want to come to the Castle at midnight or do you really want to be left out of it now?"

"The Castle at midnight. Shouldn't it be the graveyard to discover whether vampires really exist? Of course I want to come."

"I've invited Mary, too."

Bridget nodded, a faint smile on her face. It was better than her smirk.

"What do you intend to do until then?" she asked innocently, or rather with an approximation of innocence.

"I thought I'd take Mary back to the apartment to look at the photographs. Do you want to come?"

The smirk was back.

"I'll join you there later. You're a naughty, naughty boy, Mr. Madrid."

It was still light when Mary and I walked down George Street into Charlotte Square. We stopped at the crossing and waited for the lights to change. Mary touched my arm.

"You realize that if you're serious about Bradley Stokes, he must be the father of the baby?"

"That's the bit I can't see somehow. He's not exactly Mr. Sex Appeal."

"But I thought you agreed the father of the baby is the crucial person in all this."

We started walking again.

"Okay then, maybe he is. They were together at the launch party. Did you see them? Could he have been the man you overheard her talking to?"

"Don't know. But I agree with you. Besides, I'm not sure he can be the father because of his—you know—his thing."

"His thing?"

"His implant." She looked at me. "You don't know about it? I thought every journalist in the world knew about it. He's impotent but he has some kind of electro-mechanical implant in his penis to give him erections. It's one of the things that came up, so to speak, during the divorce hearings."

"You're kidding me."

"It's true." She started to laugh. "You haven't heard the story? It had a malfunction when he was appearing in Las Vegas. At his hotel, every time his neighbor used the television remote control ..."

I was still laughing when we reached the apartment. I entered nervously, hurrying to turn on all the lights. I kept Mary waiting in the corridor whilst I checked the sitting room. The snake had been removed.

Mary went to the long window and looked out at the sky darkening over the Firth of Forth. I gave her a glass of wine then went to get the photographs. When I came back she was lounging on one of the plump sofas, her dress riding high on her thighs. I sat beside her and gave her the photos. Swigging her drink she looked at each one carefully, spending the most time on the one of Cissie with the mystery man.

"I don't recognize him," she finally said. "But I don't think it can be Bradley Stokes. He's not fat enough." She put the photos down on the table. "Sorry I can't be more help."

I nodded and took a sip of my drink. I glanced at her sideways. There was a shift in the air. After a few moments we turned together, in that way two people with but a single thought do. We kissed for a long time. As we embraced she brushed her hand across my trousers.

"I think your neighbor has been changing TV channels," she murmured.

After a few more minutes she disentangled herself. "I need your bathroom."

As she went out I flashed a quick look at my watch. Ten forty five. Bridget was arriving at eleven thirty, which meant we had forty-five minutes. Ample time, in my experience, to cover all the bases from foreplay to post-coital. At least twice. I don't want to brag but I don't hang about.

Mary came back into the room wagging a finger at me.

"Nick, you little devil," she said.

"What?"

She brought her other hand out from behind her back. She was wearing on her middle finger the yellow condom with the cat's head. I felt myself flush scarlet.

"Oh, that," I said, attempting nonchalance. "That's not mine. It was in the flat when I moved in."

"Really?"

"Sure," I said, adding in my most risqué voice, "it's too small for me."

She looked at it, then at me.

"I doubt it," she said, dropping it on the telephone table. She walked over and sank back into the sofa beside me. As I reached for her she said, "We have to be at the Castle by midnight."

"So we shouldn't waste any more time," I said, nibbling her earlobe.

"No, no," she said, shifting her head. "I like to linger."

"What else do you like?" I said in my huskiest voice.

She told me. In great detail. I had to pause to catch my breath. Not in excitement. In panic. I couldn't do that, yoga or no yoga. She didn't need me, she needed a mechanical engineer.

"I'd hate to start something we don't have time to finish," she said.

"I agree," I said fervently. "Perhaps we'd better leave it to another time."

Maybe I was too fervent. She leaned over and kissed the tip of my nose.

"Just kidding you, Nick," she said gently. "No need to be alarmed. I like a cuddle more than anything."

Bridget's early arrival saved me further embarrassment. She was clearly disappointed not to find us sweaty and dishabille.

"Julie always said you were fast," she muttered as she came into the sitting room.

I took that as a compliment but I was indignant that my ex-girlfriend and Bridget had been discussing me.

"When?" I said, as I walked Bridget over to Mary, standing by the window.

"We had a long conversation about you once. I was curious to know how you were in bed."

"Oh really. And what else did she say?"

We reached Mary.

"She said you were thorough, sweetie."

"Thorough?" I mouthed.

"Thorough?" Mary said, looking from one to the other of us.

"Nick's research," Bridget said, giving 'smiling sweetly' her best shot. I suddenly had a vivid image of Lionel after he had eaten the cat.

"So you were Steve Hewitt's date on that infamous night," Bridget said.

"Discriminating, aren't I?"

Bridget looked me up and down.

"No comment."

I phoned for a cab and whilst we were waiting we made slightly strained conversation. On the way out, Bridget gingerly picked up the cat condom from the phone table.

"This is to save your nails when dialling the phone I suppose," she said sarcastically. "Nick, I hope the policeman interrogating you about offences to animals didn't see this."

Mary gave me a long look.

The cabbie took us over Waverley Bridge and up on to High Street in about five minutes. The pubs were still doing a roaring trade, with drinkers milling about on the pavement outside. The Edinburgh Tattoo, the great military exhibition and fireworks display, had not long finished. Discarded programs and other litter lay all around.

The cab dropped us just below Castle Hill, a couple of hundred yards from the castle gates. We were a few minutes early so we strolled slowly up the steep incline, silent except for Bridget's high heels—she'd abandoned the platforms for the evening—clacking on the broad flagstones.

There wasn't a breath of wind so the sounds of the city below were carried up to us on the soft air ... traffic and voices and snatches of music. We could smell the cordite from the big guns used in the Tattoo.

We reached the huge gates and waited. And waited. At twelve thirty, when we were just about to abandon our vigil, we heard the sound of someone hurrying along Johnston Terrace, below the south wall of the Castle. The man who had approached me in the Assembly Rooms appeared round the corner and came up to us.

"I said you, Mr. Madrid, not your fucking harem."

Mary and Bridget both stepped forward and I wondered which one would land the first punch.

"If anyone hits me again, I'm off," he said quickly. "Listen, ladies, why don't you go over there into that pub whilst I talk to your man here. 'Cos what I got to say is for his ears only."

I looked at them and shrugged.

"I'll be over in five minutes."

Bridget and Mary went remarkably meekly. I wondered what revenge they would plan. The man pulled me into the shadows of the gatehouse.

"Well?"

"I have something you may want to buy from me. A piece of information."

"I don't have money to buy anything."

"Your paper, I mean."

"You saw Cissie Parker die," I said flatly.

"Clever man," he said.

"What were you doing in Montreal and what are you doing here in Edinburgh?"

"I'm a street performer. Human Blockhead. Hammer nails up my nose, all that stuff. You should write about me some time."

"Yeah. Some time. Why didn't you go to the police with your information?"

"I've got a living to make. I figured I could get money from a certain person who wouldn't want the information to be known or from others who would."

"You saw who pushed her?"

"We haven't discussed money yet."

"I need to know roughly what I'm buying."

"Fair enough. I saw where from and I saw she was being helped."

"Who were the heavies in the Assembly Rooms?"

"I'm Dick Francis and these gents are Harvey and Ronnie," a voice said.

I jerked round. Two men I recognized from earlier in the evening were standing a few yards away, with a third man hovering just behind them.

"Harvey who?" I said.

"Just Harvey," one of the men from the Assembly Rooms said, his voice a deep rumble. A bodybuilder by the thickness of his neck and the width of his shoulders. He was only about five feet eight but he looked the same width. It was only when I started using a gym where guys like this hung out that I understood what physical jerks were. I looked at Ronnie. He was the man who had tried to burgle my apartment the previous night.

"Nice to see you again," I said.

"How ya doin', wasp willy?" Ronnie replied. Bastard.

"What do you want?" I said.

"We want to escort Mr. Pace here somewhere we can have a quiet talk."

I looked at the Human Blockhead and summoned up a bravado I didn't feel. "Mr. Pace has already told me everything."

Francis looked at me. Shook his head.

"I'm sorry to hear that," he said. "Very sorry." He half turned to Ronnie. "Bring the car round."

"Are you going to be all fucking night?" someone screeched. My first thought was, who'd be selling fish at this hour? My second was, Bridget, bless her. The three heavies turned to see her standing with Mary in the doorway of the pub. Pace took advantage of their distraction to sprint off down the street. From a standing start his turn of speed was impressive, but I was only ten yards behind him as he turned down towards the Grassmarket.

He slowed to allow me to catch up and together we zigzagged through narrow cobblestoned alleys, tall tenements hemming us in. Our pursuers may have been a trifle slower but they were persistent. And they seemed to know the turf far better than we did. Twice we lurched into blind alleys, losing precious seconds as we retraced our steps and started out again.

The second time, we missed colliding with Harvey and Francis by yards. "Split up," Pace hissed, pushing me into an opening to my left whilst he continued on up the street. I ran down the steeply cobbled alley, picking up speed as I went. I could hear the clatter of feet behind me. Someone was still in pursuit. Narrow alleys opened to left and right but I didn't dare go down them in case they were dead ends.

I saw a pair of double doors, opened outwards, on my left. Almost overshooting, I veered through them, ricocheting off the far wall of a corridor. I raced down the corridor and flung open a door. A harassed looking man was on the other side, deep in conversation with a couple of worried looking women. When I burst through the door he looked startled, angry, and relieved, all at the same time.

"Sorry," I said, trying to push past him to a door with a red exit sign above it.

"This way," he said, yanking me by the arm towards a grubby set of curtains. "The natives are getting restless."

He pushed me through the curtains. I stumbled forward a few yards, blinded by bright lights shining in my face. I looked round wild-eyed, frozen in place. I heard desultory laughter. I could make out the silhouette of a microphone stand. Shit. I turned and groped for the curtains. Scattered laughter.

I found the gap in the curtain. Opened it. Dick Francis was holding the harassed guy up against the wall by the throat. He looked more harassed. I dropped the curtain and turned back towards the lights, shielding my eyes with my hand. I moved across what I now recognized as a stage to the far side. I was breathing heavily. I parted the curtain. No way out.

"Shit," I said, audibly this time.

"Lee Evans did it funnier," someone called out from what I knew, with a sinking heart, to be an audience.

I moved gingerly towards the microphone, trying to get my breath. I don't know who they were expecting but he must have been a midget. I wrestled for a moment trying to get the microphone off the stand but my hands were shaking too much. I crouched therefore, trying to slow my speeding brain.

'Yeah, I know," I finally said, my mouth too close to the microphone so that my voice boomed out. "But I was thinking …"What was I thinking? I was thinking I hated speaking in public. As my eyes adjusted to the chiaroscuro I could make out about forty silhouettes. A good turn-out at this time of night for whoever I was supposed to be, especially as no one seemed to know what he looked like.

"I was thinking about mistaken identity." I glanced to my right. Francis was talking into his mobile phone. "I often get mistaken for a member of the aristocracy," I said, "… though whose member no one will say." Silence. "This reminds me of the time I was a nude model at an art evening class. I'd just failed the physical for a blue movie. They wanted a man." Silence. "Anyway, at this evening class—you know, life drawing—and I'd never done anything like this before—"

This was a true story. I took a breath and tried to slow my delivery.

"My first night I arrived early. Thought I'd get a psychological advantage. Stripped off, settled myself on the table at the front of the room, and waited for the class to arrive. Few minutes later they all filed in, glanced over at me. Sat down at their desks and opened their *Spanish for Beginners* textbooks."

Silence. "I was in the wrong classroom," I added unnecessarily.

Okay, so maybe stand-up wasn't my forte, but this was more

improv. Plus I was slightly distracted by the hoodlum behind the curtains. I could see a single exit at the back of the cramped auditorium. As I watched, a bulky silhouette blocked it.

"Evening classes, eh?" I blurted out. "I'm a sucker for them. I went to be an actor once. Drama classes. But space is so tight. We had to share with an arboricultural studies group. You know: trees. Everything got very mixed up. All these trees standing around pretending to be actors."

I shaded my eyes and looked at the audience. Not a titter, as Frankie Howerd used to say. I'm dying but at least I'm alive. Ha. So far. I cast around for something else to say as I heard mutterings, beginnings of conversations in the audience, and the shuffling of feet. Whose jokes could I nick? The only ones that came to my mind were ones that had lodged there since my schooldays. The green ping-pong ball. The polar bear. I was aware of the sweat soaking into my shirt and pouring down my face.

"You're rubbish, you are," somebody called out.

"I'm working class. The real thing. My grandfather used to keep whippets. Used to tie messages to their legs and throw them out of his bedroom window."

A snort of laughter from somewhere in the room.

"I love late night films. I was watching one set in Egypt last night. It was a big genre at one time. Copts and robbers. You won't see that on the fringe—or probably you will. The shows people come up with. You've seen that *Hamlet* is being done by a bunch of Sioux Indians? They couldn't decide where to stay. Tepee or not tepee? *Waiting For Godot On Ice*—that looks like a winner."

"Why don't you do us all a favor and get off the stage?' the guy with the big mouth hollered again.

"I wish I could," I said. I had an idea about how I might manage it.

"You with the big mouth, what's your name?"

"Robin Williams," he said, guffawing. Something else I'd never heard before.

"In your dreams, pal. I think you're a Doug. Where are you from, Doug?"

I looked to the side of the stage as I was talking to him. Dick Francis beckoned.

"What's up—is there someone funnier waiting to come on?" Doug said.

"See what happens when cousins marry," I said, nicking someone else's putdown. More laughter. "Where you from Doug? Let's get that accent nailed."

"Who gives a toss?" he said belligerently.

The object was to get out of the auditorium without being either lynched by the audience or grabbed by the heavies. Which sounds rudely painful, don't you think? I saw a comedian once leave the auditorium, taking the mike with him, to follow a guy who was going to the toilet. But I seemed to be the only person round here who needed the loo. Steve Martin, to whom by now I felt almost related, was famous for leading his entire audience out of the stadium where he was playing to a local fast food place for a takeaway.

I just needed to get past the exit sign then I'd take my chances.

"You fancy a bevvy, Doug?" I said. Silence. "Come on. Who fancies a pint?"

"It's gotta be better than this shit," Doug yelled.

"My feeling entirely," I said, jumping down off the stage and squinting beneath the lights towards the exit. The bulky silhouette was still there. "Start from the back row, and that bloke at the exit can you get the doors opened please?"

A dozen or so people started milling in the side aisle. I plunged in among them, pushing a couple of them ahead of me.

"It's no gimmick, this is the real thing—I'm paying," I said, glancing back at the stage. The formerly harassed, now frightened and perplexed, manager was standing on stage next to Francis. I waved.

"Ta, ta."

The heavy at the exit, a man I'd not seen before, was buffeted by the crowd of people. He tried to grab for my shoulder but missed by a good yard. We came out into Cowgate. There was a pub on the other side of the street.

"Doug, hold the traffic will you, boy, whilst we all go across crocodile fashion, shoes and handbags first."

Doug marched into what traffic there was and held up his arms. Asshole. He was a big guy and the traffic did as it was told. I looked back to the door to the theater where Dick Francis and the other heavy were hovering behind my audience. I dashed ahead and into the pub. I saw the signs for the toilets.

"Mine's a beer," Doug said over my shoulder. He wasn't taking any chances.

"Sure. Look, take everyone's order. I need the loo. Back in a minute."

The toilet window was big enough to wriggle through. Within two minutes I was puffing and panting up a steep incline to get back to High Street. Gasping open-mouthed I dashed into the pub where I'd left Mary and Bridget. No sign of them.

I jogged back along High Street and cut off to the left down a steep set of steps, heading for the park below the castle. I sprinted down Market Street and along the Mound, the Castle looming large above me. Dropping over a wall into the park, I misjudged the distance and landed with an almighty thump in the shrubbery.

Winded, I crawled slowly through the undergrowth. Right into a fat bloke with a pair of night glasses strapped to his head.

"Shit!" I yelled, falling backwards, convinced I'd bumped into Buffalo Bill from *The Silence of the Lambs*.

"Wist!" the guy hissed. "D'ya want them to hear?"

I looked past him. A big man with his trousers round his ankles stood up in front of me. Well, he was on his knees actually but you get my meaning.

"What the fuck are you doing?" he snarled. Beside him I caught a flash of bare breasts and thighs as his girlfriend pulled her dress up around her. The man with the night glasses scarpered.

"Just passing through, mate," I said cheerily. "Don't mind me."

I plunged on through the shrubbery. For ten minutes I looked for somewhere to hide and rest but everywhere I turned it was the same. Courting couples—love that phrase—going in for advanced courting. All of them having sex: noisily, energetically, drunkenly, single-mindedly, heterosexually, homosexually, profitably—you name it they were doing it. I didn't know where to look first.

I needed to use my phone but somehow didn't think that would go down too well here. I left the safety of the undergrowth and walked up out of the park. I came onto the pavement beside the Scott monument. Making sure the coast was clear, I scurried across the road and up towards Charlotte Square. I sheltered in a shop doorway to make my call.

"Mary, it's Nick. Nick Madrid. What? M-A-D-R—very funny. Well, I'm sorry I ran out on you too but I didn't have much choice. Yes I know what time it is. That's why I'm calling. I daren't go back to my apartment. I wondered if I could sleep with—sleep on your floor. No, I don't snore. Have you ever seen me dribble in the short time we've known each other? Well, drooling isn't the same as dribbling. Of course I don't have pajamas with me. Would I consider what? It depends what color the nightdress is. Thank you. Thank you very much."

SEVEN

I woke just as Mary was sliding out of bed.

"Where are you going?" I said drowsily. "The best is yet to come."

"I certainly hope so," she said, disappearing into the bathroom.

Her remark confirmed my suspicion that my lovemaking hadn't exactly wowed her. I hadn't been able to forget that I was seen as "thorough"—which I took as a compliment—so it had been a little bit of this, a little bit of that.

"Are you using some kind of checklist?" Mary gasped at one point.

When eventually I slumped down beside her ready for sleep she gazed at me with what, at first, I took to be wide-eyed admiration.

"Is that it?" she said.

"Well, yes," I said. "How was it?"

"Brief," she replied, rather acidly I thought.

She came out of the bathroom in running gear.

"Should I put the nightdress on now?" I mumbled waggishly.

"You need your rest," she said shortly. "I'll be back in an hour."

I dozed for a while when she'd gone then I got up. It was six thirty. I opened the curtains on another sunny day and looked down through the trees at the tents in Charlotte Square. I wondered if Mr. Pace, the blackmailing street performer, had got away from our pursuers. When I had asked Mary how Bridget had reacted to my peril she said Bridget had suggested they go and have dinner.

"How caring," I said.

"She'd only had a sandwich for lunch," Mary said, missing the point somewhat.

On a table by the window, alongside her tape recorder, filofax, notebook, and the other paraphernalia of a journalist's life, Mary had a copy of the Fringe brochure. I flipped through it looking for Pace's name to see where he was supposed to be performing.

I wasn't clear what Pace was up to. I thought blackmailers were supposed to set things up so that heavies couldn't threaten them: the incriminating-evidence-lodged-with-the-solicitor-to-be-released-to-the-press-in-case-of-accident scenario. Maybe he was new at the game. Or just incompetent. Didn't Lenny Bruce do a routine about incompetent kidnappers who thought the point of the operation was not to get ransom money but merely to kidnap somebody? "If you just keep 'em …"

Not strictly relevant to Pace, I know, but I'm pleased to have been able to mention Lenny Bruce. My hip credentials are now assured. If I can mention Joyce Grenfell too, everybody will be happy.

The brochure didn't name street performers. I idly picked up the literature program to see what I ought to be covering today. "Drop In!" I read. "Drop in on the Edinburgh City Libraries Youth Service Team for fun games and activities." I didn't think so. I flipped through some more. At the back, Mary had scrawled a name and an Edinburgh phone number in the margin in pencil. I looked, then looked again. The name was John Rolfe.

When I got back to Cathay Place I tiptoed up the stairs and let myself into the apartment very cautiously. I checked each room. The place was deserted. Sliding the bolts on the front door I showered, changed, and got some breakfast. I should have done my yoga—I hadn't done it for days—but now wasn't the time.

Of course, it could be perfectly innocent that Mary had John Rolfe's number in Edinburgh. Rolfe was the assistant of Juliette Smith, an important U. S. agent. And Mary was a journalist, after all. But it was strange she hadn't mentioned it. I recalled her looking away when she'd seen him in the Assembly Rooms bar. Could she be in cahoots with Rolfe and Juliette? Had she got to know me on their instructions?

If she had she now knew that the photographs were unhelpful. In fact she now knew everything—i.e., hardly anything. But why, then, did she sleep with me? I'm not exactly irresistible. Well, not very.

I was watching the clouds shifting lazily over the hills beyond the Firth when the phone rang.

"You ran out on me," Mary said quietly.

"No, no. I left you a note. Didn't you read my *billet doux*?"

"I'm not sure a *billet doux* is usually signed Yours Faithfully."

I giggled nervously.

There was silence on the line for a moment.

"So that's it?" she said. "I'm cast off?"

"I said I'd call you later. I just had to get one or two things moving."

"I thought we had one or two things already moving."

"You were the one who went for a run," I said defensively.

"I figured after last night you needed your rest."

"You mean my performance?" I said sharply.

"I mean being chased by hoodlums," she said gently. "Making love last night was, well, it was a start."

"A start." I did like her. It wasn't just the knockout body, no honestly. She was bright, warm, and funny too. But I didn't want to end up betrayed and broken hearted. Beneath this cool exterior beats a heart of mush.

"I'm having lunch with Billy Cash today," I said.

"So you said in your note."

"I expect Juliette Smith and her man Rolfe will be there," I said casually.

"Really."

"Do you know them?"

"I met Rolfe in Montreal," she said, without hesitation.

"Oh, right. What do you think of him?"

"Great body."

"Looks a bit big to me."

"I like 'em big," she said throatily.

I laughed nervously. "Right. What exactly does Rolfe do for Juliette, do you know?"

"He's her assistant. I guess he, erm, assists."

"Right."

I cleared my throat. She laughed again.

"Is there something you want to ask me, Nick? About Rolfe, me, and the beast with two backs maybe?"

"Since you brought it up," I said, with a lightness I didn't feel.

"We almost got it together but I guess my luck was out in Montreal when it came to men. Trust me to pick a guy with a Prince Albert. I hate that shit."

"A Prince Albert?"

"Nick, love, there's a whole world out there about which you clearly know nothing. A Prince Albert is what you Brits call a certain kind of penis pierce."

"A penis pierce. Of course."

Actually, I knew about penis piercing. I'd done an article about mutilation as art the previous year. I quoted the Jim Rose Circus. One of its performers lifted heavy weights suspended from a ring inserted through his penis. How should I know why? He was called, for obvious reasons, The Amazing Mister Lifto. The Tokyo Shock Boys, when they weren't setting fire to their farts or swallowing scorpions, used thongs around their testicles to pull a weighted chair across the room. Excuse me a moment whilst I cross my legs and wince.

"John Rolfe has a ring through his johnson?" I said.

"Yup. So I said thanks but no thanks. As it was I could barely stand the rings through his nipples. Besides, he was your typical tragic weightlifter: big muscles, small schlong. Hung like a hamster in fact."

"How come you know so much about penises?"

She laughed. "Just lucky, I guess."

After a moment I said, "So you've not seen him over here?"

"He wanted me to. I bumped into him in the bar and took his number out of politeness. That's it. I'm more interested in where we're at. Am I going to see you again? Seems to me we've got some unfinished business."

We arranged to meet mid-afternoon at her hotel. It was only nine now. Far too early to call Bridget. I phoned the Fringe press office to find out where Pace was performing. Eleven every day outside the National Gallery.

I thought about going to see a film. Every morning there were a dozen or so festival film previews in various cinemas around Lothian Road. However, I was here to interview directors. I'd found in previous years it wasn't strictly necessary to see any movies to do that. The high standards of modern journalism.

I decided I had time for a walk before I went over there. One of the reasons Edinburgh is such a great city is that within ten minutes of Cathay Place there's a beautiful wooded ravine that runs along the river from the old industrial village of Deal through Stockbridge down to the port at Leith.

I kept my eyes peeled to make sure no one was taking an unusual interest in me as I headed towards the Queensferry Road Bridge. Traffic surged in both directions across the viaduct. I glanced over the parapet. There was a vertiginous drop some three hundred feet to the waters of the River Leith.

I came off the bridge and followed the narrow, cobbled road down to Deal village. As the road dropped steeply the sounds of the city were replaced by birdsong, the rustle of the wind in the trees, and, shortly, the rush of the weir beside the little bridge at Deal. The village—a cluster of old workers' houses and converted factory buildings—was deserted. Before the bridge I turned to the right and walked past the weir on to the road that ran alongside the river.

The air was very still beneath the canopy of tall trees. The water gurgled and, if you will, giggled over soft outbreaks of rock. I flared my nostrils at the smell of the trees and the damp earth. I always enjoyed coming here. It seemed so strange to have a ravine that seemed to be in deep country actually right on the edge of a city. Looking up I could see rows of houses way above me.

Soon I came to the round, stone building that formerly housed a mineral well. I came off the road and down half a dozen rough stone steps to a large flat slab of rock sticking out into the river. I stood for a few minutes, brooding.

I was thinking about my dad again. He'd loved being in the country, but I think that was because he reckoned it was a great place for tripping. We'd go out on a Saturday or a Sunday for what he liked to call a country trip. He'd drop a tab of acid on the bus then spend all afternoon in a field reading the grass. I'd wander off looking for animals to stroke. Any animal, I wasn't fussy.

"Nick?" I heard a timid voice call. I looked over my shoulder.

Hilly was standing on the road, hands stuffed in jean pockets, shoulders hunched. A tall, gawky-looking man stood beside her. He was holding a long pole. When I joined them I saw the pole had a sign attached to one end. It looked like one of those triangular red road signs. Inside the triangle was a drawing of a frog.

"This is Ewan, my fiancé," Hilly said shyly. I assumed she meant the man not the frog, so I shook his bony hand. Bearded, wearing thick glasses and what we used to call a windcheater, Ewan was the epitome of the word nerd. I couldn't help noticing he had enormous feet, however, which probably explained what she saw in him. I've observed that the old rule Big Feet, Massive Mocamba holds true in most cases. Sadly not in all. I have very large feet.

"Are you here to picket frogs or warn us against them?" I said.

Hilly giggled.

"It's a toad, not a frog. We're here from the Edinburgh Amphibian Group. Ewan's the chairman. That's where we met actually, isn't it, Ewan? We're putting signs up warning people about the toad crossing."

"Zebras and pelicans outmoded now, are they?"

"No, no it's a crossing *for* toads, Mr. Madrid," Ewan said, adding eagerly, "although frogs will use it too."

"Of course they will, old chap, of course they will," I said soothingly. I turned to Hilly, assuming her to be marginally the saner of the two. "How come toads and frogs get this preferential treatment?"

"Shall I start at the beginning?" Ewan broke in, proceeding to tell me what fascinating creatures these warty amphibians actually are. He told me about habitat (woodland and wetland for the common toad, somewhere drier for the presumably snootier natterjack toad), food (woodlice and insects), lifespan (up to thirty years), and much, much more. When I already knew more than anyone other than a toad could possibly wish to know he still showed no sign of slacking.

"On second thought, Ewan," I interrupted, "start at the end. Why do they need their own road crossing? And do they get a lollipop person thrown in?"

"We've just discovered a community of toads on the land over here," Hilly said, pointing to the wooded slope on our right. "Unfortunately, its breeding ground is a toad pond across the road over there on the left. Usually they breed in the spring but the weather has been so mucked up this year they haven't started yet. We think they are about to."

"Got it. You're worried this family of toads will come hopping over the road here and get squished by the traffic."

"They don't hop, actually," Ewan said. "The common toad does a kind of cross between a walk and a jump. It waddles, really. The natterjack, of course, simply runs.'

I sighed. "Thank you, Ewan. But it is the traffic you're worried about?"

"Exactly," said Hilly. "You see the female lays her eggs at the pond and the male then fertilizes them. But some males try to get a jump ahead—ha, ha—and wait in open spaces for the female. They jump on her back so they are ready when the eggs come out. They can be there for weeks waiting for the eggs to drop."

"Amazing," I said, trying to glance at my watch without appearing rude.

"Well, of course, a road is a perfect open space and often the males sit for hours waiting for the first female to come along."

"But a car may come along first," I said.

"Quite," Ewan said.

"It's jolly thrilling when the migration starts," Hilly said, getting as excited as Ewan. "We come down when we think it's going to happen—warm wettish nights usually—and we act, well actually, almost as you said, as lollipop people, shepherding them across. You could come and see if you'd like."

"Love to," I said, "work-load permitting." I looked at my watch more obviously. "Look at the time, got to see a man with a nail up his nose."

I left them there and climbed the steep hill back to the bridge. I was sweating heavily by the time I got to Charlotte Square. I made a dash through the rush of traffic, past the encampment of Book Festival tents, and down on to Princes Street.

Hot weather is the last thing you need during the festival. Most of the Fringe venues are disgusting enough at the cool-est of times but sitting through an indifferent performance in a sauna is a horrible experience. The heat had spoiled Billy Cash's gig for me the previous night.

As I walked towards the National Gallery I tried to remember something of Cash's act. I seemed to have seen the show weeks ago. He'd been quite funny in a laid-back, seen it all, done it all kind of way. The difference between British and U. S. perform-ers on the whole is that the British present themselves as imper-fect and make jokes against themselves whilst the Americans have more confident personae and make jokes about other people.

The courtyard in front of the gallery was crowded, people clustering around various street performers: a fire swallower, a unicyclist, a juggler. No man with a hammer, nostrils, and nails, though. It was eleven forty. I threaded my way through in search of Pace. I climbed to the entrance of the Gallery for a clearer vantage point and scanned the crowd. No sign of him.

I bought an ice cream and found a place among the people sitting on the steps. There was a carnival atmosphere around me. It was so hot the scoop of ice cream was melting within moments, running down the side of the cone and on to my fin-gers. I tilted the cone to lick my fingers. I heard a sharp intake of breath somewhere below me. I examined the cone.

A young woman who looked no better than she should be was glaring at me. I glanced down at the large amount of cleavage on display above her skimpy T-shirt. Ah. I'd been wondering where my scoop had gone. Should I offer to retrieve it? I looked again at her pinched face and her mouth about to spout something, I'm sure, obscene. Perhaps not. I smiled weakly and moved away.

At twelve fifteen I did one more sweep of the courtyard just in case I'd missed Pace then wandered over to the Traverse Theatre for my lunch with Billy Cash. The Forum was a dark, candlelit restaurant along one side of the ground floor. Cash walked in moments after I claimed our table.

I was prejudiced against Cash because I didn't like the thought that Amanda, my favorite U. S. comedian had been willing to sleep with him to get on his cable show. But I didn't suspect him of involvement in Cissie Parker's fall to her death. However, I hoped he might let something slip about Bradley Stokes, whom I did suspect. I assumed that since they shared the same agent they came across each other from time to time.

"So how do you get on with Bradley Stokes?" I said, once we were seated.

"Hitman? He's okay," he said in his gravelly voice. "Don't see much of him."

"I asked because I always wondered how much people mix who share the same agent."

"Well, you know, agents don't have regular little get-togethers of all their clients. It don't work like that. Juliette has clients I never ever met—some I never even heard of, but don't say I said that. Just happens Brad and I know each other from the circuit."

"Nice guy is he?"

"Sure," Cash gave me a shrewd look. "This interview about me or him?"

"Oh, you, of course. I was just, you know, settling you in."

"I'm settled in fine, thank you."

Cash was a good-looking man, tall with a rangy physique. His presence reminded me of Kris Kristofferson. I had a flash back to Jilly Dougan.

We'd both ordered hot chicken salads and mineral water. The restaurant was full but nobody paid any attention to us, although the waiter glanced at my tape recorder and microphone set out beside the ashtray.

"Hoped to catch your act in Montreal but I hear you were ill."

"Sick as a dog. Damned shame to disappoint all those people but I just couldn't do it. I promised I'd go back next year, make up for it."

"If you're not making movies back to back by then."

"Even if. I gave my word."

Cash wasn't overly friendly but he was open and answered all my questions conscientiously. Like most comics in interview, he rarely said anything funny. He ran through his bio. Born in Texas, left school and home at fourteen to do a Jimi Hendrix and tour the county fairs in some cover band. Had a couple of minor hits with original material then the band broke up. He carried on as a solo performer, playing the clubs and making the occasional album.

"I toured for twenty years. Got no illusions. I made a living but I know that until I turned to comedy, hardly anybody out there knew I so much as existed. Then in the eighties a lot of the clubs I regularly performed in were turning themselves into comedy clubs. Comedy spread like an epidemic—got so I was finding it hard to find clubs that still played music. I'd always told stories between my songs, established a good rapport with my audiences. So I made the switch."

"And now that comedy's dying you're switching again," I said helpfully.

He gave me a level look.

"Well, not exactly. If that were the case I guess I'd be switching back to music. No, some of these Hollywood guys think I'll look pretty in pictures, so that's the avenue I'll pursue."

"I hear Juliette got you a good deal. Lot of money."

"No comment on the money but she's a smart operator, all right. Been looking after me for over twenty five years."

We carried on over coffee and pudding circling around his youth of drink and drugs and a roistering lifestyle.

"Are you settled now?" I said. "Do you have a partner?"

He shook his head slowly.

"Not right now. So if you know of anyone, Nick, on the lookout for an old man who'd treat her good—what say you let me know."

He grinned and sat back from the table.

"What kind of woman do you like?" I said, smiling back.

"Anything with a pulse," a woman's voice said.

I looked around. Juliette was standing beside me. She had the kind of smile on her face made me wonder who she'd just devoured.

"Now this is the kind of restaurant I like," she said. "Gloomy and candlelit even in the day—very flattering for a woman."

She sat down in the chair beside Cash and launched into a story about Cash and a well-known country and western singer he'd pursued. She told it with brio. I'd never seen her being vivacious before. It was quite terrifying. When she'd finished and I was laughing and Cash was attempting to look sheepish, she looked fondly at Billy but spoke to me.

"About done, Nick?"

"Believe so," Cash said, smiling as he carefully folded his napkin by his plate. "Very pleased to have your company, Nick."

"My pleasure," I said as Cash got to his feet. I started to rise.

"No, no you stay here and finish your coffee," Cash said,

leaning over to offer his hand. "I have to go and rest before the show tonight." He walked from the restaurant, half turning to call back to Juliette. "See you later, Toots."

Juliette called over the waiter and ordered us both another coffee. Then she clasped her hands on the table in front of her, looked around the room, then at me. She had gone back to being her normal, icy self.

"I've given you an hour with Bradley tomorrow but there are some ground rules we have to establish."

I nodded. "Sure."

"No questions about his divorce or his wife. Any questions about either and the interview is over. That clear?"

I nodded. Juliette unclasped and reclasped her hands. She seemed uneasy. Did she know about my suspicions? If Mary really was working with her—I stifled the thought. Besides, I wouldn't be allowed anywhere near Stokes if that were the case. Juliette cleared her throat.

"You know he's enjoyed his career as a comic but he's been looking for straight acting roles lately."

"Don't they all?" I muttered.

"He's just finished his first one, as a drug dealer in this low-budget movie. He's got no acting training, you know. Until now he's been going off his instincts." She hesitated again. What was the problem? I smiled encouragingly.

"There's no need to smirk," she said sharply. "You've heard then?"

I assumed she wasn't talking about the penis implant. I shook my head.

"Well, the way he's working is to immerse himself in the part. Immerse himself. And he's only just finished the film and, well ..." She trailed off.

Now I understood.

"He has a bad case of the Method," I said flatly.

"Just one or two mannerisms he hasn't been able to shake yet. Speech patterns. An attitude …"

"Is he going to try to sell me drugs?"

Juliette gave me a withering look.

"I'm telling you as a courtesy, to warn you that the Bradley Stokes you meet tomorrow isn't quite the usual Bradley Stokes. Okay?"

I held my hands out, palms up. "Okay. No problem." And there wasn't. After all, she hadn't said I couldn't ask about Cissie Parker.

Walking back up Lothian Road, lorries and buses grinding by, I replayed our conversation in my head. I really didn't think she suspected that I was curious about Bradley Stokes. Or if she did, she wasn't worried about it. I needed to talk to Pace, the street performer, about what he'd seen in Montreal. I wondered where he was lying low. I cut off through the park so I could use my mobile phone and called the Fringe press office again, asking if they had a contact number or address for him.

I sat on a bench and tried the number they gave me. It rang and rang. The address was somewhere in Deal. I may well have walked past his house earlier in the day. I doubted he'd still be there. If I could get his address so easily, so could Dick Francis, Harvey, and Ronnie.

A storm was coming, black clouds piled up in the sky and the air was still and very humid. I was sweating again when I approached the Rathbone. I hung back on the pavement when I saw Francis leave the hotel and hurry off into George Street.

I was wondering who he'd been visiting when I almost collided with Loud Lenny in the hotel lobby.

"Nick! How's it hanging, buddy?"

"It's hanging reasonably well, thank you. This your hotel?"

"Nah. Just visiting. I'm staying at some real old place on the edge of town. Got me the James I Suite, whoever he is. They said, 'James I slept here.' I said, 'I hope you changed the sheets.' You having a good time? Just had lunch down on the Firth. That's a neat bunch of water. You know it?"

I nodded.

"How's the show going?" I said.

"Great. I hear they're putting me and Rich Hall forward for one of them Perrier Awards. Have you seen it yet?" I shook my head. "It's a sell-out but let me know when you wanna come and I'll leave tickets for you. Hey, I'd love to keep gabbing but I'm going off to buy me one of those kilts. How d'you think I'll look? I mean if Mel Gibson could wear one …"

"The Clan Finnegan," I said. "Has a ring to it."

"Well, figure I can get a few laughs in the act. And that's what it's all about."

Lenny went off, leaving me pondering the coincidence of Dick Francis and Lenny Finnegan being in such close proximity. I stopped pondering when Mary let me into her room, took my hand, and led me to her bed. Turning, she stood on tiptoe and murmured to me, "This time, let me show you how it's done."

"I know how it's done," I said, bridling slightly.

How wrong can a chap be?

It was raining hard when I left the hotel but I didn't notice as I floated several inches off the ground across to the Book Festival. I meandered down the wooden walkway to the spiegeltent, the rain drumming on the canvas above my head, a stupid grin on my face.

"If the wind changes you'll stay like that," Bridget said. I looked around. She was standing in the doorway of one of the tents where publishers each had stands for selling their wares.

Now Bridget has about as much affinity to literature as a vampire to a crucifix.

"You can't be here for books. You've been looking for me?" I said.

She held up two books and tottered across to me.

"*With Knobs On*," I read off the spine of one of the books. "Is that the sequel to Paula Yates' book of photographs of rock star's underpants? And *The Definitive Van Morrison Joke Book*? Interesting."

Bridget took my arm.

"And it's obvious what you've been doing. Just discovered there's more than the one position have you?"

"Very funny," I said, blushing. How did she know me so well? "So what's happening?"

"I phoned you this morning," she said accusingly.

"I went for a walk," I said. "I think better when I walk, a lot like Nietzsche."

"Nietzsche?"

"Well, not a *lot* like Nietzsche. Obviously, he was a great thinker and I'm—"

"—an idiot. Quite. I was worried about you."

"Oh, really. How was your supper?"

"Very tasty," she said, blithely ignoring my sarcasm. "So what happened to the seedy street performer?"

"Dunno. I've got his address. He's somewhere down in Deal. I could have called in this morning if I'd known. I was going to go back later."

"I'll come with you."

"I thought you didn't want to be involved."

"I am involved, whether I like it or not. I'm not going to let you have such a big story all to yourself. Especially as you'll only make a hash of things." Bridget looked round. "Let's have a drink until the rain stops then we'll go down."

"Been to any shows today?" I said as we sat down.

"I've been to two whilst you've been getting your hat blocked. I don't understand why they always seem to put the noisy shows right next door to the quiet ones, with only a cardboard partition between. They might as well put all the noisy shows together and let them fight it out like a psychotic Battle of the Bands."

"What did you see?"

"I saw a musical about Robert Burns. I thought I was seeing one about Rasputin but I went next door by mistake. The accents of the actors were so thick it took me twenty minutes to realize. It was only when Rasputin started reciting a poem to a haggis I twigged anything was amiss. I'd thought the kilts were making a statement about universal experience."

It was two hours before the rain stopped, by which time we were both well lubricated. We got a taxi in the Square. In the back, Bridget rummaged in her shoulder bag and came up with a pair of plimsolls in place of the platforms she had been staggering around in.

We had the taxi drop us on Queensferry Road so that we could walk down to Deal. It was very humid, the road steaming gently as the rain dried. Dusk was falling early tonight. As we neared the bottom it got increasingly gloomy under the canopy of dripping trees.

When we got to the bridge we saw a car standing in front of a house some fifty yards up the road on the other side of the bridge. Its sidelights were on and we could hear its engine running. As we came on to the bridge, Harvey and Dick Francis came out of the house and started to get in the back of the car.

At that moment, the streetlights on the bridge and the road popped on. Harvey glanced up as he was getting into the car. He did a double take. I grabbed Bridget and pulled her back across the bridge. We instinctively lurched off to our left, hurrying onto the road I had strolled down in the morning. I heard the car move off.

Bridget was surprisingly fast on her feet and I had to struggle to keep up with her. Not only that, she was running whilst keeping her cigarillo in the corner of her mouth.

"Where are we going?" she said.

"This road goes down to Stockbridge but we can cut off and come up somewhere behind Cathay Place."

"It'll take a bit of manoeuvring to get the car on to this road," Bridget said.

"Not necessarily," I said, looking back over my shoulder. The car, its headlights on full beam, was picking up speed some three hundred yards behind us.

Ahead of us a thick shadow spread across the road. As we ran nearer there seemed to be something odd about it.

"Why's that shadow moving?" Bridget gasped.

"I was just wondering that myself," I said, catching sight of Ewan's sign. I managed a jerky laugh. "That's all we need."

"What the fuck is this?" Bridget yelped, coming to an abrupt halt.

"Did I ever tell you about toad crossings?" I said, stopping beside her.

When Hilly and Ewan had been talking earlier in the day I hadn't really understood why they were making such a fuss about a couple of dozen toads hopping—excuse me, waddling—across the road. A couple of thousand though, that was something else again.

Spread in front of us and for about fifteen yards down the road were more toads than you could ever wish to see, certainly when you were being chased by three hoodlums. Big toads, little toads, piggybacking toads—a seething mass of them, tumbling over each other to get across the road.

I looked to the right and the wide procession was emerging

from the undergrowth, seemingly without end. I looked to the left and a similar procession was disappearing into the gloom. I looked behind us and the car screeched to a halt some ten yards away.

"Bridget," I said.

Bridget looked around, then gave a little, squirming jump as a female toad waddled over her feet, a male hitching a lift on its back. She looked at me, "No way I'm wading through these buggers."

I looked at the pulsating mass before us.

"They're packed so tightly together I don't think there's any question of wading, we'd have to walk on—"

"I know what we'd have to do," Bridget said quickly. "And I don't intend to do it."

Harvey and Dick Francis were swaggering towards us.

"Did you ever see that Michael Winner film *The Nightcomers*?" I said.

"No, but I'm glad you brought it up at this particular juncture in my soon to end life."

"Oh, they won't kill us," I said. Harvey pulled a knife from his jacket pocket.

"How does it feel to be right all the time?" Bridget said.

"Pick one of the toads up," I said, in a more panicky voice than I would have liked.

"You pick one of the bloody toads up," she snapped. "This is no time to be slaking your perverted lusts."

I bent and grabbed one of the passing toads in both hands. It felt like wet leather. Holding it firmly I grabbed Bridget's cigarillo and pushed it in the toad's mouth.

"I don't care if he only wants one drag, I don't want that back," Bridget said. Then her eyes widened as she saw the toad taking in the smoke and starting to ... swell.

Harvey and Francis had stopped about five yards away. Grinning at the sight of all the toads, they looked intrigued as the toad in my hand expanded rapidly.

"Wha—" Harvey started to say as I lobbed the toad, its skin by now as taut as a balloon, at head height between them. They instinctively drew back their heads. But not far enough to evade the fall out as the toad exploded with a surprisingly loud bang.

"Come on," I shouted, taking advantage of Harvey's surprise to deadleg him. As he fell down I was thinking I should kick him in the head to make sure. But I wasn't sure how hard and I didn't want to risk killing him. More to the point, it might not be hard enough and I didn't want him to get up even more pissed off than he would already be.

I turned to Francis but Bridget was there before me, a toad in one hand, a platform shoe in the other. I thought she was trying to decide which to sock him with but then she swung the shoe at his face. There was a loud crack as she made contact with his nose, then she dropped down a little to execute a really beautiful knee to the groin.

Francis grunted and crumpled to the road. Ronnie started to get out of the driver's door of the car. He was still half in and half out when Bridget shouted "Catch!" in her most imperious voice and tossed the toad to him. Instinctively, Ronnie cupped his hands and caught the toad close to his chest. When he looked down to see what it was, Bridget slammed the door on him with the flat of her foot.

Overwhelmed with guilt as I am about what I did to the first toad, I'm sorry to say the second one didn't come out of our meeting too well either.

Bridget's blood was up. She grabbed the car door, pulled it open and swung it shut on Ronnie again, catching his legs against the sill. He bellowed in pain. She swung it a final time just to make sure.

Legging it back up the road to the bridge, I glanced at her in amazement.

"Where did you learn to fight like that?" I said between breaths.

"One of the benefits of a convent education. There were girls at my school could have taken all three of them. Why didn't you kick that guy in the head?"

"Generosity of spirit."

"So what about this *Nightcomers* film?" she gasped as we neared the bridge.

"Marlon Brando does that to a toad in it. Something to do with toads not being able to breathe through their skins."

"Perverse memory you have."

We ducked down behind the bridge's parapet and looked back. It was getting too dark to see very far but by the interior light of the car I saw Harvey bundle Ronnie into the back seat. Francis was slumped in the front. Harvey hobbled to the driver's door and climbed in. Slamming the door he revved the engine for a moment.

"Do you think they'll come after us?" I said to Bridget. The headlights brightened and the car shot forward towards the migrating toads. And kept on going.

"Ouch," Bridget said after a few moments.

"I don't think the Edinburgh Amphibians Group is going to be very happy about that," I said.

"Toad Rage in Edinburgh. I can see the headline now: Toad Killers Hop It."

We stood up and looked towards the house we'd seen the two men leaving.

"Since we're here," Bridget said, leading the way across the bridge.

The house looked like a squat. Windows poster-painted in psychedelic colors, metal sculptures rusting in the garden.

I knocked on the door. No answer. It was remarkably quiet, the last of the birds just knocking off for the night. Bridget disappeared around the side of the house. I knocked again, then called through the letterbox.

"Pace, it's Nick Madrid. Pace!"

Nothing. I pushed at the door. It seemed to be held only by a Yale lock. Bridget came back.

"The back door's locked and bolted."

"There's only a Yale lock here. You can spring them with your credit card."

"That presupposes I have a credit card," Bridget said.

"You haven't?"

"Bank manager cut it up in front of me. May as well have stabbed me in the heart with the scissors when he cut up my Harvey Nick's card too, the sadistic bastard."

"But, Bridget, I thought you were earning really well."

"Back tax and booze, sweetie. I can't abide the thought of drinking anything but champagne at home, can you? Where's your credit card?"

Ten minutes later we were still standing outside the house. I looked sadly at the mangled credit card, NUJ membership card, and phone card in my hand. So much for received truths. I leaned back and gave the door a sharp kick right against the lock. It sprang open.

"I'm as surprised as you are," I said quickly before Bridget could make a comment.

I stepped in and felt unsuccessfully for a light switch. There was light coming under a door at the far end of the hallway. We hung together as we tiptoed towards it through the darkness. When we reached it, we stopped and looked at each other. Bridget stretched out her palm and pushed the door gently. It swung open silently.

Pace was sprawled in an old armchair facing the door. I noticed the mallet first, lying carelessly in his lap. My eyes travelled up his body to the thick pool of blood coagulating on his chest. There was blood on his chin and mouth and upper lip. Yet more blood encrusted the fat handle of the screwdriver protruding from his right nostril—the screwdriver someone had hammered up into his brain.

EIGHT

"It's usually an easy enough trick to perform," I said. "We've all got empty space up by the sinuses, a cavity that serves no purpose. Human Blockheads—that's what these guys were called in the forties in the States when this was a classic human marvel stunt—start off inserting a small nail into this cavity and keeping it there, then they progress to bigger and bigger nails. By enlarging the cavity, they can eventually hammer a screwdriver up there quite safely."

"Clearly not," Mary said.

"Oh yes. Whoever did that to Pace wasn't aiming for the cavity. I would imagine they split the septum and went straight up into the brain."

"Godammit," Bridget said, lighting up a fag from the stub of the last one. "I'd just about given up smoking again until all this happened." She expelled a lungful of air. "Nick, how come you know such things?"

I raised my head from the thick cushion on one of Hilly's sofas and looked across to Bridget lounging on the other.

"James Bond books, I think. For a hippy pacifist, my dad seemed to read an awful lot of thrillers and spy books. When he died I got his entire collection. I read in one of them that the quickest way to kill someone is to whack them hard under the nose, angling upwards so that you drive a splinter of bone up into the brain."

"Jesus," Mary said, looking at me askance.

"I've read how to do it, I didn't say I'd done it," I said mildly.

Mary was propped up on the sofa beside me. She nudged me in the ribs.

"Even so, this probably isn't the time to be so graphic. You've both experienced a terrible thing."

"The terrible thing was he didn't tell us what he knew before he copped it," Bridget said, examining her plimsolled foot. Mary looked across at her.

"That's an awful thing to say. A man has died."

"What, sweetie?" Bridget said. "Sorry, dear, I didn't catch what you said. I was wondering if this toad grunge will come out of canvas easily with soap and water. Nick, did you ever wash your hands?"

Mary gave her a look of disgust. I gave Mary a squeeze.

"Coping mechanism," I said.

"Don't try to psychoanalyze me," Bridget said sharply, wetting a tissue with her tongue and dabbing at her plimsoll with it.

"Why not?" I said.

"If anyone needs examining it's you, Nick," she said, looking at the tissue and grimacing. She tossed it into the fireplace. "Did you tell Mary about the exploding toad? You're telling me the person who thought of that is normal? I don't think so."

"Saved your ass," I said shortly. I turned to Mary. "Have you come across Mark Borkowski? Great showman PR. I saw him bung a long nail up his nose at his Christmas party. Jim Rose had shown him how to do it when Mark had done his publicity."

"You Brits," Mary said, climbing off the sofa. "You haven't a clue how to show your emotions." I watched her walk to the door. She turned for a moment, a puzzled look on her face. "An exploding toad?" she said, leaving the room without waiting for an answer. I heard the apartment door close.

Bridget had been watching me. She shrugged and reached for the bottle of wine near her head.

"Great ass," she said, matter-of-factly.

I looked up at the ceiling and yawned.

"Be blasé then," she said.

"Just tired," I said. It wasn't midnight yet but I was knackered. All the drama of earlier in the evening.

"So what are we going to do?" I said.

"Well, I'm going to get through this bottle of wine then pass out on this sofa, if that's all right with you," Bridget said.

"I mean about the hole we're in."

"Well, I'm going to get through this bottle of wine then pass out—"

"Bridget! We just discovered a murdered street performer. In the past few weeks we've had a pile of dead bodies slowly accumulating around us. I would have thought that worthy of discussion."

"A murdered street performer? We should encourage that. I volunteer to compile a hit list of mimes." She lifted her head to gulp her drink then lay back again. "It's the toads I worry about. Toads in Real Hole in Edinburgh."

"Bridget!"

"What? You think I like seeing blokes with their brains hanging down their noses any more than you do? I'm sorry for Pace but I don't know the man. I vaguely knew Cissie Parker. I didn't know Ruthie but you did a little so I'm sorry for that. Frank I knew and I know how I feel about that. So I don't need you or some ring-a-ding, New Age biddy telling me what I'm supposed to be feeling. I know what I feel."

"Mary isn't New Age," I said mildly. "Okay, okay. It's just that as long as I've lived I've never seen violent death—I've rarely seen violence. None of this is what I'm used to. And we need to figure out what we're going to do."

Bridget looked across at me and shrugged again.

"How the fuck should I know?"

I'd called the police from the bridge, Bridget sitting on the road beside me. Three cop cars came grinding down the steep road about ten minutes later, sirens and lights going. The first car stopped on the bridge a few yards short of us. Three uniformed cops and a fourth in a crumpled suit got out. The plain-clothes cop was big and lumpy with a droopy moustache circa 1969. He walked stiffly over to us as the other three trotted by. Although he looked no older than thirty he wore the dolorous expression of a man who had suffered much. When he introduced himself as D. I. Condon, I understood why.

"Is that as in—" I started to say.

"As in ConDON," he said, glaring at me. Poor chap. I could imagine a lifetime of puerile jokes about his name, especially in the police canteen where they'd go on about precautions rather than cautions. Whatever his first name was I was willing to bet everybody called him Johnny. Like or dislike them, you can't say policemen ever overlook the obvious.

"—as in the Metropolitan Police Commissioner in London," I finished. He glared at me again, gave a quick nod, tugged his moustache, then looked at the pool of vomit a few yards to Bridget's left.

"The lady not feeling too good?"

Bridget looked up at him. "The lady's fine. It's the gentleman who isn't feeling too good."

The policeman glanced my way.

"It's been a bit of a messy evening, one way and the other," I said, instinctively glancing at my palm and wiping it on my trousers.

"These men you allege chased you ..."

"Allege?" Bridget said, flaring.

"They went that away," I said quickly, pointing to the toad crossing. "Along the river towards Stockbridge."

"Did you set up roadblocks?" Bridget said.

Condon ignored her as he looked across the river and spoke into his radio. The third car in the queue reversed, then split off to the right. Condon excused himself and ambled off towards the house. He didn't seem to be in too much of a hurry but then I guess Pace wasn't going anywhere.

"We should have searched for clues whilst we had the chance, shouldn't we?" Bridget said.

"That would have been fun," I said, grimacing. "You know, Bridget, I don't think I'm cut out for this. It seemed a bit of a lark at the very start in Montreal. It hasn't seemed like that for a long time now."

The third police car halted somewhere near the toad crossing. A policeman passed across the headlight beam carrying a torch. I leaned back and looked up at the darkening sky. After a few minutes, I became aware of Condon glaring down again.

"I'm assuming you're Mr. Madrid and you're Bridget Frost. You both know the dead man?"

"I do, vaguely," I said. "Bridget doesn't. He's a street performer, name of Pace. Hammers nails up his nose for a living."

Condon tugged on his moustache. "Say again?"

"He's a Human Blockhead. Blokes like him used to be the staple of the old American 'ten in one' thrill shows. Their act is hammering nails, spikes, and screwdrivers up their noses."

"What, so you're saying—he could have—it might just be his aim was a bit off?"

"You tell me," I said. "But I think it unlikely those three thugs just happened to be here."

Condon nodded, reached for his moustache but opted this time just to finger it. "Tell me more."

"The old thrill shows were essentially freak shows where the attractions would include armless and legless wonders, giants, dwarfs, fat ladies, bearded ladies, living skeletons, Siamese twins, and the occasional pinhead. Tattooed men and women and people able to push spikes up their noses or hammer nails into their flesh were acceptable alternatives to the 'freaks..'"

Condon sighed. "I meant about the three men you say chased you."

"We say chased us?" Bridget said, scrambling to her feet to stand pugnaciously in front of him.

"Local lads were they, would you guess?" he continued calmly.

"Sounded London to me," I said. "But I think they knew their way around."

"What makes you say that?" Condon had an unwavering stare. I bet he practiced in front of the mirror each day. His hostility had thrown me at first. But I'd realized the glare and the moustache tugging was a gimmick, part of a set of defining mannerisms that he imagined, from watching TV policemen, he ought to have. I even wondered if the moustache was a prop, glued on for effect. I mean, nobody but Sean Connery grew one like that willingly these days.

He gave me another searching look. He was really quite good at it, I felt hideously guilty. Before he could speak, a second policeman joined us. We looked at each other with mutual recognition. He kept his eyes on me as he said to Condon, "Been a bit of a wildlife massacre on the road there, sir. Hundreds of frogs."

"Toads," Bridget said, still standing in front of Condon.

"What's happened to them?" Condon said, looking impassively down at her—she only came up to his chest.

"Been run over I'd say."

"Hundreds of them?" Condon looked at me.

"They were migrating," I said. "The getaway car …"

"Could I have a word with you a moment, sir," the policeman said to Condon, drawing him away from Bridget and me.

I got to my feet and stood beside Bridget as the two policemen conferred, both of them shooting me hard looks. Condon's face took on an expression of distaste.

"What's his problem?" Bridget said.

"That policeman is the one who came round to the flat and found me just after the snake had eaten the cat."

The policeman murmured something else to Condon. Did I imagine they both looked at my crotch before they started sniggering?

Condon came back over. "We're going to need descriptions from you of these men and there's other paperwork to do. Would you mind coming down to the station?"

"What are the chances of getting these hoodlums? They've threatened me before, you know. Your policeman knows all about one incident."

"Ah, yes." Condon paused. He was clearly grateful for the chance to look sagacious. He tugged his ear, stroked his moustache, rocked on his heels, sucked on his teeth. "I wouldn't like to commit myself at this stage, sir," he finally said, somewhat pathetically, in my view.

I slept badly. I couldn't get Pace out of my mind. At five I gave up and went to make myself a drink. I heard Bridget whimpering in her sleep. I looked in on her. Bad dreams for her, too. She had thrown her blanket to the floor. I tiptoed across and put it back over her. At six I phoned Mary at her hotel. When I heard no answer I assumed she was running up Arthur's Seat, if you'll pardon the expression, on the edge of Edinburgh.

I put on my tracksuit and called a taxi to take me there. Whilst I waited for her to arrive, I jogged in a large circle, my attention drifting every so often to the lovely view of Edinburgh below me, wreathed in morning mist.

I saw Mary approaching some ten minutes later, face flushed, legs pumping hard as she powered up the hill. She was looking at the ground in front of her feet so she was almost on top of me without having seen me when I called:

"I suppose a fuck's out of the question."

With hindsight, I can see that was a *really* stupid thing to shout. She was alone, early in the morning, miles from anywhere, not expecting to come across anyone she knew.

"You know Mace is illegal in this country," I wheezed, some fifteen minutes later, still startled at the amount of liquid that was gushing out of my nose.

"You'd be dead if you were in my country," she said coolly. "I carry a gun, not Mace, when I'm running in NY."

I lay doubled up on the wet grass. Every so often I got another whiff of the tear gas and started to retch. Mary patted my back.

"Must be really good for my sinuses though," I said, as more goo discharged itself down my nose.

"What are you doing here, Nick?"

"I came to apologize. About last night."

"For what?"

"Well, you came round expecting to have me to yourself and there were Bridget and I suffering post-murder trauma."

"Hardly your fault."

"So why'd you leave?"

"Because I felt like a spare wheel. You and your tough buddy don't leave much room for anyone else."

"I was so pleased when you turned up."

"Nick, I like you, too. And we had fun. But I'm just a farm

girl. I'm not into threesomes. I didn't realize you were already spoken for."

"Bridget? It's not like that. We're just friends."

"Boy, you do need therapy. Looks to me like you're all but man and wife."

"We've never slept together."

"Then it's long overdue. That's all that's missing from your little twosome."

I managed to sit up straight.

"All my life I've yearned for domesticity. The pipe, the slippers by the fire." I wiped away a tear. It would have been more moving if it hadn't been accompanied by more yellow gunk rolling on to my top lip. "Mary?" I said.

"What?"

"You don't smoke a pipe, do you?"

She looked at me.

"No. Why?"

I looked at her sadly.

"Nothing."

Bridget was still asleep when I got back. I stopped in the doorway and watched her for a few moments. Did I want a proper relationship with her? I was pretty sure I didn't. Had I been hoping for one with Mary? I didn't think so, although I'd grown very fond of her. But then, I grow fond of people very easily. For me love is a once in a lifetime experience I have about every fortnight.

I tried to sleep for a couple of hours before my meeting with Bradley Stokes but it didn't really take. I was curious to know how Juliette would treat me, especially if she had hired Dick Francis and his heavies and if Pace the street performer had been trying to blackmail her.

I was dozing when the phone rang. It was Hilly. She sounded upset.

"Nick, I have to ask. Do you have a problem with animals?"

"I like animals," I said drowsily.

"But Kevin—"

"I didn't eat him," I said indignantly.

"The toads?"

"Ah, yes, the toads."

"The police called Ewan this morning to say what had happened at the toad crossing. They mentioned your name. Said you had the details."

I was midway through my explanation when Bridget wandered into the room. She sat on the bed, yawning, waiting for me to finish.

"Who's that you're trying to placate?" she said when I put the phone down. "The horsy one?"

I nodded. She yawned again.

"I'm going back to my flat to change my clothes. How are you going to play it if you see Juliette? She'll be wondering what Pace might have told you."

"I'll see how she is. Do you think we're still in danger from those blokes?"

"Shouldn't think so. I imagine they're lying low. They might even have left Edinburgh, with D. I. Condon in hot pursuit. Call me later. I've got a piece to write today so I'll be at the flat."

She leaned over and kissed me brusquely on the mouth.

"What?" she said as she stood up. "Why the odd expression?"

"Nothing," I said, thinking about what Mary had said.

Bradley Stokes was staying at the Caledonian Hotel. I called his room from the lobby. Juliette answered. She told me to come right up. When I got to the room John Rolfe let me in. He gave me a small smile and ushered me through into a living area with a desk, sofas, and big, comfortable armchairs. All the curtains were drawn and the only light came from a couple of standard lamps.

Peering through the gloom I could see Juliette standing in the middle of the room. Stokes was taking up most of a sofa. He was enormous. He was wearing what appeared to be a bedspread but on closer examination proved to be a kaftan. My God. A kaftan. Tears in my eyes, I looked at it as you would an ancient relic.

Juliette was her usual cold self.

"Bradley, this is Nick Madrid. He'll be with you for the next hour. John and I will be sitting just over here in case you need anything."

I took the seat opposite Stokes and smiled at him. His lips twitched in return.

"Hi," I said. "Almost met you in Montreal. I was there to cover the Festival."

He tilted his head. He looked remarkable. He was wearing wraparound shades so dark I couldn't see his eyes at all. His hair was greased back and drawn up into a bow on top of his head, like a Sumo wrestler's. In fact, he looked remarkably like a Sumo wrestler, with folds of fat around his neck and settled under the kaftan around his middle. He had big pinkie rings on his fingers. His feet were bare and I caught a glimpse of white, swollen ankles. I couldn't conceive of him and Cissie Parker together.

"Nice suite," I remarked as I was setting up my tape and microphone. Stokes nodded again. "Not as nice as the suites at that great hotel in Montreal, though. I interviewed Phyllis Diller in hers. It was great. Yours was next door I believe. Great views."

Stokes didn't say anything. I could see this was going to be one of those teeth-pulling jobs. I started the interview proper and for the next forty minutes pretended extreme interest in every facet of Stokes's professional life, his every banal pronouncement. His pronouncements were even less interesting than the usual banal movie star profundities because of the role he was playing.

He really did have a bad case of the Method. He was in drug dealing hepcat mode. Whether he had been able to speak in complete sentences before he became a hepcat I have no idea. But as Mr. Cool his responses, if they weren't limited to "You in the groove, daddyo" and "Ring a ding dong, toots," rambled on without form or content. A stream of consciousness—extremely limited consciousness—flow. He went off at tangents then forgot what question he was answering. I wondered if he was high on something.

It didn't help that he couldn't see a bloody thing through those shades. I thought he might take them off once he'd knocked over the bottle of mineral water and spilled his coffee down his kaftan. But no, Stokes persisted.

I'd also been hoping to lull Juliette into boredom with the dull way the interview was going but she remained as alert as she had been at the start. When I mentioned Cissie Parker, therefore, I was half expecting an explosion behind me. We'd been talking about Stokes's experience making his first straight film.

"One of our English performers is in it with you, isn't she?" I said. "Cissie Parker."

"Cissie. Poor, tragic Cissie," he said huskily.

"Tragic," I agreed. "Boy, I bet she was excited to be making movies."

"You're in the groove, jackson. She was kissing the moon, man. She might have appeared tough but performers, let me tell you Nick, we're ... vulnerable. That girl knew how to feel. Sure did."

With an effort Stokes reached to put his coffee cup on the

table. He missed and the cup landed with a soft thud on the thick carpet. He ignored it, looked down at his large hands.

"Makes it even stranger she killed herself, don't you think?" I said quickly.

"I don't think Bradley wants to get into that at this time, Nick," Juliette called across the room, a warning note in her voice.

"Sure," I said, glancing at my watch. If you have a nasty question you always save it to last. 'So tell me about your relationship with gerbils, Richard,' is likely to result in the interviewee abruptly quitting the room. (The more intrepid reporter will hope to be punched in the mouth to give his story a bit of color but that kind of verite I can do without.)

"You must have got to know Cissie pretty well on the film."

"Nick—"Juliette started. Stokes tilted his head to give me a peculiar up from under look.

"Cissie, my tragical girl. An incandescent talent, daddyo. Snuffed out." He clicked his fingers. "Like that. We mourn, we mourn. But …"

His voice drifted away. Here we go.

"Were you lovers?" I said. "Did she visit you in your penthouse suite in Montreal? Was she carrying your baby?"

Juliette moved very quickly for someone in such a tight skirt. She had scooped my tape and microphone up and was moving to the door with it even before Rolfe had levered me out of the chair and strong-armed me away from Stokes.

"Interview over," she said firmly, pulling open the door.

Just as I was being ejected from the room I twisted my head to get a last look at Stokes. He was still sitting on the sofa, looking down at his big hands. I could hear him slowly repeating to himself:

"We mourn, daddyo, we mourn …"

Rolfe let go of me once we were in the corridor. Juliette handed me my tape and microphone.

"You put anything about Bradley Stokes and Cissie Parker in your article and we'll sue you for more money than you could ever imagine," Juliette said icily. "Nick, you disappoint me. I thought you were a responsible journalist but here you are making malicious and wholly irresponsible accusations."

"I wasn't accusing, I was just asking," I mumbled, immediately on the defensive.

Juliette nodded to Rolfe. He gave me a long, hard look then went back into Stokes' room. Juliette leaned against the wall.

"I'm sure I remember a conversation in Club Soda about people who can be good friends and people who make very bad enemies."

"I recall that conversation too," I said. "It was the night Amanda Colgate performed at the Lost In the Translation gig. Why? Have I been making enemies?"

She examined my face.

"Somebody has been trying to fuck with us," she finally said, her voice steely. "I hope for your sake you aren't involved."

She had to mean Pace, the blackmailing street performer. Ex-blackmailing street performer. In that case, Dick Francis and the other heavies must have been working for her.

"Fuck with who exactly, in what way exactly?" I said, sounding calmer than I felt. I'm hopeless at dealing with angry people.

"If you are involved, you know. If you aren't, you don't need to know."

"Are you talking about a guy with a screwdriver banged up his nose? Street performer called Pace?"

She didn't so much as blink. "What I'm talking about is your future career. Colluding with others in wild allegations against any of my clients could land you in serious shit."

"Colluding? If you're talking about Pace, I've seen him three times for a total of five minutes. The third time he wasn't saying much. Three hard men had seen to that. Your hard men?"

"If you continue to act irrationally you'll see what hard men our lawyers are."

"Look, I just wondered if Stokes had seen Cissie around the time of her death. That's a legitimate concern."

"If you were the cops, maybe. But they don't seem concerned so why should you? You're just looking for a sleazy story."

"I'm *in* a sleazy story. I'm just trying to find who's writing it. The police here are looking for three hoodlums called Dick, Harvey, and Ronnie. Should I suggest they contact you for references?"

Juliette's eyes blazed. She leaned forward and hissed, "Nick, I can't believe you would be so stupid as to do that."

I tried to hold her stare but couldn't. Mr. Macho. After a moment she reached out and squeezed my arm.

"I don't know what to make of you, Nick."

"I'm pretty straightforward," I said sulkily.

"I can't work out if you're what you seem—an incredibly naive chancer—or a very smart operator."

"Those are the only options?" I said, attempting a grin. She ignored me.

"Whichever you are, if you are involved in trying to fuck with us, you'd do well to desist. I work with guys who, one way or another, play for keeps."

I wandered up the Royal Mile, past the Fringe offices. Half a dozen leaflets were thrust into my hand by various enthusiastic actors promoting their shows. I was looking for a pub where I could have a quiet drink and a think. Not just any old pub. The pub I like has bare boards, smoke darkened ceilings, wooden panelling and pews, no one-armed bandits, no piped music, no jukebox, no loudmouths. Unfortunately, it doesn't exist.

I went into the pub I'd left by the toilet window a couple of nights before. Ten minutes later I was sitting with a pint of beer and a plate of haggis and neeps in front of me. Yes, I do enjoy haggis, give or take the sheep's bladder.

My tape and mobile phone were on the table beside my plate. I thought back over my morning with Bradley Stokes. Definitely doolally but did that make him a murderer? I felt I could forget him as the father of the child. But maybe he and Cissie were doing drugs together. Then there was Juliette. If Bradley Stokes wasn't involved, why was she being such a hardass? I was pleased I'd left my tape running during our conversation.

If I got no breaks in Edinburgh, I was either going to have to forget the whole thing or follow Stokes, Juliette, and Rolfe back to Los Angeles at the end of the festival, in the hope of finding something incriminating there.

It was quiet in the back room of the pub but as I was pondering this option I became aware of an old couple some yards away having an argument. The thin faced, sharp-nosed old woman said querulously, "You will not have another. "You said your pacemaker was acting up. Are you wanting to give it more work than it already has to do?"

The old man had watery eyes and ill-fitting dentures.

"Go your own way, woman," he snarled, "and let me go mine."

He pushed himself to his feet and staggered over to the bar.

"That's it, you bloody old fool, see if I care," the woman said, as much to herself as to him. She caught my eye. "His pacemaker's giving him gip as it is."

I smiled sympathetically and concentrated on my haggis. More people drifted in to the back room. The old geezer returned to his wife. His wife looked sourly at him. "Pint for me, a dram for you," he said. "Jimmy is next door. Let's shift in there."

I watched as they made their slow way into the next room.

After the haggis and another couple of pints I was ready to phone Mary. Foolish, I know, but I was in that kind of mood, even though she'd failed my humor test. I dialed her hotel and asked for her room, not really expecting an answer. She picked up her phone on the fifth ring.

"Mary, Nick. Am I disturbing you?"

"I was taking a shower," she said.

"Perfect timing," I said, dimly aware of some kind of echo on the line. "I wondered if I could see you later."

"Why?"

"Why?" I said. "Because I thought we had something going."

Although I was speaking quietly I was aware that my voice seemed to be echoing loudly somewhere in the next room of the pub. I looked round bemused.

"I think that the something has gone," she said.

"You weren't serious about me and Bridget were you?"

"Very," she said.

"But I thought you wanted to track down Cissie Parker's murderer."

"I'll wait to read your article."

I dropped my voice even lower.

"I want to make love with you," I said. I heard catcalls from a gang of men in the next room. I was more specific. There were more hoots.

"What's that in the background?" Mary said.

"I think someone has just won at darts. Listen. Can I come over?"

Bizarrely, as I said it, I heard my question echoing back at me from off to my right. I looked up. The old geezer and his wife were standing in the doorway looking wildly round. He had one hand on his chest and he looked very peeved.

A group of young men was crowding round him looking into the room.

"No point," Mary said, both in my ear and, remarkably, in the old man's chest.

"Some buggers using a mobile phone," the old man said, glaring at me and clutching himself.

"That does it," his wife said. "We're going back with that sodding pacemaker tomorrow. You wanted something to sort your heart out, not a bloody public address system."

As I sat, temporarily dumbfounded, a familiar figure separated itself from the group of men.

"You owe me for seventeen pints of beer, fifteen pints of lager, a gin and tonic, and a Long Slow Comfortable Screw," Doug, for it was he, bellowed at me, his face contorted in anger.

Obvious witty responses rose to my lips but I settled for, "Oh buggeration."

"What's happening?" Mary said, her voice reverberating round the room.

"A minor electrical malfunction," I said, grabbing my things and heading for the toilet as my favorite member of the audience on the night of my ill-fated comedy debut pushed through the crowd in the doorway, an empty glass clutched in his fist.

I was out of the toilet window and halfway down the cobbled street to Waverley Bridge in double quick time. I saw a crowd of very trendy leather clad people standing on the pavement outside a cafe-cum-gallery. I went in.

I looked at a sign on the wall as I caught my breath. There was a quote from someone called Paul Gabriel Bouce, from an essay of his called "Chthonic and Pelagic Metaphorisation in 18th Century Erotica. "How should I know what it meant?

It referred to rhetorical epiphenomenons, bellicose lexis, and poliorcetics.

"You're darn tootin'," I said, bemused.

"You have trouble with that?" a young woman beside me murmured. I looked down at her, registered sixties long straight blonde hair and pale face. She flicked a glance at me.

"What makes you think so?" I said.

"You were mouthing the words as you read them."

"Only to see if there was any possible way to pronounce 'Chthonic.' No one should be allowed so many consonants together in one word."

"You just pronounced it."

"Yeah. If I knew what it meant I'd be well away."

"He's saying aggressive metaphors are often used in describing sex in erotica."

"Oh, well, sure. I knew that. So you know this guy Bouce?"

"It's a great essay. For him a snatch isn't a snatch, it's a thesaurus of metaphors."

"I see."

"And a penis is an encyclopaedia of natural history."

"Aha."

"Are you gay?"

"No. Why, do only gays say 'Aha'?" I looked down at her. "You?"

"No. Some of my best friends are. Were."

"They converted?"

"They died."

I nodded then, for good measure, shook my head, too.

"Are you an artist?" I said.

"We're all artists."

"Of course."

"My body is my work of art."

I peeked down the front of her dress.

"It's very nice."

"I'm into corporeal modification."

"Aha—I mean, I see."

"I started with tattoos and body piercing. Now I'm turning to scarification, tribal markings and branding."

"Branding? Isn't that dangerous?"

She shrugged. "Third degree burns. I may try minor amputations next—a toe here, a little finger there."

"Wow," I said, looking for some way out. "Why would you put yourself through that?"

"My boyfriend Lee is aiming at self crucifixion. Pain for him has a spiritual purpose. When you experience pain, you gain knowledge and control of yourself. For Lee its a rite of passage along the lines of Mayan blood-letting ceremonies."

"But self crucifixion!"

"Oh, he's being sensible about it. He's arranging for someone to look after his business while he's being crucified."

"A sensible self crucifixion sounds like an oxymoron," I said.

"What you doing calling the nice young lady a moron," a deep voice intruded.

"Doug," I said, turning to where he was standing beside me with half a dozen of his mates. "How—"

Then he hit me.

"The Amazing Mister Lifto exercises his eleven pierced body parts like a weightlifter," a familiar voice said. "With a hook through his nose, ear, tongue, nipples, or penis he's now able to lift enormous weights."

When I opened my eyes D. I. Condon was sitting beside me, reading from a sheet of paper to a uniformed policeman. He caught the movement as I shifted my head and looked across at me.

"See, I've been swotting up on your thrill show entertainers, Mr. Madrid."

"That's very impressive," I said, my nose feeling as if it was stuffed with cotton wool.

"Toads too. They're parotoid you know."

"Are you daking the biss?" I said. "You should dry dalking with a swollen dose. Why are they parodoid?"

"Paranoid? Wouldn't you be if you were a toad living round here after what happened the other night?" Condon threw back his head and let out a loud laugh. It was a frightening sound. When he had recovered he said, "But I meant *parotoid*. It's the term applied to the glands that form the warts round their ears. It's in one of your books here."

D. I. Condon held up one of Hilly's textbooks for me to see. I sighed and closed my eyes.

"Have you found them yet?" I said.

"Which ones? The ones who chased you in Deal or the ones who beat the living daylights out of you in the Old Town?"

"Any of them. I'm not fussy."

"We think your Mr. Francis and his colleagues are back in London. We're still on the lookout for the gang that attacked you in the art gallery. You got off lucky, you know."

"Lucky?" I said, wincing as I breathed in. "I've got a badly bruised nose, four cracked ribs, a dwisted ankle, and I'm black and blue all over. Thad's lucky?"

"If they'd got any more of those coins down your throat you'd have either choked to death or ruptured your spleen."

"Don't remind me of the coins," I said, instinctively clutching my buttocks together at the memory.

When Doug had smacked me in the mouth I'd gone down, of course. Doug, however, had not been able to follow up immediately because the girl got in the way. Catching sight of the size of the lads Doug had with him, I'd scrambled off into the next room. The walls were coated with thick brown chocolate. At least I hoped it was chocolate. After Gilbert and George had exhibited their own faeces you couldn't be sure any more.

The room beyond that had a weird floor. According to the sign on the wall, it was a shifting metal floor, made up of thousands of coins. I hate conceptual art. I headed through the coins towards a fire exit door, slipped, and felt my ankle go. When they caught up, Doug and his mates thought it was a good idea to make me eat some of the coins. When they got bored filling my mouth with them they kicked me instead. I'd lost consciousness with a horrible metallic taste in my mouth.

At the hospital they told me I'd swallowed half a dozen of the coins.

"How will you get them out?" I said.

"Good dose of syrup of figs," they said. "Then you'll pass them naturally."

Not *that* naturally given the size of the coins. It brought tears to my eyes to think of it.

In shock, I'd been laid up in bed, first in the hospital then in Hilly's flat, for nearly a week. In that time the bulk of the festival had passed me by. Although it still had a week to run a lot of people had finished their stint there. Mary had come round to say goodbye on the day she was flying back to New York for her next assignment. Bradley Stokes, Billy Cash, Juliette, and Rolfe were all back in Los Angeles. If I intended to continue my investigations, I would have to follow them there.

Bridget had been popping in every so often and Hilly had been looking after me for the past couple of days. We'd got quite close—no, not like that. I'd even told her about blowing up the toad. I think she had to struggle to keep a straight face. Hilly and Bridget both advised me to drop the whole thing and get on with my life. So did D. I. Condon.

"You should just go home, Mr. Madrid," he said now, eying me dolefully. "And leave everything to us."

I nodded wearily. I was feeling pretty *parotoid* myself. It probably was best to leave well alone. But when had I ever done what was best for me? Three weeks later I was on a plane to Los Angeles.

LOS ANGELES

NINE

The girl in the bikini briefs reclined on the lounger all day doing her knitting. As her needles clacked away she was scrutinized closely by five British journalists. Behind their Reactolite sunglasses they had growled and lusted, as men in packs do, over all the women frolicking in the kidney-shaped pool. But their attention always came back to her.

One by one, the five found excuses to walk slowly by her so that each in turn could ask as an opening gambit what it was she was knitting. Each received the same considered reply. Fuck off, limey.

I was the sixth journalist. I wasn't growling. The best I could do was gurgle. Cheap sunglasses. And I didn't bother to make the journey over to the girl with her knitting. Occasionally, even I know when I'm on a loser. I'd seen the guy she'd been with earlier. Good looking. Rich looking. Tough looking. Besides, my thoughts were elsewhere. I looked down again at the Los Angeles paper I held in my hand and snickered.

I like Thomas Hardy novels but I don't like the way his plots often hinge on unlikely coincidences or twists of fate: you know, the note pushed under the door getting lost under the doormat for months. But here was something right out of *The Thomas Hardy Bumper Book of Unlikely Coincidences*.

I'd been thinking about Amanda Colgate ever since I got on the plane at Heathrow the previous morning. I hadn't really been able to get her out of my mind since Montreal. The memory of abandoning her on the brink of sex to follow up the new clue about Frank's death was seared into my brain.

I hadn't a clue where she lived in California but when I came over I'd felt sure that somehow we'd meet up. And virtually the first thing I'd seen in the L.A. daily was this ad for a gig she was doing that night at the Comedy Attic on Sunset Boulevard.

I'd spent the three weeks after my return from Edinburgh trying to get someone else to pay for me to come here. A travel PR mate told me he was putting together a press trip for a holiday company that specialized in deluxe camping tours around the States. The trip would start in Los Angeles.

I'd done a deal with my friend that in return for a piece about the second week of the trip I could stay in Los Angeles in the first week whilst the other journalists headed off to Yosemite. I'd expected to spend it in some downtown roach motel but my friend had managed to get me a great deal here at the Century. It used to be Ronald Reagan's favorite hotel but, hey, nobody's perfect.

I'd been ready to give up my amateur sleuthing after Pace's death—as far as I'm concerned fear is a healthy emotion and I didn't mind admitting I was damned scared. But, strangely, the anger I felt about my beating by Doug and his mates expressed itself in a determination to find out exactly what had happened to Cissie Parker. I would spend this week alone in L.A. pursuing my investigations.

"What investigations, exactly?" Bridget had asked before I came away, over a bottle of wine in St. John, my favorite restaurant in London's Smithfields. "You went for broke with that fat bastard, Bradley Stokes, and came up with nothing. The Edinburgh cops aren't going to tie Juliette Smith in with Dick Francis and those other hoodlums who killed Pace. Pace is the only person who may have seen who threw Cissie Parker out of a window. So where's that leave you?"

"Stokes is a couple of laughs short of a punchline. He's vulnerable. If I can get to him again who knows what might spill out?"

"He's the one you're concentrating on?"

"Yeah. I was suspicious about seeing Lenny Finnegan in the Rathbone at the same time as Dick Francis but I think that was just coincidence. I checked on Loud Lenny with good old Gerard, the deputy manager of our hotel in Montreal. Lenny was on the same floor as me in the hotel. If it was him with Cissie they must have been using someone else's room."

"I'd already discounted him."

"How come?"

"I asked him." There was something odd about Bridget's tone of voice.

"When?" I said casually.

"Well, I, er—we hung out a bit in Edinburgh."

I was startled to see Bridget blush. Bridget embarrassed? She avoided my eyes and looked over at another table, where a well-known TV actor was canoodling with a pretty woman I somehow didn't think was his wife.

"Bridget. You and Lenny? Lenny and you?"

She looked at me defiantly. "Well, you weren't around to keep me company. He's very nice under that loud exterior."

"But Bridget, I thought you had rules. He's married."

"Yes, but he only married her because she's rich."

I looked at her blankly.

"That justification has stumped me," I said eventually. "But okay. I want details. When? How often? How big?"

"Phil Peters and I were in the Gilded Balloon having a drink at the Late 'n' Live show. We met up there."

"Where was I?"

"Unconscious, I think. It was the day after you were beaten up. I didn't mention it because I knew you'd be upset you couldn't be there, too."

"How thoughtful. I thought you hated Phil Peters' guts."

"Life's too short for all that. Forgive and forget, that's what I say."

I slumped back in my chair.

"Since when? You're the woman with 'Revenge is Sweet' tattooed on your forehead." Realization dawned. "Bridget, you're soft on Lenny Finnegan."

Bridget looked away.

"He's cute."

"Cute? Loud Lenny?"

"He's keen," she said. "He's touring Australia and New Zealand for six weeks. Wants me to go along."

"I bet he does. You laughed in his face of course. Didn't you?"

"I said yes," Bridget said meekly, not an adverb I'd ever associated with her before. She was looking almost soft, almost vulnerable. Unexpectedly tears welled up in my eyes. I reached over and squeezed her hand.

"Well, that's great Bridget, if you're sure. Really great."

"I was feeling low. Seeing Pace murdered in such a horrible way so soon after Frank's death. Then seeing you all beaten up."

"You don't have to excuse yourself to me," I said softly. "When do you go?"

"Next week. But I'm not happy about you going off alone whilst I'm away. Forget Bradley Stokes."

"Why?"

"It's career suicide, that's why. There's millions of pounds invested in Stokes, a lot of people with a lot to lose if his career comes to an abrupt end. They won't let you get near. You've already seen what they're capable of."

"I just want to go and nose around. Talk to Cissie's agent about her movements the past few weeks, talk to her friends. Talk to her father."

"Her father?"

"Mick Gaven. Jilly gave me his phone number."

I'd called Gaven as soon as we'd arrived in Los Angeles and left a message on his service. I'd also arranged to have breakfast the next day with Cissie's agent, Jeffrey Green. He'd sounded guarded but friendly.

Until that meeting I intended to spend my time lounging by the pool. Although I was pretty much recovered physically from the beating I'd received, emotionally I was still pretty shaky. Anger, anxiety, and despair had been chasing each other around me for the past weeks. I had bad dreams: Ruthie, Pace, Frank, Cissie, and Doug all mixed up together in them. My yoga would have helped to calm me but I couldn't seem to get started with it.

That evening, after a hurried dinner with my colleagues, I made my farewells and took a cab to the Comedy Attic. I love Los Angeles at night. The tatty daytime sprawl is transformed by the lights into a fantasy city. On Sunset Boulevard I leaned out of the window to goggle at the billboards for this summer's block-buster movies. The cab pulled up between massive hoardings for Kubrick's *Artificial Intelligence* and Schwarzenegger's medieval epic, *The Crusades*. Across the board was the monochrome bill-board for the remake of *Citizen Kane*.

I was on an unprepossessing, shadowy stretch of the Boule-vard. The Comedy Attic was in a wooden building above a bar. Painted on the side of the low building beside it was a boastful sign: Getting Rid of Unwanted Tenants Is Our Business.

Inside it wasn't so seedy. Worn but well swept wooden floor, solid chairs and tables, and a big wooden bar at one end. It was only half full. At the other end was an open triangular stage with a microphone on a stand at its apex.

"Hi, " I said, smiling at the barmaid.

"I live with my boyfriend," she said.

I bought a beer and settled myself at a table near the back. A compere with some kind of hook where his hand should be bounded on stage. He proceeded to talk about the problems of having his artificial limb. I was impatient for Amanda to appear so didn't find it easy to concentrate on him or the other acts.

Amanda came on last. God, it was great to see her. She looked very slinky in a short, tight dress. She saw me when she had the lights man swing the spot round on the audience. She looked, did a double take, then got on with the routine. Every so often she glanced my way. When the lights went up I ordered another beer and stayed in my seat. Eventually she came over, acknowledging people at other tables on the way. She slipped into the chair opposite me.

"You're not a stalker are you, Nick?" she said lightly, showing the tip of her tongue between her teeth.

"Just serendipity," I said. I smiled and examined her face, framed by her Louise Brooks bob. I was thinking of her kissing me ardently in the back of a Montreal taxi. I was imagining her with Phil Peters. She looked very pale and there were hollows beneath her eyes. She reached over and tapped my spectacles.

"Didn't know you wore glasses, Nick."

I blushed. I was wearing a pair of recently purchased wire framed specs.

"Erm, I don't actually—they're clear glass. Thought I'd join the in-crowd. I've noticed that all the stars—Costner, Schwarzenegger, Stallone, Liam Neeson, whoever—are wearing them for that intellectual Los Angelino look."

"A Los Angeles intellectual," she said, grimacing. "There's a contradiction in terms."

"Yeah, a real … oxymoron," I said, the word flashing up all sorts of bad memories.

"But anyway, you're about three years out of date, Nick."

"Story of my life. So what's hip now?"

"Big cigars still are—just—but you can hardly carry a humidor around with you. I'll get back to you on the latest trend."

There was a silence.

"In Montreal—"

"I don't want to talk about Montreal," she said sharply. She smiled too brightly. "Tell me the latest Royal gossip. Tell me about Di and Fergie."

"I tried to call you in Montreal. Left messages—"

"Okay then, I'll tell you about which movie stars are lesbians. Shall I start with the men?"

"I heard about you and Phil Peters."

She stiffened and looked at me suspiciously.

"Word gets around."

"Not really. I found out by accident. Made me feel rather silly."

"So you know about the detox retox?"

I nodded slowly. Actually, I hadn't a clue what she meant.

"Detox retox?" I finally said.

"Detox retox," she said patiently, as if speaking to an imbecile—no cheap comments, please. "I'd been in recovery for drug addiction and in Montreal I went back to my old ways. With a vengeance. Thanks to Phil."

"He told me he was clean," I said indignantly.

"He'll tell you what you want to hear," Amanda said. "He's a brilliant manipulator. Absolutely brilliant."

I looked at her pale face again. "And now?"

She looked at her empty glass. "Hey, Chrissie," she called to the barmaid, "gimme a double Stoli over here." She gave me a sour look. "Now? Now I'm clean as ... clean."

There was a hard edge to her I hadn't seen before. Or maybe once, when she'd made the decision to sleep with Billy Cash to get on his show.

"Is your appearance on *Prize Cash* sorted?" I said.

"A couple of days from now. Live in front of twenty million people."

She grimaced. I smiled.

A moment later she reached over and touched my hand. I liquefied.

"Why are you out here, for God's sake? Are you on a story?"

"I've got a few people I want to see about Cissie Parker."

"Jeez, Nick." She shot me a sour look. "You're not still messing around with that, are you? I thought that Canadian PR, Steve Hewitt, had done it?"

"Apparently not. The killer is still on the loose."

"So what has it got to do with you?"

I looked again at her. Could I trust her?

"Well, I seem to be on the right track judging from the troubles I've been having. Juliette—"

"You'd do better staying away from Juliette," she said quickly. "Especially in Los Angeles. She's got powerful friends."

"I've just got to check a few things out."

"Well, leave me out of it. I don't want to hear and I certainly don't want to be involved. Not when my big break is about to happen."

"I understand. It looks like things are going well for you. Top billing here."

"Yeah," she said, looking a little embarrassed. She finished her drink. "I oughta be going."

"Maybe I could come and see you on *Prize Cash.*"

"Not if Juliette's pissed with you, you can't."

"Can I see you tomorrow?" I said, reaching to touch her hand. She gave me a small smile.

"I'm free in the day. I'm housesitting for a friend of mine in Brentwood. You can come over and help me walk her dog. I'll show you where Nicole Simpson was murdered and where Jim Carrey lives."

She scribbled down the phone number on the back of a coaster. Abruptly she got to her feet. She put a hand on my shoulder when I tried to get up too.

"Finish your beer," she said, dipping down to kiss me lightly on the cheek. "Call me in the morning."

It was still early and, jet-lagged again, I was wide awake. Mention of Nicole Simpson made me wonder whether to do the ghouls tour, get a cabbie to take me to Chateau Marmont where John Belushi died of a drug overdose; then to Johnny Depp's Viper Club where River Phoenix spent his last night on earth; the Menendez house where the brothers murdered their parents; finishing with the stretch of street where L. A.'s finest beat the bejesus out of Rodney King. Instead I went back to the hotel, hoping to catch the other guys in the bar.

In the lobby I almost collided with a long-legged black girl wearing a short dress that ended where her legs started.

"Can you tell me where the bar is?" I asked politely.

"Ugh?"

"Where's the bar?"

"Bah?" She looked blank.

"Bar?" I repeated, feeling increasingly, well, sheepish.

"Oh you mean *bar*," she said, twigging.

"That's what I—do you speak English?" I said.

She giggled then stared at me for a moment with huge, huge eyes.

"Do you want to fuck me?"

My mind went into panic mode. Was that a trick question? I mean I know I'd just left Amanda but this woman was beautiful. Of course I wanted to fuck her.

"Five hundred dollars for half an hour, baby."

"Oh, I see," I said, blushing. "Erm, no thanks."

When I found the others in the bar I told them what had happened.

"Do I look like the kind of guy who has to pay for sex?" I said indignantly. They all looked into their drinks. Bastards.

I was up by six and already the traffic was piling along Century Boulevard outside the hotel. I was expecting to be hit by air pollution—the birds coughing in the trees and all that—but it was a soft morning, the smell of jasmine wafting through my open window.

I attempted some basic yoga whilst watching TV. Some little curly-haired guy, hosting a combination chat and exercise show, was dispensing advice about Life to American matrons. He was chatting to an old guy who had just walked from New York to Los Angeles (some 3,000 miles) to protest about something or other (I had my ear tucked somewhere under my knee when he said).

Presumably to keep the show peppy, the host was interviewing him whilst cooking a meal. So the guy was explaining his reasons for the walk with great sincerity whilst the host was rolling and dipping and rubbing ingredients. And when the old guy gave his final tearful appeal and threw his hands out to indicate the distance he had walked to get this message across, the host popped a kebab stick into the nearest hand and said, 'Taste this, isn't it delicious?'

I phoned the front desk to order a rental car—I love being on expenses—then went down to the pool for a swim. I'd been dreaming of driving a convertible but they didn't have any so I settled for something standard with air conditioning.

I'd driven in London for nearly ten years so I had no fears about driving in any other city in the world. Sure, Los Angeles drivers might shoot each other on the freeway, but as far as driving skills were concerned, forget it. I made an easy way along wide streets lined with palm trees up into Beverley Hills.

Two blocks south of Rodeo Drive I saw my destination, a restaurant called Lot 49. This place was purportedly hip for movieland breakfasts. I was expecting huddles of film stars talking about the arc of the characters they were playing and how as craftspeople or artists they were their own tools.

A pretty, extremely slender waitress in a white shirt and short shorts led me into a courtyard. I scanned the place for film stars. Not a one. A man and a woman were in deep discussion at a table in the shade of a massive palm tree. The woman was drawing heavily on a cigarette. They both stood to greet me as I approached.

"Nick, hi. I'm Jeffrey Green. My assistant, Anna Leone." The man thrust out both hands. He took my hand in one and my elbow in the other, giving both a strong squeeze whilst looking me straight in the eye. He was in his thirties, medium height, regular features, with slicked back blond hair. He was wearing a cream shirt, with an Armani tie, and baggy navy trousers.

The woman offered me a limp hand. She was small and plain with stiffly lacquered hair. The ashtray in front of her had half a dozen cigarette stubs in it.

"Take a seat, Nicky," Anna said. "You're kinda late so we started breakfast without you. Would you like to order?"

"Just orange—"

"Good. Honey, could you clear these things away then bring our guest here a fresh orange? I'll take a double decaf espresso with a twist of lemon and Mr. Green here will have his bulb." She turned to me. "So, Nicky."

I glanced at my watch. It was two minutes after the time we'd arranged to meet. "Sorry I'm late."

"Never apologize, mister, it's a sign of weakness," Jeffrey said, revealing velvet slip-on shoes as he crossed his legs beside the table. The waitress brought him something small and white on a plate. "Thanks, honey. Garlic, Nick, good for your testosterone."

He bit into the peeled bulb and began to chew. He talked as he did so.

"Okay, Nick, I like to fuck on my first date. What say you tell us exactly what you're up to and I'll tell you if we can help."

"I just wanted to ask you some questions about Cissie."

"Why?"

"I'm not happy about the way she died."

"You think I'm happy about the way she died? It's tragic. It's tragic, it's tawdry, and it's a damned waste of a life. But what's to say? She either killed herself or died accidentally whilst under the influence of drugs."

"I'm not so sure her death was either of those things."

"Murder? I don't buy it."

"Three other people have died since her death. A journalist friend of mine who was curious about the circumstances of her death. A photographer who had taken some shots of her just before Cissie died. And a street performer who saw something he shouldn't have seen in connection with her death. I find that suspicious."

"You're sure you're not just looking for a juicy scandal, get you on the cover of the *National Enquirer*?" Jeffrey said, impatience in his voice.

"I'm sure. Will you answer some questions?"

"I don't know about those other deaths and I don't know that they are necessarily linked." Green sat back in his chair. He looked at his watch, glanced quickly round the room. "But go ahead."

"Do you know who the father of Cissie's child was?"

"No," Green said. He took another bite of his garlic bulb.

"No? That's it?"

"Cissie kept her private life to herself. I handled her career. Anything you want to know about that I can help you with. Anything personal is a no-no."

"Okay. When did you take her on your books?"

"Few months ago. I'm very much a see it and you can achieve it kinda guy. My background is marketing and I had an entre-preneurial perception the time was right for someone like her. Cissie had something—sassiness and smarts—that could take her all the way. She coulda' been the next Sandra Bullock."

"You must be sorry she's dead."

"Sure I'm sorry. I invested a lot of money in her. But hey, do you see me crying? In business, those are the breaks."

"Was she working six or seven weeks before Montreal?"

"I should have her engagement book memorized?"

"She wasn't, Jeffrey," Leone said. "Remember she took that time off. Went off with a friend somewhere."

"Do you know what friend?"

"I told you—" Jeffrey was impatient again.

"Okay, but who in general did she hang out with in Hol-lywood?"

Jeffrey sighed, re-crossed his ankles, glanced at his velvet slip-ons.

"I don't know. I guess the Brit Pack. Probably the SPEDs."

"The SPEDS?"

"Is there an echo in here, Anna? SPEDs—Stupid Pretentious English Directors."

"Did she know Bradley Stokes?"

"Where do you think you're going with that kind of ques-tion?"

"I think he might be implicated in her death."

Green looked round the courtyard, laughed mirthlessly, and looked at Anna.

"Phew. Huh, Anna? What'd I say? Didn't I warn you about this guy?"

"What do you mean?" I said.

"After I got your call I phoned up a coupla people I knew in

England, find out about you. They said you were a bit of a loose cannon. But I work a lot on vibe. When we spoke on the phone I had a good vibe about you. Now you make me kinda nervous. Not exactly nervous. Anxious. Yeah, I'm anxious. What is it that worries me, Anna?"

Anna exhaled smoke. "That British reserve."

Green laughed. "That British reserve. Right. That's what it is."

"Did she know Bradley Stokes?"

Green leaned forward.

"Mister, look around you," he said fiercely. "You're in a room full of green lights. A dozen people in this room have films in production. There are heavy hitters here. Any one of another dozen can give the go-ahead to movies that might cost a hundred million dollars. Between them they've got the budget of a small nation. Guys like Bradley Stokes make money for them. Have you any idea how much money his three *Hitman* films made?" I shook my head. "Well, I haven't either but I'm damned sure it was a lot. And they don't want anything to harm their investment. Hollywood's a small community. We work together. You come into town, a guy looks to me is all hat and no cattle, and at my table—at *my* table—you go making that sort of remark about one of their investments." He shook his head in disgust. "You Brits, you slay me."

I sipped my orange juice, focusing on Green's velvet clad foot as he jiggled it impatiently.

"Sorry," I said.

"As I said, never apologize, it's a sign of weakness—you know that John Wayne film?"

"Er, no. I don't. But I saw his footprints outside Graumann's Chinese Theatre. He had tiny feet. No wonder he always walked as if he was about to fall over."

Green looked at me blankly.

"Where was she living in Los Angeles?" I said.

Green and Leone looked at each other.

"Guy doesn't give up," Jeffrey said. "Gotta admire him for that." He nodded to Leone, who scribbled down an address on a piece of paper and handed it to me.

"You would have got it from the L.A. papers anyway," Jeffrey said, seriously overestimating my investigative ingenuity. He and Leone got to their feet.

"Maybe see you around," he said. "Oh and Juliette asked to be remembered to you when we saw you. But then, who needs to remember? She's not a lady you're about to forget."

I stayed on when they left and ordered a coffee. I was feeling very stupid. Hollywood is indeed a tight knit community and small fish like Green depended on the bigger ones like Juliette for survival. He would have been got at long before I even phoned him. Now Juliette would know I was in town and—since I'd given Green my phone number—even where I was.

I picked up a copy of *Variety* someone had left at a nearby table and flicked through it, doing a little yoga breathing to calm myself down. Dicky Attenborough had finally got funding in place for his Thomas Paine film. There was a lot of hoopla about the remake of *Citizen Kane* by an unknown Seattle film director after Branagh and Tarantino had both turned it down. Rosebud the sled was now Rosebud the skateboard. Billy Cash's first film in his three-film contract was finishing preproduction. The cameras were expected to start turning in a month's time. Bradley Stokes was about to start work on the fourth of the *Hitman* films.

I left the cafe around ten and reached Santa Monica by eleven. It was so hot even the ocean breeze couldn't stop the sun burning. Cissie's apartment was a couple of blocks back from the beach. I was hoping the apartment building would have a caretaker but there was no one listed on the door and nobody else in the block was answering the bell.

I phoned Amanda from a booth on the street and suggested she come down to Santa Monica for lunch. She couldn't make lunch but she said she'd be down mid-afternoon. I'd noticed an English pub across the street so I suggested we meet there.

I wandered over. It was pretty low rental but at least I could get a drink without anyone looking askance. In L. A. these days the waiters tut-tut if two people order a whole bottle of wine with lunch. A couple of Mexican guys were playing darts. Two women were sitting at a table by the door. Good looking, thirties, tanned, and tough.

One was speaking in a kind of squeaky Minnie Mouse voice. "So he says 'Do you want to know my credo? It's something of Joe Namath's that I've paraphrased.' Sure, I say, thrill me. He puts on this deep voice: 'I can't wait for tomorrow, because I get better looking every day.' I mean, when was the last time he looked in a mirror, right?"

The two women cracked up. They were still laughing when I walked over. They looked me up and down. None too friendly.

"Are you regulars here?" I said.

"Nice glasses," Minnie Mouse said, tittering.

"Who wants to know?" the other one said in a smoke-damaged, husky voice.

"I'm an English journalist," I said, putting my glass down on their table. "Wanted to ask you a couple of things. Perhaps I could buy you a drink?"

"Depends what you want to ask," Minnie Mouse said.

"I'm doing an article on a woman called Cissie Parker. She lived down the street. Wondered if she ever came in here."

"You doing a number on her?" the one with the husky voice said.

"No. She's dead. I just wanted to find out about her."

"I read she was dead," Minnie Mouse said. "We'll both have large vodka tonics."

"I'm Suzi with a Z I," the one with the husky voice said when I brought their drinks back. "And this is Sharyn."

"With a Y," Minnie Mouse added.

"Well, Suzi with a Z I and Sharyn with a Y, your good health."

I raised my glass to them and sipped my beer. They downed their drinks in one.

"Here, let me get you another," I said quickly.

They each finished off three large vodkas without apparent ill-effect before I had a chance to ask them any questions. This was worse than being out with Bridget.

"You look a bit like Liam Neeson with those glasses on," Suzi said. "You packing a pistol like his?"

Sharyn leaned round the table to look at my feet.

"He's got big enough feet," she said. "You know what that means?"

"Yes," I said hastily. "I know what that means. Usually."

There was a bowl of peanuts on the table. I grabbed a handful and started munching.

"Liam Neeson, Jimmie Woods, and Willem Dafoe. Some actress once said with those three in a room there wasn't room for anyone else." She smirked at me. "Usually?"

"So did you know Cissie Parker?" I persisted.

"She used to come in from time to time," Suzi said, lighting up a cigarette. "Said hi. She knew we were actresses. Actress-models actually."

"Are you working at the moment?" I asked politely.

"Sharyn here is—what's that word you Limeys use—'resting.' I've just been picked for a new horror film. Only two days filming but it's an important part. And a start. I'm only eighteen after all."

I tried not to look astonished. Suzi looked thirty if she was a day.

"How old are you, Sharyn?"

"In my mid-twenties," she said coyly. I added ten years.

Another couple of drinks and I was getting their stories. Didn't matter they weren't talking about Cissie yet. I'd got three or four hours before Amanda came down here. From the way they both spoke I guessed they'd done some therapy, or drug counselling, or maybe just read the right books.

They were typical of so many good-looking girls who came to Hollywood looking for fame and fortune. Their looks got them only so far then they were paying the rent with a bit of part time hooking. They became party girls, constantly in demand at big shot parties where all they had to do was look great—and do whatever any of the guests wanted them to do.

"We don't really do the paid stuff anymore," Sharyn said. "For the money we do phone jobs."

I nodded.

"How were the parties?"

"Everyone wants beautiful girls at parties. Sometimes we got paid, sometimes we didn't. If the guys were real handjobs we made 'em pay."

"They're all handjobs," Sharyn said sourly.

"If a big star was interested in us," Suzi continued. "Well, they never have to pay for sex. Except if they want us to perform."

"Perform?"

"Sure," Suzi looked at me, raised her eyebrows. "Together. And the perverted ideas they got—there are some sick fucks out there, Nick, smiling down at you from the biggest billboards in town."

"You'd be surprised how popular the plexiglass platform is," Sharyn chipped in. I nodded wisely. Out of my depth again.

Sharyn sighed. "For a journalist you're pretty wet behind the ears. Guy erects it above his bed. He lies underneath. Two girls get on the glass. He watches."

I must have looked as shocked as I felt.

"What, guys don't get turned on by that in Britain?" Suzi said scornfully. "I've heard you're all butt-burglars."

"It's always sounded like a pain in the ass to me," I said, grinning nervously.

"Well, sugar," Sharyn said, leaning forward with a horrible leer on her face. "If it's a pain in the neck you know you're doing it wrong."

I tittered—she had me doing it now—nervously.

"The Don Simpsons of this world, they're into toilet sex big time," Suzi continued. Simpson was the producer of mega-hits like *Top Gun* and *Crimson Tide* who had died, appropriately enough, sitting on the toilet. There were some terrible stories about him.

"You've done all that?" I said, hoping I didn't sound prurient.

Suzi leaned into my face as she stood up. "I've done it all, honey," she hissed, heading for the loo. I scooped another handful of peanuts into my mouth. Sharyn, who was pretty drunk, eyed me for a moment then slid across and kissed me open-mouthed, sticking her tongue halfway down my throat. I blew half masticated peanuts up my nose. When I put my peanut-encrusted tongue in her mouth, she bit down. Hard. Laughing she pulled away.

Suddenly we were not alone. One of the Mexican guys, the one with the Zapata moustache, was standing looking fiercely down at me. I was drunk enough not to be scared. Much. My ribs started aching. He was about a foot shorter than me so I lurched to my feet, snorting peanuts, and put on my most macho look. Sharyn hiccuped with laughter. My tongue was like a barrage balloon in my mouth.

"Yeth?" I said, feeling I'd rather spoiled the effect. He eyed me, turned on his heel, and went out the door. I swayed for a moment, then resumed my seat.

"Don't mind him. He's a big fan of Jean Claude Van Damme."

"Can he do the moves?" I said nervously.

"That's where I knew Cissie Parker from before," Sharyn said, ignoring my last remark.

"Kick-boxing movies?"

"Naw. One of those parties. Few years ago. We did a twosome at this agent's place. Horrible little guy. A testicle on legs. Wanted oral servicing."

"Did Cissie talk much?"

"Guess we were both taught never to talk with our mouths full," she said, sniggering.

"I meant afterwards."

"Probably. I don't remember."

"Did she remember you when she came in here?"

"Didn't seem to. We were both pretty messed up that night—cocaine, 'ludes, booze. Don't know why I remembered her but it was her. Definitely."

"How was she when she was in here?"

"Friendly, you know. Nice. She'd cleaned up, I think. Was in a movie and was doing some comedy," Sharyn sighed. "She was on her way."

"Your turn will come," I said, with an encouraging smile.

"How would you know, fuckwit?" She pursed her lips and looked out of the door. Suzi returned.

"What did you make of Cissie Parker?" I said.

"Stupid cow was in love last time I saw her. An A-list party. I was there with some ancient handjob who wanted to show me off. All these creeps with all us young hard bodies. She recognized me from hanging out here. Came over to say hello."

"Who was she with?" I asked, as casually as I could.

"Bunch of people. I didn't pay much attention."

"Anybody famous?"

"They were all famous, honey. Like the man said: I was the only person I hadn't heard of."

"Was Bradley Stokes there?"

"That fat putz. He was there, sure. Tried it on."

"Was he hanging around Cissie?"

"Don't think so."

"Juliette Smith?"

"You know her?" Suzi said sharply.

"Is that a problem?"

"Well, if you're a friend of hers you're sure no friend of ours. She was there. And the big guy with the Prince Albert."

"Everybody knows about that then?"

Sharyn laughed.

"One of my girlfriends has a ring in her tongue—you know, for fellatio. Was getting it on with that guy Rolfe in some Beverley Hills hotel when their rings meshed. Had to call the hotel handyman to separate them with a file."

"Should have used a blowtorch," Suzi said sourly.

"Hey, Lauren's a good friend of mine," Sharyn said. "That would have hurt her, too."

Suzi shrugged.

"Whatever."

"Why don't you like Juliette?"

"Old history," Suzi said. "We owe her one. And we'll see that she gets hers one day."

"Cissie never came in here with anyone?"

"Nah. I occasionally saw guys come and go at her apartment but nobody I recognized as regular."

I went to the bar to get more drinks. I looked round to see what the other Mexican was up to. He was playing a video game in the corner, shrieking and baring green gums a lot. I figured I was okay as long as he didn't come over and bite me.

Sharyn was crying drunk when I got back. Suzi was idly patting her back whilst pulling on a cigarette. She looked at me, a little blearily.

"Feeling sorry for herself," Suzi said.

"I'm not a whore," Sharyn said. "I'm just an ordinary young woman with a pretty heavy past who turned a few tricks."

"Why'd you do it?" I said.

"For money, fuckwit. Why else? Men want to fuck you anyway. You may as well get paid for it. I loved this guy who used to give me hot coffee enemas whilst we were sixty-nineing. What do you think of that?"

I wasn't thinking at all. I was stunned, frankly, by people's perverted ingenuity and jaded appetites. Me, I got overexcited at the thought of the missionary position. I smiled sympathetically.

"Don't you look so fucking superior, you Limey bastard," Suzi snarled. "What's your kink—you fuck chihuahuas?"

"I wouldn't stoop so low," I said, quick as a flash, but it went over their heads. I hurried to the bar so they could drink the rest of it dry.

"But now you work in telecommunications?" I said on my return with yet more drinks.

Suzi snorted. "You could say that."

"Well, that's the future right there."

"I said we do phone jobs," Sharyn said. She gave me a withering look. "You know—phone sex. We talk dirty on the phone."

"Ah—aural sex," I said, but they didn't get that either. I coughed and cleared my throat. "So what's next for you two girls on the performance scene?"

."We're doing a couple of days at City Walk on roller-blades."

I puzzled over the sexual possibilities of rollerblades for a few moments. I didn't want to admit yet further ignorance but I couldn't get my head round what they might do.

Suzi guessed what I was thinking. "It's an acting gig, dummy. The real thing. City Walk—it's Universal Studios replica of three blocks of Los Angeles just down the road here. Venice Beach, Melrose Avenue, and Sunset Strip. Cost a fortune to build. There's a shopping mall and imitations of famous restaurants. They got streetsellers hustling celebrity autographs and astrological charts. They got weightlifters and hairdressers. And they got rollerblading."

"Why build a false Los Angeles so near the real one?"

"Risk free. You know—no drug dealers, gang bangers, thieves. No crime. It gets more tourists than the real L.A."

Suzi seemed to ponder this a moment then I realized she was drifting away. I think she'd probably popped something in the toilet. Time to go. I gave them my phone number and persuaded them to give me theirs. I left them there, leaning against each other, and emerged into the bright sunlight feeling very depressed.

A battered old convertible was parked immediately outside the pub. Amanda was standing in front of it, in shorts and a halter top. In front of her, by the curb, was a Dulux dog, a big long-haired English sheepdog, haunches lowered as it did its doggy doo.

"I bet he's hot," I said, coming up behind her and leaning on the front wing of her car. She turned.

"He should be shaved, I know," she said. "But he's not my dog."

I couldn't help noticing she was holding a roll of toilet paper.

"God, you've got him well trained," I said.

She grimaced and, as the dog finished up, started to unroll the paper. "Sadly not."

I guess I've always assumed that if a dog has long hair all over, nature has found a way to keep it clean after it does what it has to do. Taking one look at this dog's besmirched bum I could see how naive I'd been.

"You're not going to—" I said. But she was. Amanda bent and started to wipe the dog's bottom. I turned away as the smell hit me and caught sight of the Mexican with the Zapata moustache hurrying along the sidewalk towards me. He had a knife in his right hand.

"Oops," I said, moving away from the curb. "Amanda, crazed-Mexican alert."

He stopped a couple of yards from me.

"Got a problem?" I said mildly, remembering he was a big fan of Jean Claude Van Damme.

"Yeah. You."

"It's okay, Salman," I heard Sharyn call from the pub doorway. "We were just talking."

"Salman?" Amanda said, straightening up, a big wad of used toilet paper in her hand. "That's an unusual name for a Mexican."

"He's a fan of ..." I started to say.

The Mexican turned to look at Amanda. As he did so the dog gave a sudden twitch of its rump and a large piece of doggy-doo flew through the air and past the Mexican's ear.

The Mexican turned to watch its progress. He looked at me.

"The shit almost hits the fan," I murmured. I was trying to hold down a laugh but I couldn't. The Mexican's eyes opened wider, then he too started to laugh.

"D'you see that?" he said, lurching towards the dog.

"You leave him alone," Amanda said warningly.

The Mexican held his hand up, still grinning.

"It's a Dulux dog," he said, in an accent that sounded increasingly familiar. "I wouldn't harm one of them, dearie. Used to have one meself." He closed the knife and slipped it into his pocket.

"You don't sound Mexican," I said. "You sound ..."

He grinned at me. "I sound Brummie. That's because I'm not Mexican, you daft bugger. I'm from Sutton Coldfield."

He stuck his hand out, suddenly all smiles. "And you're English," he said. "Sorry mate. Thought you were a bloody yank. Can't stand them."

"Ever thought you might be in the wrong country?"

"Every day. That's why I'm off to Bombay soon."

"So how'd you end up here?"

"Got bored with Brum, didn't I? Came here to make it in the movies."

"You're an actor?"

"A gaffer. Electrician. Well, I want to be. Well, actually I want to be a soundman. I used to do it in the Midlands for the bhangra beat bands."

"So what are you now?"

"I'm a cable puller at the minute. I brown tape cable to the floor so it doesn't trip up the star of the movie."

"That's the movie business."

"Call this the movie business? Bombay. That's the movie business. They make more films there in a month than Hollywood makes in a year. I should have gone there before. It was a toss-up. But the girls here are easier—" He looked at Amanda. "'Scuse my English, miss."

Amanda shrugged. "Observant of you. Excuse me butting in on a compatriot's' get-together, but aren't we supposed to be walking a dog?"

"Not if it's going to do that again," I said, but she was already off.

"I'll be on the beach," she called back.

Salman and I looked at each other.

"So you're a journalist. You going to the San Simeon do?"

I shook my head. San Simeon, I knew, was the Hearst Castle, an enormous folly somewhere up the coast built by billionaire William Randolph Hearst for his mistress, film star Marion Davies, in the thirties. All the big stars of the day hung out there. Orson Welles' called it Xanadu in *Citizen Kane*, his fictional account of Hearst's life. Hearst himself called it "The Ranch."

"Man, you gotta go there. I'll get you a ticket. It's the least I can do for threatening you. I get out of my head sometimes."

"Is this to do with the remake of *Citizen Kane*?"

"That's it. Everybody's going to be there. Everybody. All today's stars, lookalikes for the old Hollywood folk. Staff dressed in thirties costume. Fireworks, live music, and lakes of champagne."

"Sounds great, but how do you know you can get me a ticket?"

"I'm moonlighting on the crew doing the sound system. I've got tickets for Sharyn and Suzi. I can get one for you. Where are you staying?"

I told him. As I was setting off down the sidewalk he called after me, "Only thing is—you'll have to go as something."

"Go as something?"

"It'll tell you on the ticket," he said, raising his hand in a little wave.

I caught up with Amanda on the boardwalk. We went down on the beach. It was like an outtake from Baywatch—good-looking men and women cavorting self-consciously. We walked across the sand in silence, the dog ploughing on ahead.

"Bless him," Amanda said. "Lumbering along, tongue hanging out. The dog looks pretty hot too."

We lay on the beach watching the surf come in. L. A. always

felt right to me. I'd inherited my dad's collection of pre-hippy surfing records and every time I looked at the surf I thought of Jan and Dean.

We kissed. It was bliss.

"Do you suppose I can get drunk from your breath," she said eventually.

"Am I beery?"

"Just a tad." She nuzzled my neck. "So where are you at, Nicholas?"

"Meaning?"

"This Cissie Parker thing. It's going to get in the way of us. You're messing with people I need. Hollywood's a small community."

"So I've heard."

"I'm determined to achieve my goals. I won't let anybody get in the way. Even you."

"It's Bradley Stokes I'm interested in."

"Yes, but it's Juliette you'll have to go through to get to him."

"Since when have you been so fond of Juliette?"

"Since she became my agent."

TEN

Cissie's father, Mick Gaven, lived in Rolling Hills, some thirty miles southwest of Los Angeles on the Palos Verdes peninsula. He'd left a message at my hotel inviting me over at eleven on Thursday morning.

According to *Worth* magazine, Rolling Hills was, per capita, the wealthiest city in America. Of course, a city in America isn't like a city in Europe. This one had a population of under 2,000 people. I'd read that it was one of a number of "gated communities" now prevalent in California, walled cities behind which the rich feel they can live in safety.

I did the distance English style, i.e. in about twenty minutes. It was a bright morning and as the road swept high up on to the peninsula I was aware of the great, shimmering expanse of the Pacific on three sides of me.

I was thinking about Amanda, of course. On the beach she had seemed to go back on the account she had given me in Montreal of her evening with Juliette Smith. The account that suggested that Juliette had all but raped her.

"Juliette can help me with my career," she said.

"In return for what?"

"It isn't like that. I should never have told you about that night. You got it all out of proportion."

"That's not how I remember our conversation."

She sighed. "Whatever. Juliette's a good agent. She's my agent and your blundering around won't help my career."

I didn't want to hurt her or her career but nor did I want to let Bradley Stokes off the hook. I owed it to too many people. We didn't exactly argue but there was a distance between us because of my intransigence. She'd had to leave to take the dog back to Brentwood before her gig at around six. I suggested I meet her after her gig. She said no. With regret.

"If you drop this nonsense," she said, pressing close, "things could be very different."

I stopped the car by the guard post at an enormous gate, feeling very Philip Marlowe. I used to love reading Chandler, although I thought his tough guy metaphors—all that tarantula on an angel cake stuff—a bit overwrought.

The guards waved me through when I told them who I was seeing. The road dipped steeply and for the next ten minutes I was driving through a series of canyons and gorges. I found it refreshing to see that it wasn't all manicured lawns and neat landscaping, like the wealthy parts of Los Angeles. There were hills with weeds and shrubbery growing wild on them. Every so often I'd see a house nestled among the trees or halfway up the side of a canyon.

Gaven was standing at the top of his long, steep driveway, waiting for me. I'd been half expecting a happy-clappy guy in polyester, but on first appearance it seemed he wore his religion lightly. He was trim, dapper, and dressed in expensive casuals. When I got out of the car he shook my hand briskly.

"Mr. Madrid, you found us okay. Great." He was a handsome man, a few tucks short of his real age, with a good tan and piercing eyes. He led the way into the house.

"Rolling Hills is an interesting community," he said. "It's pretty much a movie-free zone. Most people in Rolling Hills make their money in business or the professions—lawyers and accountants. It's near enough to Los Angeles to commute but far enough away to seem remote from there. Our one celebrity is Tracy Austin. You know, the tennis player? She's lived here since she was a kid."

"And you," I said.

"Nice of you to say so, Mr. Madrid, but hardly a celebrity. I had a brief moment of modest fame over thirty years ago. It was fun but I also got fucked up. Needed the Lord to help me straighten my head out." He turned and laughed genially. "He rewarded me by making me rich from his music."

He pointed through a long window to a wooden terrace.

"Let's go out to the sun deck," he said. "Mind your head. Ouch, I felt that. You okay? You know Frank Lloyd Wright's work? He had a lot of fun with this one. The guy who commissioned him was tall, like you. The story goes, Wright was having an affair with the wife, who hated her husband. So Wright put in all sorts of odd angles for the guy to bang his head on."

I followed him out on to a wooden terrace. Immediately below was a large swimming pool set into the hillside. It seemed like a perfect Los Angeles movie setting: scarcely a sound except for the sprinklers sussing, the cicadas rasping among the trees. Not a whisper of wind nor a wisp of cloud in the cobalt blue sky.

"My wife Charlene will join us shortly. She's just finishing up with a meeting of Spenders Anonymous."

"Since it's about your daughter I thought you might prefer … Spenders Anonymous?"

"It's a self-help group for people addicted to spending. My wife is in recovery. As indeed am I."

"You're addicted to spending too?"

"No, no. I'm a recovering drug, drink, and sex addict. I attend Narcotics Anonymous, Alcoholics Anonymous, and Sexaholics Anonymous." I mused on the possibilities for parties at Sexaholics

Anonymous for a moment. "SexAnon—that's where Charlene and I met, actually."

"How long have you been together?"

"Ten wonderful years."

"So Charlene knew Cissie?"

"Very well. Tried to help as much as she could. Hadn't she been through the same confusion and hurt herself? And, frankly, there was nothing Cissie could teach either of us about excess."

"You advised Cissie?"

"No one can advise you when you're going through that kind of thing. We talked to her and we prayed for her and it seemed to work." Tears came into his eyes. "Those last couple of months before she—before the accident—she really seemed to have turned herself around."

Gaven looked out across the pool.

"Charlene had a troubled childhood, too?" I said after a moment.

"Alcoholism goes way back in her family. She went from Alatot—that's a self-help group for young children of alcoholics—through Alateen—or teenage alcoholics—into AA."

Sounded a lot like Brownies and Girl Scouts to me but I didn't mention it.

"Of course, she's also in Adult Children of Alcoholics Anonymous and Grandchildren of Alcoholics now."

"Wow, poor woman."

"Hey, she's not alone." Gaven spread his hands, palms up. "Ninety-six percent of the families in the U. S. are dysfunctional to one degree or another. That's statistical fact."

"Goodness. But how does she fit all the recovery in? Those groups must be quite time consuming."

"Those aren't all of them. She goes to Debtors Anonymous and Shoplifters Anonymous, which, as you can imagine, comprise many of the people who used to attend Spenders Anonymous before they spent all their money. Then there's Emotions Anonymous, her emotions are very near the surface. Cocaine Anonymous. We go together to Recovering Couples Anonymous."

"No child abuse stuff?" I said.

"Oh, that's a given. Incest Survivors Anonymous is her lifeline there. She once misunderstood the name of a new group, Child Abusers Anonymous, and went along to talk about how she'd been abused. Freaked when she saw the strange glint coming into the other people's eyes."

"And do you attend many groups?"

He nodded slowly. "Recovery is a full-time commitment to myself, let me tell you. Oh, there's Workaholics Anonymous, too, although for obvious reasons that isn't always too well attended. So what with the ones I go to alone and the ones we share, I spend so long interacting with my inner child there's no time for anything else."

"Life is what happens when you're busy making plans, eh?"

"I'm sorry?"

"Life is what happens—it's just a quote—not particularly apt—from John Lennon, although he took it from a British astrologer called Patric Walker."

"No shit," Gaven said, cocking an ear as soft footfalls approached. A lifesize Barbie doll with what looked like full—very full—working parts pitter-pattered on to the sun deck in a wafty mini-dress. She walked in that straight back, neck stiff, arms clamped beside the body, small-neat-steps way women very conscious of themselves sometimes do. She looked about twenty-five. I dragged my eyes back to Gaven. Didn't he say they'd been together ten years? The dirty old dog.

"Charlene, honey, come and say hello to Mr. Madrid."

I stood and held out my hand but Charlene, a big smile on her face, moved past my hand to kiss me on each cheek. Only when she sat down, demurely crossing the several yards of leg on show, did I notice she was clutching a large, soft toy frog. I looked at her sharply. Had word got out about the exploding toad?

"How was Betty today, honey?" Gaven asked.

Charlene held the frog up and tilted it from side to side as she said to it: "Betty was just fine, weren't you, darling? We made some real progress today. And honey, I don't want the other colors in my car. I'm going to stay with the red."

"That's great, honey." Gaven looked at me. "See, before Spenders Anonymous, Charlene would never have said that. Then it was understood that she'd have her new car in four or five different colors. She liked to drive whichever color suited her mood that day." He turned to Charlene. "That shows real progress, baby."

Charlene twisted a lock of hair and gave a little shrug. "I thought maybe we could put the money towards a Lear jet instead."

Gaven nodded, smiling idiotically.

"I was just saying to Mick that your recovery programs must take up pretty much all of your lives," I said.

"Well, I tell you, Mr. Madrid. You know what I find the hardest? These are twelve step recovery programs and I just find it real hard to keep in step. Especially with four or five programs running together—how'm I supposed to remember which step I'm on for any one of them? Real tough for me, isn't it, honey?"

"You do just fine," Gaven said, giving her another gruesome lovey-dovey smile.

"The upside is that our social life has never been better," Charlene said. "I mean, check out these recovery groups and you're mixing with Hollywood's A list. It should help me with my career." She gave me a coy smile. "I'm an actress, you know."

"I guessed," I said. "And you're both into God, I hear."

Charlene nodded. "We found him together, didn't we, honey?" she said, in a tone of voice that made it sound like God was a great new restaurant.

"Any particular denomination?"

"Well, our God is kind of a personal God," Gaven said. "I mean I produce records for all denominations, but we don't exactly go in for churches as such. I think we all see God in our own way."

It quickly became clear that Charlene saw God as a celestial sugar daddy.

"I pray to my God every day," she said. "Mostly about stuff I want. And he provides it."

I wondered what it must have been like for Cissie going from a self-absorbed headcase like Jilly Dougan to living with a couple of recovery junkies.

"Was Cissie interested in any of this?"

"She had a lot of things to unpack, I could see that," Gaven said. "But she was in denial. Resisting. She wasn't ready yet."

"Was Cissie religious?"

"No way," Charlene said. "And we wouldn't impose that on her either. Although our God is a pretty easy-going God. You know, I'm from Georgia. Brasetown, same as Kim Basinger. My aunt went to school with her. We're pretty repressed back there. I got into some trouble in my teenage years over sex." She was absently sucking on her forefinger. "Oral sex."

"I see," I murmured, giving her what I hoped was a comforting glance and trying my hardest to keep my eyes focused on her face and not her legs, breasts, or finger.

"You know you can get a life sentence for oral sex there," Gaven said. I smiled, not sure of the joke. "Seriously. Maximum sentence. They classify it as sodomy, guess they're not too hot on anatomy. You only get a couple of years for necrophilia and only three months for bestiality."

Charlene fondled her frog.

"Makes you wonder what the guys passing those laws get up to, don't it?"

I cleared my throat.

"About Cissie …"

"She first came over here when she was thirteen or fourteen," Gaven said. "She'd just found out about the nature of her conception."

I glanced at Charlene, who smiled.

"It's okay, Mr. Madrid, I know all about it. We have no secrets about our pasts."

Gaven laughed.

"We regret the sins of our past. But we think God has a healthy, open attitude to these things. It's not something we would do now. Now we think that sex between two people is wonderful."

"Between five it's incredible," I murmured to myself, finishing off the old Woody Allen joke. Gaven smiled. Charlene sucked her finger.

"Cissie was pretty upset when she first came. She was already drinking and doing drugs—dope, amphetamines. She stayed a couple of months then split back to England."

"When did you see her again?"

"Not for a year or so. Then it was the same thing. I mean she could be a lovely girl, a free spirit but she could also take it too far."

"Tell him, Mickey."

"I should?"

Charlene nodded, clutching her frog between her breasts. Ouf.

"That first visit, she was upset, lonely, confused. I don't blame her. Don't blame her at all."

"For what?"

"Well, we know a lot of charismatic people. Some are famous, some aren't. Cissie found being in their company confusing."

"What Mick's saying is that she came on to every man who visited. Big time."

"She was lonely," Mick said.

"She was desperate to lose it," Charlene said frostily. "And she lost it."

"To someone you knew?"

Charlene stroked her frog and looked at Gaven.

"Oh, I knew him all right," he said. "One of my oldest friends. Freddy Redolo. A musician. Known him since the six-ties. We didn't see much of each other, of course. He toured a lot, I've been pretty busy with the studio. But we kept in touch off and on. Saw each other every couple of years."

"So he was much older than Cissie."

"Heck, yes. She was fourteen, he was forty-five. She seemed to dig older men. We're thirty miles from L. A. here. May as well be 3,000. We were out of the loop. That's all changed with the rehab stuff but back then AA wasn't where you went for the gossip and the business deals. So what I hadn't known was that Freddy had a reputation around L. A. As he got older he some-times went for jail-bait. Frankly, Cissie was a bit old for him, but soon as he sees her, he's sniffing around."

"Although we didn't realize it at the time," Charlene added, tight-lipped.

"So what happened?"

"They got together the first time she stayed with us. After that, he'd come around whenever he was in town. When we found out, we had it out with him and he said he'd be cool. We've never seen him since. Cissie, now, she freaked because we'd put a stop to it. She went back to England in a huff. It was a couple of years before we saw her again."

"Did she carry on seeing this Freddy Redolo?"

"Not around here," Charlene said. "And I don't think so anyway. Freddy had got what he wanted. He was the kind of guy who liked to move on."

She seemed to be more incensed than Gaven by Redolo's behavior. I wondered if it was because she'd had similar experiences in her life when she was younger.

"After that, she stayed with us every year. She wanted to be in movies so I called a few people I know in the business and one summer got her a job as a D-girl at one of the studios. It didn't take. When she came to shoot that low-budget movie she decided to stay and got an apartment in Santa Monica. She'd visit. We saw her just before she went to Montreal." Gaven paused, tears filling his eyes again. "And that was the last time we saw her."

"Did she tell you she was pregnant?" I asked after a moment.

"No," Gaven said. "Though I guessed her private life was going well. I think she was off the drugs and she didn't seem to be drinking much."

"Did she ever mention Bradley Stokes?"

"That fat comedian from those gross *Hitman* films?" Charlene shuddered. "Why don't fat people have more respect for themselves?"

"Did she ever mention him?"

"What—in terms of a relationship?" Charlene sounded appalled. "We never really discussed stuff like that. I mean I'd told her about the movie business years before. Told her only to sleep above the line. But Bradley Stokes? I don't think so."

"Sleep above the line?" I said.

"You know, only sleep with the guys on the sports list—the best talent, the guys who get their names on the screen above the title of a film."

They smiled. I smiled. Although I could have sneaked glances at Charlene for the rest of the day—and me with a university education—I couldn't think of anything else to ask. I nodded.

"Okay. Well thanks for your help. If I have any more questions perhaps I can call you?"

"So you don't believe her death was an accident?" Gaven said.

"It may have been an accident but a lot of murky things have been going on as a consequence of her death."

As I was leaving I dug out from my briefcase an A4 booklet and handed it to Gaven. He looked down at it and grinned.

"I was there as a little kid," I said. "I wondered if you'd sign it. For old times' sake."

It was my father's program for the Isle of Wight Festival. I'd found it in a pile of his stuff stored in my attic. Gaven opened it carefully and flicked through the pages.

"Are we in here?"

"Just your album cover. Near the back."

He found the page and looked at it for a long moment before scribbling his signature. When he handed it back to me he had a loopy kind of expression on his face.

"Seeing that after all these years. And knowing that Cissie's dead …" He gulped in air then leaned over and squeezed my shoulders. "I know I'm late to the game on this, Nick, but if I can help in any way just let me know."

"Do you think maybe I should try to contact Freddy Redolo?"

"Depends whether you're trying to find out what happened to Cissie or writing her life story. I've got no reason to think she saw him after that first summer."

"And you've never heard from him again?"

"Didn't expect to." He shook my hand. "Nick—keep in touch."

There was an envelope waiting for me in reception back at my hotel. Inside was a note from Salman and a pass for the party at the Ranch the night after next. In his note he suggested I call if I wanted to go with him and the girls.

I picked up some magazines from the shop and went to my room. I phoned Amanda and invited her over to have lunch by the pool. We both knew we had unfinished business to attend to.

"Leave the dog," I said.

She arrived around one thirty. She was scarcely in the room before we lunged for each other. She was a strong girl. I realized this when she picked me up and carried me over to the bed.

"Shouldn't I be doing this?" I gasped between kisses.

"Save your strength," she said. Her voice dropped a couple of octaves. "You're gonna need it."

I hobbled down to the pool around teatime. Amanda was already in the water, floating on her back. I gave her a little wave and lowered myself gingerly into a lounger. Amanda's lovemaking had been … ardent. Frankly, I'd got overexcited, even without Plexiglas.

She flipped over and started a fast crawl down the center of the pool, the sun glinting on the water she displaced. I lay back and looked between the palm trees at yet another clear blue sky.

Besotted.

Again.

You'd think I would have learned by now. But no, I'm one of those people who fall fast and deep. One of those people who hold nothing back. One of those people who'll give everything for the person they love. One of those people. A sucker.

I took my eyes off her long enough to look at the new

issue of *Vanity Fair*. Billy Cash's name leapt out from the cover. The strapline read: Billy Cashes In, Tinseltown's Tuneful Comic Comes Clean.

I turned to the interview. Read a couple of paragraphs. Standard stuff. Flicked the page. They'd dug out some pictures from Cash's rock 'n' roll past. Billy in some serious seventies wide lapels and flares. I read the captions.

Amanda slumped down beside me, shedding water. "Woho alert," she said, glancing at me. I looked at her blankly. "Proves my point," she said. "Woho. A world of your own. Share it with Amanda, Nick, there's a good boy."

"I was thinking about Billy Cash."

"Me too. My big moment."

"I didn't realize until now that he changed his stage name in the seventies."

"From what?'

"From Freddy Redolo," I said.

I showed her the photograph I'd just spotted of Billy Cash with Mick Gaven back in the seventies.

"So?" she said.

"Freddy Redolo had a thing with Cissie Parker when she was fourteen."

She sat up and lowered her sunglasses.

"Small world. Nick, why is it I feel I'm not gonna like the way this conversation is headed?"

I leaned over and kissed her. It took a couple of minutes. I'm the thorough one. In the back of my mind, though, I was wondering why Mick Gaven hadn't identified Freddy Redolo as Billy Cash for me.

"Does he still have a thing about young girls?" I said to Amanda.

"Insofar as I hear he screws anything." Amanda sighed. "Why?"

"A little too coincidental, don't you think?" I said calmly, although my mind was racing. So many questions. What if Billy had continued seeing her? What if he was the father of Cissie's child? Could he have been the guy Mary overheard Cissie with, the mystery man in Ruthie's photographs?

"Listen," I said. "Can you get me into the recording of your show? I'm not going to get anywhere with Juliette."

Amanda looked at me.

"Nick, this is my big chance. Juliette thinks I'm screwing her around she'll pull the plug and my career will go down the pan. She's got the power. If she's as pissed with you as you say she is and I get you in there, that's it."

I looked at her and nodded my head.

"You're right. Forget it. I'll have to think of something else." I leaned back and closed my eyes.

Prize Cash was recorded in a studio in Burbank, a thirty-minute drive from the hotel. The next morning I phoned the publicity unit for the show to try to blag a ticket for Amanda's appearance. I spoke to a guy called Toby, a keen type who, for an American entertainment PR, was unusually helpful.

I said I was doing a piece about American TV, emphasized I didn't need to talk to Billy or any of the guests. I just wanted to watch and get a feel for the show. He invited me down to the afternoon rehearsals.

I was sitting up in the bleachers watching Cash rehearse his intro when Amanda wandered by me. She glanced my way, did a double take then dashed across.

"What the fuck are you doing here?" she hissed. "Are you deliberately trying to spoil it for me?"

"Amanda, no, I'm not. But I have to try to find out—"

"You are so fucking naive," she said angrily. "Or do you

pretend? Do you actually know exactly what you're doing?" She turned away, her fists clenched by her side. When she turned back, her eyes were full of tears. "Jeez, Nick, if you knew what I've been through to get here. What I've put up with. And you're going to mess it up for me. You bastard. You total bastard."

"Amanda," I said, as a familiar voice resounded around the studio.

"Amanda, we need you here now, love."

We both looked round. Juliette was standing at the front of the set looking up at us. Amanda tripped down the steps but Juliette kept her eyes fixed on me. Amanda joined her and Juliette said something. Amanda shook her head. Rolfe and Cash appeared. Juliette went into a huddle with them. Amanda stood off beside them looking miserable. Billy was being very insistent. Both Juliette and Rolfe disagreed vehemently. Billy summoned Toby on to the set.

A few moments later, Toby sat down beside me.

"I wish you'd told me there was some history with you and Billy's people. I was trying to help you and well, this is my first job ..."

His voice trailed off.

"Toby, I'm sorry if I've caused you problems. I didn't mean to. If there's any way I can make it up."

"Forget it. I should know better with journalists. I just have this naive hope some of them will be straight with me."

When a PR is slagging off a journalist on the question of integrity, you know things are really bleak. I hung my head.

"They want to see you in Billy's office," he said.

They kept me waiting ten minutes. I idled away the time glancing through cuttings books about Billy. I'd just got back to the Freddy Redolo period when the door opened and Cash walked in, flanked by John Rolfe and Juliette Smith.

Juliette stood over me.

"I heard you were in town."

"I heard you heard."

"Listen, you shitheel—"

"Okay, Toots, I'll handle this." Cash was standing behind her. "You and John can wait outside." Juliette started to protest, then thought better of it. Throwing me a filthy look, she exited.

Cash sat down opposite me and started to roll a cigarette.

"I don't have to see you, Nick, but I'm choosing to," he said. "I've been asking around about you. I'm assured you have a sense of responsibility. Just goes to show you can't go by appearances. I'm going to tell you some things now. Juliette advises me strongly not to but I want to. Within limits I'm an honest man. I hear you've found out about Cissie and me."

"Mick Gaven told me you had an affair when she was fourteen."

"I figured. How is Holy Mike? And Charlene? Man, have you ever seen lovelier titties? Great in the sack, too. You lookin' at me like that for? Sure I had her. Most of the State of California did. Besides, I told you before, sonny: I had 'em all. Every which way but loose."

"Gaven said he warned you off Cissie."

"Sorta. It was Charlene who put him up to it. Got kind of pissed when she caught me in bed with Cissie. I think Cissie set me up for it, to get back at them for something. Charlene was spitting. Course she couldn't say why. But she made a big fuss to Holy Mike. He had his share when the band was together and since. It's only this God thing that has put him on the straight and narrow, if you can call Charlene either of those things. She was only fifteen when he met her. Anyways, he told me to leave Cissie alone. That I shouldn't see her anymore. Threatened me with the cops."

"Are you saying Gaven is a paedophile, too?"

"Who you calling a paedophile? She was fourteen but she

weren't like no fourteen year old you ever seen. And she was willing. Girls grow up a little faster here in California. Must be the climate. You think it unusual for grown men to go for 'em? Man, they been doing that in Hollywood since the silents. Charlie Chaplin liked 'em young. And don't you think Shirley Temple inspired a few lewd thoughts? These days it's more explicit: Jodie in *Taxi Driver*, Juliette Lewis in *Cape Fear*, that kid in *Leon*. Get real, buddy."

"So when did you bump into her again?"

"'Bout three months later."

"Three months?"

"What, you thought we took any notice of Holy Mike? When I was in England we met up. When she was in Los Angeles we met up. Almost ten years we got it together." He looked away. "I loved her in my way."

"Wasn't she a bit old for you by then?"

Cash tugged on his beard as he looked at me gravely.

"Don't knock it 'til you tried it, man. Though maybe you have. Don't look much like you could cope with a proper woman, I may say so."

"I do all right, thank you," I said stiffly.

"Not what I heard," he said slyly.

Who'd he been talking to? I blushed but blundered on.

"And she loved you?"

"Maybe. But she weren't exactly faithful, you know."

"Were you the father of her child?"

"I ain't here to lie to you, sonny. I'm here to come clean. She wanted my baby. I thought I wanted a baby. We spent a week together before Montreal."

"About six weeks before."

"If you're telling me. I wasn't counting."

"So what happened in Montreal?"

He sighed.

"I tell you, man. It was the saddest thing. She comes up to me at a party …"

He broke off, looked away again. Clenched his jaw to carry on. I tried not to strain forward in my seat.

" … and she told me she was pregnant and we should be getting together. I was right in the middle of some shit. I told her I needed some time to think. Told her to come to my suite the next night. Thought about it in the meantime. And I—I couldn't go through with it. I been a loner too long. I need my own space. Didn't want the damned baby. Told her she should get rid of it."

He put his head in his hands and started to sob. Was he acting or was this for real? If he was acting, I was impressed. The guy had talent.

"But I didn't mean for her to kill herself, man. I didn't mean for that to happen. I loved her."

I sat there being English—that's to say looking everywhere but at him. Eventually I spoke.

"You're saying she killed herself? So what happened?"

"She was devastated. Argued. Then said if I didn't want the baby, she didn't want to see me any more. I asked her what she intended to do about the baby. Said she didn't know. We hugged a lot. Cried a lot. Then she left."

"She left?"

"Walked right out the door man. And that's all she wrote. Man, if I'd known … if I'd known."

"Did she take any drugs with you?"

"No. I don't do them any more. Though when I heard the news I fell off the wagon, big time. That's why I cancelled my gigs in Montreal. Cissie killing herself on account of me just broke me up."

"What time did she leave your suite?"

"Around four thirty, I think."

"She fell to her death at five. What was she doing until then?"

"I should know? Getting high, I guess."

"Where? And whose room did she fall from? There are no windows in the public spaces that overlook the pool."

"I don't know, man. I'm just telling you the way it happened with me."

"There have been other deaths following Cissie's death," I said. "Do you know anything about them?"

"Not a thing. I'm a star. I don't hear anything without it being filtered."

Sounded about right.

"So listen, Nick, what are you going to do with what I've told you?"

"I don't know what's to be gained by the underage sex story. So I'm probably not going to do anything. But you have to tell the Canadian cops she was in your room, tell them about the most recent part of your relationship with her. Otherwise, believe me, I will."

I was working my way through a good bottle of Zinfandel when Amanda did her three minutes on Cash's show that evening. I watched it on the television in my hotel room. I hadn't been exactly welcome in the studio. She went down well. I was pleased though a bit distracted. Actually, I was thinking about Cissie.

I was inclined to believe Cash's version of events. At least now there was some kind of motive if Cissie did kill herself. Based on what Amanda had told me before about Phil Peters, I wondered if Cissie had got the drugs from him after all. Maybe used them in his room on the eighteenth floor.

I sat bolt upright. I had a sour feeling in my mouth. Amanda was Phil Peter's alibi. Had she seen Cissie that night? Was she unwilling to get involved because she actually knew a lot more than she was saying? I went over the possibilities until I was dizzy.

None the wiser, I slumped on my bed and reached for the copy of *Vanity Fair*. I read the interview with Billy Cash all the way through. I was thinking how much better I could write this shit when I was brought up short by a line about his early career. Reaching over for the phone I dialled Mick Gaven's number. I had the program Gaven had signed on my lap before me. I was looking at the album cover for his old band.

"Two things, Mick," I said, once we'd exchanged pleasantries. "First, why didn't you tell me Freddy Redolo had changed his name to Billy Cash?"

"Didn't know," Gaven said. "I'm out of the loop down here. Is the name Billy Cash significant in some way?"

"It is to me. Why didn't you tell me Freddy Redolo was in the band you performed at the Isle of Wight Festival with? Why didn't you tell me he probably had sex with Cissie's mother?"

Next morning I called my old chum, Gerard, at the hotel in Montreal. I phoned Amanda and left a message on her service congratulating her on the show and asking her to get back to me. I didn't expect that she would. I called the PRs for the Hearst bash who confirmed that Bradley Stokes, Billy Cash, and Juliette Smith would all be there. Then I called Salman.

"Nick, you're coming as something, right?"

"Sure am, Salman. You'll be knocked out. But listen, I wanted to ask a favor. How good a sound man are you?"

I went downtown to shop in a second hand clothes shop and a drug store, in preparation for the evening. I spent an hour with Salman, Suzi, and Sharyn in a bar there. Then I drove around for a couple of hours, trying to settle my nerves. I reran my conversation with Gaven as I drove through Benedict Canyon.

"I assumed you knew about Freddy," Gaven said. "He was the one with the exotic supply of condoms. Never had sex without them. Didn't Jilly tell you?"

Jilly had told me about a man who was scrupulous about wearing condoms, but she'd named no names.

"So what?" Gaven said, a little impatiently.

"So nothing, I suppose. It just seems too neat a coincidence."

Gaven sighed.

"Nick, there's something you need to know …"

How right he was.

ELEVEN

The Hearst Ranch was up in the Santa Lucia hills. Set in 160 acres it was actually a 165 room castle, furnished with European antiquities shipped over by the ton—so many of them that crates were stashed unopened in warehouses along the wharves for years. During Hollywood's Golden Age, the dozens of guest bedrooms in the Ranch were occupied by the biggest movie stars in the world, dropping in and out of a house party that went on for years.

Lookalikes of all these oldtime Hollywood movie stars would be at the party, rubbing shoulders with today's movie celebrities. The staff would be dressed in thirties gear. And some people would attend as characters from movies. Including me.

Quite a number of drivers had honked their horns at me on the drive up here along Highway 101. By the time I reached the entrance to the Ranch I was soaked in sweat. I pulled in close to some other cars and sat for a moment. I could see the Ranch, set among cypresses, oleander, and oak trees, some five miles away in the hills.

The security man grinned when he saw me.

"You could be thirsty by the end of the night," he said as he stamped my invitation. "Enjoy."

He was right. I had no worries about Juliette or anyone else recognizing me but I was wondering how I was going to get a drink. In the old days here, Hearst tried to control Marion Davies' drinking by restricting alcohol consumption to cocktails before dinner and champagne during it. Guests would stash bottles under their mattresses or in their luggage but the guest rooms were regularly searched and all booze confiscated. I didn't imagine it was going to be like that tonight. My problem was how, physically, to get a drink down my throat.

I boarded a bus already full of lookalikes and film characters. The horror movie contingent—Dracula, the Wolfman, and Frankenstein's monster—beckoned me from the back row but I sat down next to Charlie Chaplin. Veronica Lake and Alan Ladd were in front of me, a couple of Humphrey Bogarts immediately behind.

"Look, you be Sam Spade in *The Maltese Falcon* and I'll be Philip Marlowe in *The Big Sleep*," one of them was saying.

"Why should I have to hang out with Sydney Greenstreet," the other Bogart said sourly. "He sez, 'I'll tell you right out, I'm a man who likes talking to a man who likes to talk'—but you try getting a word in edgeways. Why can't I be Rick in *Casablanca* and you be Philip Marlowe and we forget Sam Spade? We don't have a Mary Astor anyway and I know for certain there are two Bacalls and a Bergman."

"'Cos Rick is up there at the front of the bus with Gable," the first one said.

"Will you two quit beefing?" Jimmy Cagney said from the seat across the aisle. "Who's gonna know the difference anyway?" He winked at me. "I hope Ladd hasn't brought his box to stand on to kiss the girls. I mean, it's funny the first time you see him do it, but for a whole party?"

I looked at the wooden box perched on the luggage rack above the diminutive Ladd, an essential prop in his movie-making days if he was to get within kissing distance of his leading ladies.

Midget tough guys like Ladd, Bogart, and Cagney have

never done anything for me. Mitchum I believe. Douglas and Lancaster I believe. But I can't take pocket private investigators seriously. They talk the talk, but who for a minute believes they can really walk the walk?

Thirties dance music cranked out of a speaker at the front of the bus. I could hear Gable, in his Rhett Butler outfit, discussing with Bogart-as-Rick the finer points of line delivery.

"'Frankly, my dear, I don't give a *damn* '—that's the logic of the line," Gable said. "But the studio said no cursing allowed so I had to put the stress somewhere else. 'Frankly, my dear, I don't *give* a damn.' "

"Sounds damned stupid to me," Bogart said. "But what about 'Here's *looking* at you, kid'? I ask you—as opposed to doing anything else to you, I suppose. No logic to that at all. Well, tonight I'm going to say it the way it should have been said: 'Here's looking at *you* kid.' "

"Strange word, *genitalia*," Chaplin suddenly said to me. "Sounds like a character in Shakespeare or an Italian town."

I nodded.

"You know why Hearst tried to stop the distribution of *Citizen Kane*?" he continued. "It wasn't because the film was about him. It wasn't because the Marion Davies character was presented as talentless. It was because of rosebud."

I nodded again. I knew.

"You know it's the last word Kane utters and everybody in the film goes crazy trying to figure out what it means. The audience knows that it's the name of the sled he had when he was a kid. In real life it was Hearst's pet name for Marion's *genitalia*. Marion Davies told Louise Brooks, Louise Brooks told Orson Welles, and Welles more or less told the world."

The bus deposited us at the front door where butlers and maids dressed in period clothes held trays of champagne. As I was climbing down, Cagney came up behind me.

"He been rabbiting about genitalia again?"

I nodded.

"Gangway, guys," Rita Hayworth said, pushing between us. She tossed her hair and looked back over her shoulder. "If I were a ranch they'd call me the Bar Nothing."

Cagney grinned and strode after her with that springy, bantam cock walk.

I heard Dracula mumbling in an artificially deep voice behind me in the queue. "I *never* drink—wine. I never *drink*—wine. I never drink—*wine*." We reached a waitress holding a tray of drinks. "Champagne," Dracula said, in a somewhat lighter voice. "Thanks ever so."

I joined the throng of people in the assembly room. Spacious didn't really describe it. The room was enormous. The ceiling was two-storeys high. Oversize Flemish tapestries hung from ceiling to floor, rows of black walnut choir stalls lined the walls. There must have been 300 people in there but it looked deserted.

There was an enormous sixteenth century fireplace—the kind you can walk into—in the center of one wall. I wandered over to it, holding my glass but unable to drink from it. I had my other hand placed lightly in my pocket.

Actually, I was feeling pretty damned Cary Grant. Not that I was being him. But in my white dinner jacket, red rose in lapel, black dress trousers, and polished black pumps I looked about as suave as a person can with fifteen feet of bandages wrapped round his head.

It had seemed like a good idea when Salman had said my class of invite meant I had to "come as something," It would mean I could stalk Billy Cash without being recognized. What I hadn't predicted was how hot I was going to get and how much I'd need a hole where my mouth was before I could either speak or—more significantly—drink.

"I guess maybe you need a straw," a breathless voice beside me said. I looked down at a passable imitation of Marilyn Monroe, wearing the dress from *The Seven Year Itch*. She pointed at my glass. I nodded.

"Oh, but then you'd need a little hole right here," she said, her finger hovering in front of my mouth. I shrugged.

"Nick?" she said in a Minnie Mouse sort of voice.

I looked more closely. It was Sharyn.

"I'm very impressed," I said.

"What?" she said. "Your voice is kind of muffled."

I leaned down and shouted close to her ear.

"I'm very impressed!"

"You look pretty good, too. *Curse of The Mummy's Tomb*, eh? But why the gloves?"

"I'm not the—never mind, I'll explain later. Where is Suzi?"

"She was with that crowd over there." She gestured at a group standing in the entrance to the refectory. A couple more Chaplins, a Marlene Dietrich in top hat and tails, two Groucho Marxes, and at least three Mae Wests. The two Al Jolsons were pushing it a bit with their boot polish faces and white lips. Half a dozen men sported thin moustaches. They could have been variously Ronald Colman, David Niven, Errol Flynn, or Tyrone Power.

"I can't see her," I said.

Sharyn gave me that trembly-lipped Marilyn smile.

"Don't worry, sugar. She's definitely here."

She looked around the room, swaying slightly to a tune we could hear drifting through the open windows. I saw Juliette, in a man's dress suit, stroll in with Rolfe and Billy Cash. Logic told me I was impossible to recognize in my disguise but my immediate instinct was to hide before they saw me. I ducked down and stepped into the fireplace.

I stood there for a moment, my head up the chimney. I

looked down to see a pair of highly polished shoes and well-cut trousers appear outside the fireplace. A head bobbed down and looked up at me.

"Hi," a good-looking young man with slicked back hair said.

I nodded, insouciantly lifting my champagne glass to my bandaged lips.

"Can I help you, sir?" he said, climbing in to join me. I observed the security badge on his lapel.

"No, no I don't think so, thank you," I shouted through the bandages. He turned his head and strained to hear me.

"I'm just admiring this fireplace here. Boy, they sure knew how to build fireplaces back then, didn't they?"

"They certainly did, sir." The man turned as another man ducked under the lip of the fireplace and joined us.

"Can I help you gentlemen? Oh, hi, Luke, what's happening?"

"This gentleman was just admiring the interior of the fireplace."

"That right. How 'bout that? Hey, never thought I'd see the Mummy in a tux."

"He's not the Mummy," Luke said.

"Really? Then who pray is he?"

"Look at the shades. Look at the gloves." I raised my white-gloved hands.

"Ooo, is this a game that anyone can join in?" I heard Marilyn squeak before she tucked in behind the security men. "There you are," she said to me. "I thought you'd left me."

She ducked down again a moment, calling: "Charlie, come on in here." I saw baggy trousers and a cane waddle over and the next minute Charlie Chaplin was tipping his hat to me.

Charlie and Marilyn looked at the three of us.

"So how do we play?" Marilyn asked, wide-eyed. "Is it sardines?"

By the time Carole Lombard, Jean Harlow, two Clark Gables, a Bogart, another Monroe, the Marx Brothers, and the Three Stooges had joined us it was really rather crowded. The two security guys, platinum blondes, and blonde bombshells pressing in on every side, didn't know whether to be thrilled or discomfited. Figuring Billy Cash and Juliette must have passed through by now, I ducked back out.

I strolled through to the dining room. It had once been a church in Spain, pulled down brick by brick, crated up, and reassembled here. Half a dozen people were sitting at the far end of a long monastery table.

One was the Bogart in the white tux. He saw me come in.

"Of all the gin joints in all the towns all over the world, he walks into mine," he called out, laughing as he raised his glass to me.

Cagney joined in, "Look at me, Mummy, top of the world."

As I passed through I heard Groucho Marx say, "He's not the Mummy. Look at the gloves."

I was getting a real thirst. I managed to scavenge a pair of nail scissors from one of the butlers and cut a hole in the bandages over my mouth without letting them unravel. A waitress provided a straw and I sucked gratefully on the champagne.

I followed the sound of dance music on to a wide terrace. People ebbed and flowed around me. A couple of dozen people were dancing. I tried not to gawk as movie stars sashayed by. Just about every major star you could think of was here. Warren and Annette talking to Kim and Alec. Tom and Nicole laughing with Paul and Joanne. Wasn't that … And that …

I knew there were lookalikes for some of the modern stars here, too. I was recovering from being on the receiving end of a huge smile from Greta Scacchi—or someone very much like her—when I realized Jack Nicholson, or someone very much like him, had materialized a few yards away.

A beautiful woman dressed as a flapper—she may have been a lookalike for the young Joan Crawford—approached the Nicholson person.

"Would you like to dance with me, Jack?" she said, giving him an enticing look.

He looked her up and down, then "That Smile" slowly appeared on his face.

"Wrong verb, honey," he drawled. "Wrong verb."

I forced myself to stop staring—it made me weep to think of all the exclusive interviews I could get here—and strolled along a walkway bordered by Mexican fan palms and purple bougainvillea. The shadows were lengthening as I reached a formal garden crowded with more movie stars. Billy Cash was among them.

I lurked among the rhododendrons until Cash moved off with two companions. I followed them, ducking behind a lemon tree as one of Cash's companions paused to admire the camellias.

They went eventually to the Neptune Pool. The large, lotus-shaped, open-air pool had tall cypresses like exclamation marks at one end and the facade of a Roman temple at the other. I noticed Alan Ladd standing on his box, looking wistfully at the women passing by. The three men stopped beside a Greek statue of a discus thrower. I loitered some yards away behind a doric pillar.

I was watching Sharyn sidle close to Cash when somebody nudged me.

"How are you, chiquito," a husky voice said. I looked round and got a face full of fruit.

"It is Nick, isn't it?" Carmen Miranda, in a tight, flowered frock, said. I nodded. "Have a banana," Suzi said, reaching up and plucking one from the back of her hat.

I looked at it. "Don't you think you should have taken the price tag off the fruit first?" I said.

"Fuck it. I had enough trouble making the damn hat."

I offered her the banana. "It'll spoil the display if you remove this one."

"Hat weighs a ton. I'm trying to offload the fruit bit by bit in the course of the evening. I can't wait to get rid of the coconut."

Not knowing what else to do with it, I slipped the banana into my inside pocket.

"Have you spoken to Salman?" I said, looking around.

"Sure. Everything is cool." She looked across the pool. "There's that bitch Juliette trying to look butch."

I followed her gaze. Juliette was standing watching the sunset with Rolfe. Amanda was standing beside them. I'd half expected Amanda to be here but seeing her still made me feel sick.

"Thanks for helping me out like this," I said to Suzi.

"Forget it. Anything we can do to fuck over Juliette is fine by me."

"What have you and Sharyn got against her?"

"She didn't keep her word," Suzi said simply. "Sharyn and I went to one of Juliette's Ladies Only nights. You'd be amazed how many familiar movie star faces were there. It got heavy but Juliette made all sorts of promises." Suzi shrugged. "She lied."

I was considering this information when I was jostled from behind.

"Hey, it's Carmen with the Mummy," the first drunk of the evening said as he wobbled by. "Way to go guys!" he called back over his shoulder.

"Typical Hollywood party," Suzi sniffed. "Actors full of booze and full of themselves."

A swing band started up on a terrace above us. I looked back at Sharyn. She had by now disentangled Cash from his companions and was on tiptoe whispering something in his ear. He was nodding slowly.

"Looks like we're on," Suzi said. She adjusted her hat, blew a kiss at me with her ruby red lips, and wiggled over to Billy Cash.

Ten minutes later, Marilyn and Carmen were leading Cash past the Casa del Mar, the most elaborate of the Ranch's guest cottages, towards the indoor swimming pool. I kept about twenty yards behind.

When I came into the room, Carmen and Marilyn were sitting on either side of Cash on a large white sofa. The only other person in the room was one of the Bogarts from the bus. He was fast asleep, snoring drunkenly in a lounger against the far wall.

The pool was lit by soft underwater lights. The ceiling, decorated with clusters of fish, shells, rocks, and seaweed, shimmered eerily. The bottom of the pool was decorated with stars and planets on blue and gold Venetian mosaic tiles. They were magnified under the water and glittered in the light. As the water dreamily shifted they seemed to float free. Diving in would be like diving into the night sky.

Cash glanced at me as I walked towards him.

"Alone at last," I said.

"That's how we'd like to be, Carmen and Marilyn and me," Cash said in a bored voice. "Don't you have a nice tomb to go play in?"

"He's not the Mummy," Sharyn said. "Look at his gloves."

"You were at the Isle of Wight Festival," I said.

Cash looked at me in surprise.

"That you, Madrid?"

"So you knew Jilly Dougan, Cissie's mom. You had mother and daughter."

Cash looked peeved.

"Sonny, how many times I got to tell you? I've had 'em all ways, all sorts of combinations. But now is not the time to talk about it."

"Talk to me now or talk to every tabloid in the country tomorrow."

"Say what?" Cash said. "You threatening me?"

"Just giving you the chance to clarify one or two things."

Cash glanced at Suzi and Sharyn as they eased away to either end of the sofa. Realizing it was a set-up, he leaned back, sighed, pushed his hands into his jacket pockets.

"Sure, I was there. Don't remember much of it, though. We were pretty wild back then. Juliette had to remind me about it."

"Juliette?"

"Yeah, Juliette. She was there, too."

"At the orgy?"

Cash shook his head.

"On the trip."

"Jilly told me about the orgy. I'm guessing you were the man insisted on wearing a condom."

Cash smirked. "I was known as the Condom King. Never had no sexual disease of any kind—and I been round the track more than a few times. Ahead of my time on that one."

"But you didn't wear one with Cissie."

He frowned. "Well, as you know, that was a special situation we had there."

"I spoke to Mick Gaven earlier today, " I said.

"Good for you," Cash said evenly.

"Told me he was sterile."

"So he and Charlene will set up Childless Anonymous. Big deal."

"It is a big deal because it means he can't be Cissie's father." I heard voices in the pool entrance. Cash looked over. Rolfe, Amanda, Juliette, and another man walked in.

" 'Bout time you got here," Cash called, starting to rise. I leaned towards him.

"And if he isn't Cissie's father—that means you are."

Cash sat back.

"Say what?" he said.

"You heard," I said as the four of them walked unhurriedly across. Juliette and Rolfe were frowning. They could tell by the look on Cash's face something was wrong.

"Who's your friend?" Juliette said, indicating me.

I had wanted it to be like in the movies. They say, "Who is this masked stranger?" I whip off my mask. They say: "You! But I thought you were—" I say: "You thought I was dead? No, I'm very much alive—no thanks to you."

But 'whipping off' bandages isn't easy. It might have gone quicker if I hadn't tied a double knot at the back of my head. Could I unknot the bloody things? Could I buggery. Especially with the gloves on. I messed around there, my fingers grappling with the knots, wishing I'd come as Zorro instead, until Rolfe came over and gave me a hand. Humiliating? I should say.

When he'd undone the knot it still took me what seemed like forever to unwind all fifteen feet of the bandages. Everybody had lost interest by the time the last roll slid from my head. Juliette raised her eyes heavenward.

"It's Junior fucking G-Man again," she said. She looked with mild distaste at my hair plastered to my forehead and the sweat running in rivulets down my face. "He looks kinda hot, John. Cool him off."

Rolfe moved very quickly for such a big man. He lifted me off my feet and the next thing I knew I was hitting the starry sky face first. I hoped for a moment Amanda might dive in and save me. She didn't, but then I was only in the shallow end.

I stood, with as much dignity as a man can have when his tuxedo pockets are full of water. I checked the rose in my lapel nervously and glanced at Carmen Miranda's hat lying on the sofa next to Cash.

"Okay, here's how I figure it," I said, stumbling up the steps out of the pool. I walked—okay, squelched—up to the sofa. "Billy, you are Cissie Parker's father. In the absence of a miraculous conception—and in Jilly Dougan's case we can certainly discard the notion of a virgin birth—it has to be you. You used a condom but something must have gone wrong. The condom split or something."

I smiled my cockiest smile.

"I think our friend is about to puke," Cash said.

"You told Cissie Parker you were her father and that was why she couldn't bear your child. She freaked and you had to shut her up."

Cash looked across at me.

"The bit you're forgetting is that I really loved her, man."

"Is someone sick enough to have a relationship with their own daughter capable of love?"

He held my gaze. "When we started the relationship I didn't know she was my daughter. I'd used a condom."

"It split."

"My condoms never split."

There were, I had to admit, large gaps in my knowledge.

"So what happened?"

"Don't tell him anything, Billy," Juliette said. "He'll use it against you."

Billy looked at her. "How? I've got nothing to hide. She killed herself."

"When did you find out she was your daughter?"

"Billy!" Juliette warned.

"A couple of weeks before Montreal."

"How come?"

"Juliette told me."

I looked at Juliette, who was staring at Billy.

"How did you know?" I said.

"You dumb bastard, Billy," she said. "You're gonna do for us all." She looked at Rolfe, looked round the room, shrugged, and looked my way. "Charlene told me. She's my friend from way back. When she found out Mick was sterile she discussed it with me. Told me about Cissie Parker and her conception, assuming I knew. First I'd heard of it. I knew immediately who Cissie's father was."

"How come?" I said.

Cash butted in.

"I hear you know about Juliette with chicks," he said, looking at Amanda. "But, you know, she didn't always swing that way. We were an item back around the time of the Isle of Wight."

"Having an affair with you is enough to turn anyone gay," Juliette said bitterly.

"I think Juliette would agree she was a jealous lover," Cash continued, ignoring her. "She was called back to London after the first night of the festival. She knew me pretty well. She knew what I'd be up to. So she chose, for reasons that are, honestly, not clear to me, to put pin pricks through all my packets of condoms."

"Hardly detectable," Juliette said with a cold smile. "Just slide the pin through the packet. Works every time."

"So I guess that's how Cissie was conceived by me," Cash said. "When I told Juliette I was trying to have a kid by Cissie, Juliette freaked. Told me why I couldn't."

"That's not quite all though, is it, Billy?" Juliette spat. "When I told you she was your daughter it turned you on more. You loved the idea. Gave you a big kick."

"Yeah, I found it exciting," Cash said evenly. "Artists don't live by other people's morality. But I drew the line at Cissie having my baby."

"Very moral of you," I said. "So what happened the night of Cissie's death?"

"Exactly what I told you," Cash said. "Except I told Cissie why she couldn't keep the baby—told her I was her father. She took it pretty badly, I guess." He lowered his voice and shook his head. "Didn't have my take on it. She was kind of disgusted, tell you the truth ..."

"So she left and, stoked up with drugs, jumped out of the nearest window?"

"That's how I figure it," Cash said quietly.

"How did she get the drugs?" I said, looking from one to the other of them. Cash shook his head. Juliette held my gaze. Amanda looked away.

I suddenly felt very sad. I was winging it but I could see how it might have happened.

"You know, don't you, Amanda?" I said sorrowfully.

Amanda hugged herself and looked at me defiantly.

"I don't get where you're headed," Cash said.

"Let's leave that for a moment," I said, turning towards Juliette. "Let's talk about you, Juliette. You were in Billy's suite before Cissie arrived. Billy told you he was going to tell Cissie the way it was. So you waited for Cissie when she left. Damage limitation, you see. That's what a good PR does. That's why Ruthie the photographer had to die, in case she had incriminating photographs of Billy and Cissie at the party. Because you and Cissie had always been discreet, hadn't you, Billy?"

Juliette didn't respond. Her face was expressionless.

"So, Juliette, you're trying to figure out what the fallout is going to be. I mean, Cissie was pretty freaked. Maybe she was saying all kinds of stupid stuff about blowing the whistle on Billy. And you couldn't allow it. A scandal like that—it would finish him and you, too. All that money, all the future possibilities. I mean Pee Wee Herman's career ended when he was caught watching a porn movie. But this, this was tabloid heaven. And all because Billy had never learned to keep his prick in his pocket.

"So what happened? You came on as Auntie Juliette, intercepted Cissie in the hallway, took her to your room, comforted her, listened to her? There was no point reasoning with her—you could see that straight away. When a girl finds she's been sleeping with her father I guess it makes her unreasonable.

"Maybe you thought the drugs would just slow her down, give you a little more time to think. Who did you know who had drugs? You knew Amanda." I looked at Amanda. "When Juliette called, you rushed over, didn't you, Amanda, your eyes on that big opportunity. Phil Peters was in your room but fortunately for you and for Juliette's plan—because Phil adored Cissie—he'd passed out. He never even knew you'd left the room."

Amanda looked from me to Juliette.

"Amanda," Juliette said, a warning tone in her voice. "He can't prove any of this. He's just guessing."

"Doesn't matter," I said. "The police will figure it out. You're an accessory to murder anyway."

Amanda looked at me with mute appeal.

"Nick, I … you wouldn't get me in trouble would you?"

I looked at her blankly. The woman I probably loved.

"I don't know what will happen if you help me," I said. "I can guess what will happen if you don't."

"Amanda," Juliette said again. "Do you want to go back to being a secretary? Your career is finished if you say one thing."

"Your career is finished if you don't," I said. "You did deliver the drugs, didn't you?"

"Nick. Please."

I held her gaze. She nodded.

"I can't hear you."

"Yes, I delivered the drugs."

"To Juliette's room?"

"Yes. But I didn't stay."

"Oh yes, the room," I said. "I called the hotel in Montreal

today. Dear old Gerard. Don't know why I didn't think of it before. Your room on the twenty second floor, Juliette, was directly above mine." I looked back at Amanda. "Did you see Cissie?"

"She was sitting on the sofa. She looked wretched. Nick, I thought Juliette just wanted to mellow her out. I didn't think ..."

"Was there anyone else in the room?"

"Rolfe was there," Amanda said in a small voice.

"What happened then?"

"I left."

Cash was looking at Juliette.

"Why didn't you tell me any of this?" he asked her.

"I was trying to protect your career. You don't have too many chances left, you know. You won't get another shot like this one."

"But she was my daughter!"

"Yeah. And your lover, I know. Cut the shit, Billy. In all the time I've known you, you've never cared about anyone but yourself. Don't go getting sentimental on me now." She looked at me. "I have no recollection of this and I'm sure neither has John. Whatever Amanda, the former comedy star, might say. But supposing what you suggest were true. Who is to say Cissie didn't take those drugs herself whilst we tried to calm her down? Then, when we were out of the room, disgusted with herself for what she'd unknowingly been doing with her father, she opened the window, climbed on the ledge, and jumped."

"Who's to say?" I said. "Well, a street performer called Pace, for one. He happened to be looking out of his window in the apartments opposite just around the time Cissie took her dive. He saw who helped her."

"Pace is dead," Juliette said. "Remember?"

"Yes, you told me you played for keeps. That's why you had Ruthie killed in Montreal. Just on the off chance she'd taken an incriminating photograph."

"You've never been formally introduced to Charlie, by the way," Juliette said, indicating the fourth person in her group. "He works with John here."

I looked at Rolfe and the new guy.

"Of course. Johnny and Charlie. Punch and Coco the Clown in the Comedy Museum."

Rolfe shrugged. Juliette glanced at her watch.

"You're cleverer than I thought to figure all this out," she said.

"Thanks."

"It's okay. I thought you were a moron. Unfortunately, nobody will know how clever you've been. John, the fireworks are about to start. No one will notice an extra couple of bangs."

Rolfe reached into his inside pocket and pulled out a gun.

"There are too many witnesses," I said nervously, my hand hovering over the rose in my lapel. Juliette followed my hand.

"John, I think he's carrying too," she said calmly. "See what's in his inside pocket."

Rolfe came towards me. My legs started to shake.

"I don't think three witnesses are too many," Juliette said, glancing down at Suzi and Sharyn.

"I wasn't just thinking of them," I said over Rolfe's shoulder as he stepped in front of me. I was aware of Suzi rummaging in the fruit in her hat.

"You mean old Bogie passed out in a lounger?" Juliette said. "We needn't disturb him. Is it a gun, John?"

Rolfe, holding his gun loosely in his left hand reached into my inside pocket with his right. Suzi hefted the coconut. Rolfe groped around then frowned. Bemused, he slowly drew out the gift Carmen Miranda had bestowed on me earlier.

"No," I said, "it's a banana."

Suzi hurled the coconut at Rolfe. She had a good arm. It hit him, with a hollow thwock, on the side of the head. His gun went off, alarmingly loud in the confined space, and he toppled sideways into the pool.

I looked round wildly to see where the bullet had gone. Nobody seemed to have been hit, although Bogart was sitting bolt upright in his lounger, his hands to his ears. Juliette was gazing blankly at the dozens of people who were peering through the glass wall separating the pool from the garden outside.

"They're the witnesses I meant," I said, as half a dozen security guards piled into the room.

I sniffed at the rose in my buttonhole. "Ah, the wonders of modern technology." I fiddled behind the stem for a moment. "Ten four, Salman. Do you copy, rubber duck, and all that CB shit?"

There was silence. Suzi leaned forward and spoke into her hat.

"You there, Salman?"

"I'm here," Salman said over a loudspeaker set in the ceiling of the pool. "Thanks for the earful of water, Nick. The mike in Carmen Miranda's hat got what yours missed. It was too good to keep to myself so I took the liberty of broadcasting your conversation over the Ranch's public address system."

"Bingo," I said, just as the first flurry of fireworks hit the night sky.

Bogart staggered over to Juliette.

"Yes, angel, I'm gonna send you over," he said. "You're taking the fall."

"Go fuck yourself, Sam Spade," Juliette snarled, "and take this fucking Mummy with you."

Rolfe had been disarmed by the security guards. Shedding water, he stood among them at the edge of the pool.

"He's not the Mummy," he said glumly, speaking for the first time since I'd known him. "You can tell by the gloves. He's the Invisible Man."

EPILOGUE

I was trying to figure out how to scratch my nose when I saw the blonde stagger along the beach, dragging behind her a recalcitrant suitcase on wheels. The Cretan sun was broiling, the sea clear blue, the sand golden. I was in the advanced yoga posture I'd last attempted on one momentous morning in Montreal.

During my practice I'd been re-running the events in Los Angeles in my head. Two days after the confrontation at the Ranch, Billy Cash had been splashed all over the tabloids. By the time I was back in Los Angeles, after a token Travel Trip, every newspaper was carrying the story. I assumed that meant his movie career was over. I can't say I shed a tear.

I'd sent copies of the tape Salman had made to the police in Montreal and Edinburgh. I wasn't sure what action they would take, or when they would take it.

"Of course, Juliette could still walk," Suzi said over a jug of margaritas in the pub in Santa Monica. "She can lay it all off on Rolfe."

The same thought had occurred to me. I guessed both she and Rolfe would argue, in the absence of any living witnesses, that Cissie's death was an accident. And unless Rolfe implicated Juliette it was difficult to see how she could suffer for the deaths of Ruthie and Pace.

"But her career's over," I said. "No one in Hollywood will do business with her now."

Sharyn gave me an arch look.

"For a couple of years, anyway," she said.

She was looking very stylish. She was seeing a producer later in the day for the Monroe part in a film about the Kennedys. The press had made minor celebrities out of Sharyn and Suzi for their part in the Ranch Sting, as it was known. Talk shows, book deals, and film offers were flooding in. Salman had become a talk show celeb too, so he had temporarily abandoned his plans to go to Bombay.

Sharyn and Suzi had been so grateful they'd offered me certain favors as a thank you. I declined. I'd like to think I was being honorable but really it was because I knew I wouldn't be able to live up to their expectations.

"What expectations?' Sharyn said, laughing hysterically, when I told them thanks but no thanks. "It was going to be a treat for you—we didn't expect to get any pleasure from it."

Thanks a bunch.

I had three book deals on the table, if I ever felt like writing the story. I'd decided to go to the yoga retreat in Crete for a couple of weeks to think about it. It and Amanda. Amanda wasn't returning my calls, which I thought was a bit rich considering she'd got a book deal out of it too.

I'd phoned Bridget's ansaphone just before I set off for Crete, told her where I was going and given her a brief resume of events. Lenny's tour wasn't due to finish for another three weeks but my message would be waiting for her when she got back.

"What a fucking farce," I heard the blonde say as she got nearer. "Haven't they heard of piers or jetties—oh no, just drop into three feet of water with your Louis Vuitton bags, madam. Thanks very fucking much. And I thought the Outback was primitive."

Bridget wasn't naked but she was a sight for sore eyes. I laughed in delight. As I did so I felt my balance go. There was a certain inevitability about it. I fell over backwards. I lay there unable to move, sinking into the soft sand, as she marched towards me lugging her case.

"Why I ever thought I was in love with a bloody self-centered, fat, American, *married* comic, God alone knows," she said as she drew level. She glanced down at me but didn't slow her pace. "And as for you—you look a right bloody plonker."

A Ghost of a Chance
by Peter Guttridge

Nick Madrid isn't exactly thrilled when his best friend in journalism—OK, his *only* friend in journalism—the "Bitch of the Broadsheets," Bridget Frost, commissions him to spend a night in a haunted place on the Sussex Downs and live to tell the tale. Especially as living to tell the tale isn't made an urgent priority.

But Nick stumbles on a hotter story when he discovers a dead man hanging upside down from an ancient oak. Why was he killed? Is there a connection to the nearby New Age conference center? Or to *The Great Beast*, the Hollywood movie about Aleister Crowley, filming down in Brighton?

New Age meets The Old Religion as Nick is bothered, bewildered, but not necessarily bewitched by pagans, satanists, and a host of assorted metaphysicians. Séances, sabbats, a horse-ride from hell, and a kick-boxing zebra all come Nick's way as he obstinately tracks a treasure once in the possession of Crowley.

0-9725776-8-8

speck

Bullets

by Steve Brewer

When a contract killer bumps off a high roller in a Las Vegas casino, a tangle of romance, gambling, and gunplay follows. The killer, Lily Marsden, is a mysterious and cold woman who is a true professional. But soon, the casino owner, his henchmen, and the victim's two brothers are on Lily's trail.

Former Chicago cop Joe Riley is pursuing Lily, too. She cost him his job as a homicide investigator when suspicion of a bookie's murder fell on him. Joe is certain Lily killed the bookie, and he's tracked her across the country to Vegas.

Throw in some local cops, a playboy, a new widow, a rug merchant, a harridan, and a couple of idiot gamblers named Delbert and Mookie, and the mixture soon boils with intrigue and murder. Add a dash of romance as a strange magnetism develops between Lily and Joe, dust the whole concoction with Steve Brewer's trademark humor, and you end up with *Bullets*—a crime novel you won't soon forget.

0-9725776-7-X

DeKok and the Geese of Death

by Baantjer

"Baantjer has created an odd police detective who roams Amsterdam interacting with the widest possible range of antisocial types. This series is the answer to an insomniac's worst fears."

—*The Boston Globe*

Renowned author Baantjer brings to life Inspector DeKok in another stirring potboiler full of suspenseful twists and unusual conclusions.

In *The Geese of Death*, DeKok takes on Igor Stablinsky, a man accused of bludgeoning a wealthy old man and his wife. To DeKok's unfailing eye the killing urge is visibly present in the suspect during questioning, but did he commit this particular crime?

All signs point to one of the few remaining estates in Holland. The answer lies within a strange family, suspicions of incest, deadly geese, and a horrifying mansion. Baantjer's perceptive style brings to light the essences of his characters, touching his audience with subtle wit and irony.

0-9725776-6-1

speck

For a complete catalog of *speck press* books please contact us at
the following:

speck press
po box 102004
denver, co 80250, usa
e: books@speckpress.com
t: 800-996-9783
f: 303-756-8011
w: speckpress.com

All of our books are available through your local bookseller.